I had such high hopes for my.

I was going to stay at home for the first year or so. Maybe take in an extra kid or two for babysitting. I was going to give Natalie everything I never got at that age — a home, a sense of belonging, affection.

That was the plan.

And now look what I've got. A kid who doesn't even recognize me. A kid who can't make eye contact. A kid who won't even live to see her first birthday.

Praise for *Beauty from Ashes* by Alana Terry

" ... a story that is **both heart-wrenching and heartwarming**." ~ Jaime Hampton, award-winning author of *Malnourished*

"*Beauty from Ashes* **stole my heart and made me cry**. The writing was so real." ~ Helen, The Book Club Network

"Alana Terry **takes you into the heart, soul and mind of her characters**. If I could I would give copies of this book to every woman I know." ~ Kim Persalis, Book Reviewer

"I didn't think it was possible that the author could write any better than she already does. **This is a book I will never forget**." ~ Deana Dick, Texas Bookaholic

"By far **some of the best Christian fiction I've read**." ~ Amy L.

There was silence for such a long time Kennedy wondered if there was a problem with Carl's antique cell phone. Finally, Rose asked, "And so what happens if you get pregnant, and you're too young to actually have a baby?"

Defying all laws of inertia, the acceleration of Kennedy's heart rate crashed to a halt like a car plowing into a brick wall. "What do you mean?"

"Like, what if you're too young but you still get pregnant?"

"How young?" Kennedy spoke both words clearly and slowly, as if rushing might drive the timid voice away for good.

"Like thirteen."

Praise for *Unplanned* by Alana Terry

"Deals with **one of the most difficult situations a pregnancy center could ever face**. The message is **powerful** and the story-telling **compelling**." ~ William Donovan, *Executive Director Anchorage Community Pregnancy Center*

"Alana Terry does an amazing job tackling a very **sensitive subject from the mother's perspective**." ~ Pamela McDonald, *Director Okanogan CareNet Pregnancy Center*

"**Thought-provoking** and intense ... Shows **different sides of the abortion argument**." ~ Sharee Stover, *Wordy Nerdy*

"Alana has a way of sharing the gospel **without being preachy**." ~ Phyllis Sather, *Purposeful Planning*

"Chung-Cha belongs to Christ," Father declared. "Even if you destroy me, God will still watch over my daughter."

The agent chuckled.

"And what if I destroy her?"

Praise for *The Beloved Daughter* by Alana Terry

Grace Awards, First Place

IndieFab Finalist, Religious Fiction

Women of Faith Writing Contest, Second Place

Book Club Network Book of the Month, First Place

Reader's Favorite Gold Medal, Christian Fiction

"...an ***engaging plot that reads like a story out of today's headlines****..." ~ Women of Faith Writing Contest*

"In this meticulously researched novel, ***Terry gives readers everything a good novel should have*** *— a gripping story, an uplifting theme, encouragement in their own faith, and exquisite writing." ~ Grace Awards Judges' Panel*

"The Beloved Daughter is ***a beautifully written story****." ~ Sarah Palmer, Liberty in North Korea*

Without warning, the officer punched Reuben in the gut. Reuben doubled over as the cop brought his knee up to his face. Reuben staggered.

"You dirty n—." Without warning, the cop whipped out his pistol and smashed its butt against Reuben's head. He crumpled to the ground, where the officer's boots were ready to meet him with several well-placed kicks.

Throwing all rational thoughts aside, Kennedy jumped on his back. Anything to get him to stop beating Reuben. The officer swore and swatted at her. Kennedy heard herself screaming but had no idea what she was saying. She couldn't see anything else, nor could she understand how it was that when her normal vision returned, she was lying on her back, but the officer and Reuben were nowhere to be seen.

Praise for *Policed*

by Alana Terry

"*Policed* could be taken **from the headlines of today's news**." ~ Meagan Myhren-Bennett, *Blooming with Books*

"**A provocative story** with authentic characters." ~ Sheila McIntyre, *Book Reviewer*

"It is important for Christian novelists to address today's issues like police misconduct and racism. Too often writers tiptoe around **serious issues faced by society**." ~ Wesley Harris, *Law Enforcement Veteran*

"Focuses on a prevalent issue in today's society. Alana **pushes the boundaries more than any other Christian writer**." ~ Angie Stormer, *Readaholic Zone*

Simon exhaled as he stretched his arms. "I wish we didn't have to say good-bye." His voice was distant.

Hannah stared at the moon. She would never sit here beside him again in this garden. "There are no good-byes in the kingdom of heaven," she whispered, hoping her words carried the conviction her soul lacked.

Praise for *Torn Asunder* by Alana Terry

"Filled with suffering, yet ultimately has a **resounding message of hope**." ~ Sarah Palmer, Liberty in North Korea

"Alana has a **great heart for the persecuted church** that comes out in her writing." ~ Jeff King, President of International Christian Concern

"Faith and love are tested beyond comprehension in this **beautifully written Christian novel**." ~ Kathryn Chastain Treat, Allergic to Life: My Battle for Survival, Courage, and Hope

"**Not your average love story** - wrapped in suspense, this story of faith will stop your heart as you hope and weep right along with the characters." ~ Nat Davis, Our Faith Renewed

"Torn Asunder is an **enthralling, heart-aching novel** that calls your heart to action." ~ Katie Edgar, KTs Life of Books

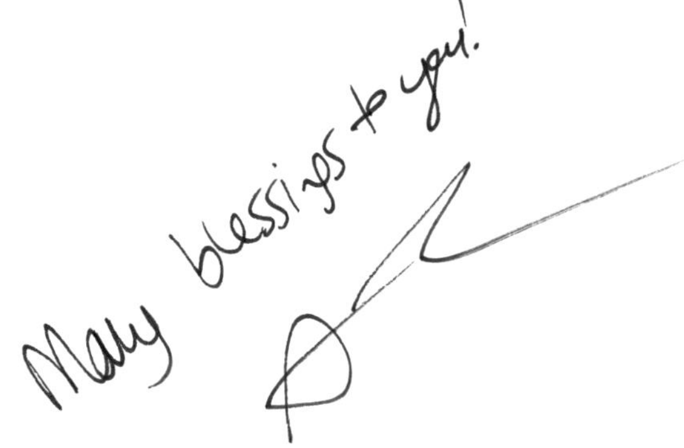

Before the Dawn

a novel by Alana Terry

Note: The views of the characters in this novel do not necessarily reflect the views of the author.

Before the Dawn

978-1-941735-39-8
October, 2017

Cover design by Victoria Cooper.

www.alanaterry.com

CHAPTER 1

I wasn't always like this, you know. Wasn't always such a mess. Back in high school — you might have a hard time believing me — but back then I was this big overachiever. Straight As, college scholarships, you name it. But you're not here to talk about the glory days, are you?

You asked for the details, the gritty, hideous truth, the shame-filled reality of my past that's too difficult to speak of. Which explains why I'm writing it all out. You said you wanted to understand better. Figure out why I've made the choices I have, as much as it hurts us both. So here I am, baring my entire soul to you.

I'm ready.

I just wonder if you are.

When I asked you what I was supposed to write, you answered with a very cryptic, "Whatever you think's important," and I've spent the past week trying to figure out what that means. You already know a lot of it. How long ago did we first meet? Time feels a little weird to me lately. I'm never really sure what day I'm in. There's old Halloween candy on discount in the stores, but I'd have to consult a calendar to tell you if we've had Christmas yet or not.

But that's all irrelevant. It has nothing to do with me or you or the daughter I've lost. You asked about the past. About the things that led up to where I am today. I guess you're trying to figure out how someone like me ended up where I am.

Where did it all go wrong?

I could tell you about the first crash. I mean, when it comes down to it, that's when it technically began. But that's like starting *Les Misérables* in the chapter where Fantine's already walking the streets and dying from tuberculosis. If you don't know how far she fell, you don't care how low she ended up, right?

Anyway, you didn't ask me about Victor Hugo. You asked about my history. So here it goes.

I'm going to start with school, because you know what? It's the last time I can remember being truly happy.

Who would have thought it'd be hard to write about those days? Seriously, though, who wants to admit they peaked at the age of seventeen, and everything went downhill from there? Still, sometimes it's comforting to remember what you once had. Even if the memories themselves are torture.

Which they are.

Chris and I, we met all the way back in junior high when his family moved to central Washington. I guess technically we may have even known each other in kindergarten, because his family used to live here then. But I don't remember him, and he doesn't remember me, so even if we might have been around each other when we were just starting out school, I have no memory of meeting him until seventh grade. That's when his parents moved back to Orchard Grove.

It's a long, complicated story — his family's, I mean. His mom was a migrant worker, fell in love or had some sort of fling with the son of an apple orchardist — Montague and Capulet stuff, seriously, except without the poison or the well-meaning albeit horrifically meddling friar. Which maybe explains why both of Chris's parents are alive today.

Anyway, Chris was born in Orchard Grove, moved away for a while, then came back halfway into our seventh-grade year. I was on the pom squad then. Think cheerleader but it's more like dance, not standing there yelling and doing a few toe-touches. I was co-captain at that point — the first Chinese co-captain in the history of Orchard Grove, as my mom would always boast. (Apparently she's forgotten that the only other Chinese-American student who ever walked the halls of Orchard Grove was my older brother who graduated ten years before I did, so it's honestly not that huge of an accomplishment.) Well, part of my job was to show the new kids around. I don't know. I guess the guidance counselor thought it'd be a nice way to boost school spirit, which is really what the pom squad was all about. That and the dancing, of course.

So when Chris moved back to town in the middle of the year, it was my responsibility to make sure he could find all his classes, sit with him the first few days at lunch if he was by himself, help him out with his locker if he couldn't get his combination working right. That sort of thing, and that's how our relationship started. Call it cheesy if you want. If this were all written out in a book, I wouldn't read another page. It'd be like those trashy teen love series that do nothing but prepare little girls to grow up and devour bodice-ripping romances. But I'm not writing a piece of literature here. I'm writing my story, so you don't get to tell me if it's an overused motif or not.

Chris and I dated officially for five straight years. Six if you count seventh grade, where technically neither one of us was allowed to date, but we were already mushy-gushy at that point, even if the kissing and stuff didn't come until later.

But that's just the thing. With Chris and me, it wasn't the physical. Not all of it. We were both active in youth group at the time. Chris, he was Mr. Sunday School through and through. Knew better than to go messing around too much. A lot of people wouldn't believe us because it's not like we made it this big announcement or anything, but we both graduated high school virgins. I'm only telling you this because some folks see a couple where things go bad, and they immediately ask, *Well, what did you do wrong?* and the whole sex before marriage thing comes up a lot, especially if you grow up in a church as strict as Orchard Grove Bible.

I'm not saying we were perfect. I just want you to know we had something more than hormones between us. Young love gets such a bad rap these days, you know that? Sometimes I think, *yeah, that's probably for good reason.* Then every once in a while I wonder if that's because all the old people are jealous.

But I'm getting ahead of myself. A lot happened those first two years after we graduated. A lot. It's too much to write about in one sitting. This is going to drain my energy, I know it. Way more so than I initially expected. Just this little rambling introduction, it's taken me two days, and I swear I could lay down for a five-hour nap right about now.

I'm sure as I keep on writing, I'll be tempted to skip over some of the more difficult parts. Jump to the good stuff. Because hard as my life's been lately, it's been sprinkled with blessings as well. So please don't start feeling sorry for me. I couldn't stand your pity on top of everything else that's passed between us.

Just like good old Robert Frost had to pause where those two roads diverged into that yellow wood, and he couldn't transport himself to the end of his journey without explaining to us why he stopped there to wrestle with his destiny, I've got to tell you everything. Got to be thorough. So help me God because he alone knows how hard this is going to be.

He alone knows all the secrets I've been carrying around like that sack on Christian's back in *Pilgrim's Progress*. Except unlike John Bunyan's hero, I'm still waiting for my Evangelist, my messenger to tell me where to get rid of these burdens. Who knows, maybe that's why God brought me here to talk to you.

One could always hope, right?

So don't worry, I'll tell you everything. Well, at least the parts I'm able to get out. I don't make promises beyond that. I'm like Tolstoy. He said he could sum up everything he'd learned about life in just three words. I may not be as experienced as some, but I've walked through more despair and heartache than my burdened soul knows what to do with. Like Tolstoy, I can also summarize everything I've learned about life as concisely as he did:

It goes on.

Life goes on. In spite of the secrets we're destined to carry to the grave, heavy and cumbersome though our load may be.

In spite of the squalid human condition, the wretchedness that pierces your soul until you imagine you're staring at some phantom or demon in the mirror and not yourself at all.

In spite of the excruciating sadness, the grief that can consume you for weeks, months at a time, until you don't just lose track of the days but of the seasons and years, too.

In spite of it all, life goes on.

And all you have to hold onto is the hope that maybe, by God's grace or some miraculous intervention on your behalf, you'll find release from your burdens.

You'll find peace for your soul.

I pray that I will. I hope that I will. Because sometimes, truth be told, it's tempting to think about giving up. Just like Frost said, the woods are lovely in their darkness and depth. It's tempting to think of staying here forever, but I have promises to keep.

Promises to myself. Promises to my daughter.

I can't fail. Not again.

But I'm so tired. So bone-weary, soul-draining tired.

With miles to go before I sleep.

And miles to go before I sleep.

CHAPTER 2

I've found that I have unconventional tastes when it comes to literary match-making. Rhett Butler? Ok, so maybe he and Scarlett deserve each other, but I certainly don't mean that as a compliment.

And Mr. Darcy? Awkward, eccentric introvert? Umm, excuse me, but exactly what does he have going for him? Other than his fortune, I mean. If I wanted to read billionaire love stories, I'd find them a dime a dozen in the erotica section.

And what's up with Rochester? I don't mean that rhetorically either. I seriously want to ask Jane Eyre and her myriad fans what's the deal with him.

I suppose I'm more of the boy-next-door kind of girl. Which is why when I read *Little Women*, I rooted for Laurie, the quintessential (and literal) boy next door. And Jo turned him down and married the professor. Seriously? I threw the book against the wall. Still refuse to reread it.

I'm not much of a *Lord of the Rings* fan, but I worked

my way through the entire series. I'd read Austen and Bronte and all the others by then but didn't experience my first literary crush until I met Samwise Gamgee.

Now there's a boy next door for you.

So I've been thinking about Chris a lot. Not Chris, the reason my entire life's turned into one giant train wreck, or Chris the man who destroyed my faith in happily ever afters. Not Chris, the reason I've been spending my nights in and out of different battered women's shelters. I'm thinking about Chris as he was back then.

In that time in the not-too-distant past when he was everything.

Chris the football kicker, because he was destined to be a star in our small town, but he wasn't big enough for defense or fast enough for offense. Chris the homecoming king, because he and I were on court all four years of high school, so it would have been basically an impossibility for us not to get ourselves crowned as seniors.

And maybe you look at all that, you see me with my pom-pons and him in his football uniform, you walk through Orchard Grove High School and see the framed pictures of us in our homecoming crown and sash, and maybe you think we were that shallow, flighty couple you meet in teen romances or whatever.

Maybe you see him as Chris the jock or Chris the kid who probably peaked in high school and wouldn't ever go on to do anything else of significance in his entire life.

But I see Chris, the boy who sprinted across the street to the gas station in between second and third period to buy me an emergency supply of pads. Chris, the boy who planned a scavenger hunt that stretched across the entire town to celebrate my sixteenth birthday and who graffitied his next-door neighbor's broken-down shed (with permission) to invite me to our senior prom.

Sure, we were both athletic, but guess what? We worked our butts off on the school newspaper, too. We kept going to youth group, and when he was a senior, Chris even helped out with this junior high Bible study just for boys at his church. When he and I got together Friday nights, it usually wasn't to party. It was to talk about our AP literature class or to work on layout for the school paper. We even started writing a play together. Never finished it, but that's not the point. The point is we weren't just some flaky high school power couple.

That's why it's so hard to remember, you know? Remember what we used to have. People say memories are supposed to comfort, but they're wrong.

Dead wrong.

Chris was my Gilbert Blythe, and I was his Anne Shirley, so convinced, so confident that wherever our future would bring us, we would be together.

He was Count Vrosnky, and I was Anna Karenina, and our love was just as fierce and passionate, except it wasn't tainted. It wasn't taboo.

It should have turned out so differently.

Which is what makes it so hard to talk about.

I didn't just lose a high-school crush. I didn't just lose my first love.

I lost my stinking soul.

CHAPTER 3

I'm like a time bomb these days. I really am. Like I can feel the next crash creeping up on me centimeter by deadly centimeter. I look back and think about those days when I was happy, those days when Chris and I would stay up until one or two in the morning, working on the school paper, laughing at our stupid typos, talking about all our plans for college and beyond. That's the worst of it. I can remember when I actually felt like a person. A person with a life to live. A reason to exist.

At least the suicidal side of it is gone. I know it's no reason to boast, but I never actually made an attempt, even when things were at their worst. Through it all, I've maintained a shred of my dignity. The irony is the only reason I didn't try to kill myself was because I was too tired to form any sort of cohesive plan. But I did think about it.

A lot.

You don't need all the details, I'm sure. Even now, I can't believe how much I'm already telling you. I spent two full months in bed. I didn't technically sleep that entire time, but I was about as mentally useful as a coma patient. I still remember the way it felt. Heaviness. Brain smog. That thick, pea-soup mental fog. It doesn't just sap your strength. It feeds on your exhaustion. You're so sluggish, which is exactly how it wants you. So your thoughts aren't your own, because you don't even think anymore in words or pictures, just in primitive sensations. Sensations of tiredness. Of nothing. Of death.

I was still a mess when I returned to Orchard Grove. It was Christmas break my sophomore year of college. Daddy was a saint. Got me audiobook after audiobook, and he'd sit by my bedside listening with me so I wouldn't feel lonely. Mom thought I had mono. It was easier to explain it that way. Explain why I didn't just refuse to get out of bed, I literally couldn't lift my legs off the mattress.

She clucked and fretted. Mom's like that, you know. Chiding me in English, then muttering to herself in Cantonese. You want to know about my relationship with my mother? I swear all you've got to do is read an Amy Tan book. It doesn't even matter which one. In Mom's professional opinion, mental illness isn't illness at all. It's not caused by a germ, and therefore it doesn't exist. And on top of all her quintessential Chinese-American mothering tactics, she goes to Orchard Grove Bible Church, so she's got theology on her side backing her up.

Because of course, *God helps those who help themselves.* She quotes it so many times she actually believes it's written right there in red letters. Hers is that old-school, bootstrap sort of Christianity, where you take a little bit of the Bible, a heavy dose of puritanical ideals, and pour out the American Protestant work ethic on top. So you're constantly pulling yourself up by your bootstraps, quoting Philippians 4:13 to yourself like you're some heavyweight champion wrestler, and you conquer anything and everything that stands between you and your goal, which is a mix between a traditional family, a comfortable retirement, and eternal security.

That's why it was so much easier to tell her I was recovering from mono.

Which didn't keep Chris from stopping by to see me, even though I'd broken up with him over a year earlier.

And then the fog lifted. Gloriously. Miraculously. I was myself again. So much so that I started to wonder if maybe I did catch a virus, and it just took my immune system longer than expected to fight it off. Of course, reconnecting with Chris didn't hurt. It didn't hurt that we were talking about the future, even mentioning the word engagement. It was like I'd been asleep for the past year and a half and was just now waking up.

I mean seriously, I looked at the way I was at the start of my first year of college, and I had no idea who that girl was. The girl who called her long-time boyfriend one week after freshman orientation, begging him through tears to understand why she was dumping him. The girl who tossed all his old love letters — five whole years' worth — into the recycling bin because she was certain that it was in both of their best interests to move on.

The girl who couldn't get out of bed until Prince Charming swept in and woke up her exhausted soul with his kiss.

That girl was gone, and good riddance to her. Once again the future was promising and glorious and everything Chris and I had hoped it would be when we celebrated our high-school graduation.

He forgave me for breaking up with him. He even said it was good, said that our year and a half experiment of living apart from each other helped us to grow and mature, so now our love was destined to be even stronger.

I wish to God he'd been right.

CHAPTER 4

I knew writing this out would take a lot of my energy. I'm surprised I haven't crashed yet. I've always dreamed of being a novelist one day. I've lived the past decade in that perpetual pre-aspiring author stage. Problem is I either write absolute fluff (the kind that would make even a teen-romance junkie gag), or I create something so real it sends me to bed for a week or two at a time.

Move over, J. K. Rowling, I'm hot on your heels.

As soon as I finish this month-long nap.

Once I woke up from my semester-long sleep, I tried hard for Chris. I'd swear on Gutenberg's printing press how hard I tried. At first, things were going so well. Looking back, it was the dumbest breakup to start with. I thought we both needed time to focus on our studies. It was difficult maintaining a relationship when he was in Seattle and I was all the way on the other side of the state in Spokane. That was all there was to it. I started to think that's what my first crash was all about, that after trying to survive without him, my body and mind finally gave up and refused to function anymore.

So Chris and I had a blissful New Year's together, then I went back to Spokane. Went back to my studies, got more involved in church because I'm always inspired to grow closer to God when I'm with him. And things were so good. I can't explain it. Can't explain how the only time I seriously know who I am is when I'm with Chris. It's like we were together for so long we were the equivalent of octogenarians married for six decades by the time we got to college. I can just picture the way you're rolling your eyes right now. Don't think I can't. But I've got to talk to someone about all this, and awkward as it's going to be for both of us, that someone is you.

Don't forget that you're the one who asked for it.

I've still got that time-bomb ticking inside me. Still know that at some point, maybe tomorrow, maybe three months from now, my body's going to wake up, but my brain's going to decide to hibernate for however long it sees fit. I'm so ashamed of this mess I've turned into. I try to hide it well, I really do. I try to make up for my dysfunction by overcompensating the rest of the time. I go overboard on self-care because I know at any moment, I might lose the energy to bring a brush to my hair. Seriously, have you ever been so exhausted that Germ-X becomes your best friend because getting a squirt of soap *and* having to rinse your hands is too taxing?

Maybe that's a calloused question for me to ask, and I'm sorry. You know what I've gone through. But I think about you, and it makes me feel even more wretched.

We shouldn't have ever met, you and I. You know that, don't you? Of course, you're too much of a gentleman to come out and say it, so I'll do it for the both of us. I wish you'd never stepped into my life.

Because you're the reason for that next crash, and all the ones that came after it.

CHAPTER 5

I've heard people say that folks who struggle with mental illness are the strongest out of everybody because what's scarier than fighting with your own mind day in and day out? And I suppose if I was an inspirational-calendar-quotes kind of girl, that sort of thinking might give me a little perk when things get hard.

The funny thing is when I function, I function fine. You would never look at me and guess that by tomorrow my brain might go on strike for three or four weeks. When I'm busy with life and being productive, you could never imagine the demons that I've battled.

Both the demons I've conquered and the ones that I'm sure will plague me for the rest of my life.

It's a curse, really, because when you do that well ten months out of the year, nobody worries about you during the two when you disappear. They just think, *oh, I wonder where she is. Probably off traveling and forgot to tell me, or writing that great American novel she's always talked about.*

So, I know there's this stereotype about authors, and really all artists in general. It's this idea that depression is the muse of creative geniuses, and without their beloved mental illnesses, they'd never be able to create the masterpieces they do. Case in point: My high-school English teacher had a comic taped on the chalkboard. There's a black-haired man with a pen sitting at his desk, smiling at the raven who just landed on his windowsill and greeting him with a cheerful, "Hello, birdie." Caption? *Edgar Allen Poe on Prozac.*

I'm not knocking Prozac, by the way. My mom does enough of that for the both of us. What I'm saying is that as a culture we've got this idealized notion that a mentally stable Edgar Allen Poe would have never penned the haunting cadences in *The Raven* or the chilling, tragic story of *Annabelle Lee* in her kingdom by the sea. Tchaikovsky could have never dived into the depths of human emotion and experience to birth his fifth symphony in all its melancholic, awe-inspiring grandeur. Vincent Van Gogh cut off his ear half a year before painting *Starry Night.* Coincidence?

Not according to the experts in their ivory towers.

So the artists are left to suffer as martyrs because who besides nursery-school kids wants to read a poem about a little birdie visiting a cheerful human in his well-lit chambers?

The problem with that line of reasoning is that for every Van Gogh, for every unstable artist who manages to surface from the depths of mental illness to create such lasting masterpieces, there are twenty or thirty or maybe a hundred artists who die without having the strength to lift up their pens or their paintbrushes and show the world the haunting, spirit-aching beauty that's in their souls.

I could write. I know I could. If it weren't for the fact that every time I try to jot something down, it lays me up in bed for weeks.

But I'm done complaining. Really I am. There are some things that if they could be fixed, they would have been fixed already. There's a grand, universal reason for it all, I'm sure, and don't try to wax eloquent and tell me what that reason might be. Like I said, if I wanted inspirational platitudes, I'd buy a cheap wall calendar.

You know, I started off ripping on folks who say that people with mental illness are stronger than average, but maybe there's something to it. I mean, the fact that I'm alive is pretty startling. Not only that, but in spite of everything I've got going against me, I haven't thought of killing myself since the very first crash.

Since I met you.

I guess you could call me theologically eclectic if you

were to gauge it by the different churches I've attended. Orchard Grove, as you're well aware, is extremely conservative. Bunch of old, retired orchardists and not too many young folks. And Valley Tabernacle, the one Chris and his family went to across the river, that was something different. Words of encouragement, apostolic testimonies, all that Holy Spirit stuff. Some of it I could do without, like the raising your hands out to your sides and spinning around in circles in the aisle. Or getting slain in the Spirit. Don't even get me started on that.

I think if I were to look at that strain of Christianity with a critical eye, my biggest complaint would be how they make everything boil down to spiritual attacks. You get a bad case of indigestion — the devil must be fed up with you. You can't find a parking spot at the post office, and all of a sudden you're wondering if you invited demons into your life through some unconscious sin or other.

The problem with that demon-behind-every-bush theology, at least as far as I see it, is it takes responsibility away from the Christian and thrusts it onto the shoulders of Satan and his legions of minions. Kind of convenient if you want to look at your own sin patterns and offer up that all-too-common *the devil made me do it* excuse, but that's about all I see going for it.

But I certainly won't knock Valley Tabernacle either. Orchard Grove will never come close to creating that experience of deep, intensely personal worship. And it's because of my time there that I'm free from my suicidal thoughts. I would have never really believed in that sort of immediate deliverance if it hadn't happened to me firsthand. I'm not into the bells-and-whistles style of Christianity. Give me Jesus, give me the cross, give me Easter Sunday, and I'm ready to call it good. I don't need a dramatic testimony every weekend, a brand-new belted-out chorus every service.

I'm not saying I was skeptical, but I certainly wasn't looking for a miracle when I went to Valley Tabernacle with Chris that Sunday. We were both home for spring break our sophomore year, enjoying our last weekend together before we headed back to our respective campuses. It was hard because I hated the thought of being far from him, but we had so much future to plan, I was hopeful that the days would pass quickly. We'd both be back in Orchard Grove again by summer, and we were already in that pre-engagement stage where there's no ring yet, no date, but you're still walking through each day knowing you're going to end up together.

I honestly thought my depression was gone for good. I'd been stupid to break up with Chris to start with. I could see that now. Best I could figure, my body and brain eventually decided to conspire against me to prove what a dumb decision I'd made, and now that the two of us were together, there was nothing but joy waiting ahead.

Ok, so maybe I wasn't that naïve. I knew our future wouldn't be without obstacles, but seriously, when you love as deeply as we did, you feel completely invincible against whatever the world may throw at you.

I already mentioned how the times I've been closest to God are when I'm with Chris. And even though it would be hard to say goodbye, I felt more hopeful that Sunday, more alive than I had since my high-school graduation. So I was at Valley Tabernacle, and who do you think it was who showed up as the new pastor? You know, I'm one of those old-school types who gets used to one preacher's style of teaching, so if I hadn't wanted to spend every possible minute with Chris, I might not have bothered to even show up that day. No offense, but I remember feeling antsy because I was in the middle of rereading *The Grapes of Wrath*, and it's one of those books I like to finish in as few sittings as possible. That's why I hoped your sermon wouldn't last all that long.

And you got to talking, and it was *deliverance this* and *Holy Ghost that*, and I was half paying attention to you and half thinking about Ma and Pa Joad. I'd just gotten to the part where they bury Grampa, so I wasn't even that far into it yet but really wanted to finish up before I headed back to campus.

But then something you said caught my attention, and I couldn't help but sit there mesmerized, and you were all Holy-Spirit-fired up, shouting and even spitting on the congregants unfortunate enough to sit in the front row. And you were up there with your hands raised high, shouting, "My God is a God of DELIVERANCE!" and I was surprised you didn't thump your fist onto your Bible at that point, but Valley Tabernacle's the kind of church that doesn't really see the need for a pulpit, so it wasn't nearly as dramatic as you might have liked it to be.

And you were hollering, "My JESUS will heal every wound you bring to him," and women in front of me were swaying, and folks were clasping their hands to their chests, and you were going at it with, "In JESUS' name, we banish strongholds," and "In JESUS' name, we tear down barriers," and something told me to leave. Told me to get back home, pick up my book, and forget about the screaming preacher in his thousand-dollar suit.

But there you were, spraying us all with your holy spittle, yelling at us to be washed clean of our infirmities *in JESUS' name* and declaring the blood of JESUS over the whole lot of us, and something started quivering in my core. This shaking, trembling feeling I hadn't experienced before and haven't since. And you said in that booming voice, "SOMEONE here is tormented by a demon of suicide." I've already told you my general thoughts regarding that demons-in-the-bushes style of Christianity, and something in my gut was prompting me to get out of there, but some weight on my shoulders was keeping me planted in my chair, and I'm not kidding when I tell you it was like a hand was holding me down.

And you said, "Someone here is in need of God's DELIVERANCE," and that word sent this icy chill down my spine, like whatever monster was trying to get me to leave was terrified of even the suggestion that I might find my freedom. I remember it vividly. You were shaking your fist, and our eyes met, and I was certain at that minute that something was going to happen between us. I couldn't say what, I couldn't even have told you if it would be good or bad. I just knew that this one, single look would *make all the difference*, like old Robert Frost would put it.

It's bizarre because just as soon as your eye caught mine, I couldn't look away from you. It was like my whole soul was being drawn to you one word at a time. Then you started to pray. You didn't shut your eyes, and I didn't either, but you prayed and asked God that "the person here looking for their deliverance would find it in JESUS' name." You were so bold, that's what I remember most apart from that look. None of the typical *if it's your will, Lord*, or anything like that. You gave God an ultimatum that Sunday. You gave him an ultimatum to deliver me from the spirit of suicide, and I'm way more conservative theologically than the typical Valley Tabernacle congregant, but I still can't explain what happened to me. You said the word *suicide*, and something ripped out of my spine. That's the only way to put it. Just ripped right out. Excruciatingly painful, but freeing, too. Like that boy in *Voyage of the Dawn Treader* who has to peel off his dragon scales to become human again.

That's what was happening to me. Peeling off, removing that old self, that suicidal self, that part of me that had whispered that the world would be better off without me, that I would be better off without it. All those self-destructive tendencies of mine, the same self-loathing that made me break up with Chris when we started our first year of college. Those lies. I could see them now so clearly for what they were. Lies from the pit of hell. Lies telling me I was wretched, I was unlovable, I was unworthy of any happiness.

And in a few seconds, because that's all the time your thundering prayer took, I was free.

Since that day, I've never — not even once — thought of ending my life. Even those times when I'm at my lowest. Before there was always that little whisper, that quiet voice telling me I should just end it all because what was the use. But you silenced that deceiver forever and freed me from my chains.

Free at last.

Free at last.

Thank God Almighty, I'm free at last.

You should have left it at that.

I should have left it at that.

My life would be so much better off now if you had.

CHAPTER 6

Spending the next summer back in Orchard Grove with Chris was as marvelous as I expected it to be. I think we averaged about four hours of sleep a night. I told him all about my deliverance experience. He was more open-minded about that sort of stuff than I was, and he was happy for me. Even then, he didn't really know how far I'd sunk that fall. I really glossed it over when I explained it to him because remember, in my head the only reason I crashed that hard to start with was because the two of us weren't together. So now that we were a couple again and even more in love than before, I was certain I wouldn't crash again.

You know how it is when you step into the sunshine after being shut up in the dark all day? As glorious as the light is, it's painful, that much brightness. That's what it was like for me coming out of my crash. Spending every minute of that summer with Chris. Looking forward to an entire lifetime together with him. To dream together. Laugh together.

Love together.

My grades had slipped, obviously, at the start of my sophomore year, but second semester turned out fine. I had just declared my major in English literature with a minor in creative writing. Chris was doing well in his pre-law stuff, too, and we were engaged in lively discussions about whether it would make more sense for him to transfer from Seattle to Spokane for our junior year or the other way around.

We acted as though we had all the time in the world. We acted as though nothing lay ahead of us except more togetherness, more romance, more joy.

We fully expected to spend the rest of eternity together, rejoicing in our love, indulging in our passion, dreaming of our future.

Neither of us could have foreseen all those catastrophes that would ultimately destroy us.

You know, the Bible gets a bad rap sometimes. People call it outdated. Archaic. I wonder how many folks realize the depth of romance that pours out of some of those stories. *So Jacob served seven years to get Rachel, but they seemed like only a few days to him because of his love for her.* Seriously, how can you not read the romance, the passion, the longing glaring at you so overtly in the subtext?

And don't even get me started on Song of Solomon. I

mean, I don't read erotica as a personal preference, but how can you say God is anti-sex when it's his Holy Word that has verses like *I have come into my garden, my sister, my bride*? Can someone say euphemism? Or here's one that should make all the boys in youth group chuckle. *I will climb the tree; I will take hold of its fruit.* You ever wonder exactly what fruit he's talking about there? Oranges? Grapefruit? Maybe some melons?

Anyway, we've all heard those folks who say there's nothing in the Song of Solomon but allegory, how it's all this big, platonic metaphor for Christ and the church. I don't buy it, but if that's your conviction, all the more power to you. What I mean to say is if God's in all the details of our lives, that includes the romance, too. And the sex. And everything else that goes with it.

So anyway, like Jacob serving those seven years for Rachel and it seeming like such a short time, that's how life felt for Chris and me once we started our junior year in Spokane. Seriously. I remember how thankful I felt those days, how many times I dropped to my knees (figuratively at least) to praise God for his deliverance. It's like when you've been fighting a cold for a few weeks, and then one morning you wake up perfectly healthy and don't realize until then how poorly you'd been feeling. I was a totally new person, spirit, mind, and body. A new person ready to take on the world, ready to join my life with Chris's, ready to give God the glory for freeing me from my depression, for healing me from whatever horrible mental illness had hooked its talons into me when I was foolish enough to think I could live without my only love.

I walked through life with the conviction that my mental health was perfectly restored. Perfectly healed.

But apparently not quite as healed as I had hoped.

CHAPTER 7

Do you ever feel guilty at times for being happy? When with the brutal assistance of hindsight, you realize you were just setting yourself up for misery? I think about that sometimes. Or how God feels when we're about to destroy our lives, but we're so excited about it. Like Chris's parents. They had that storybook romance going on, the whole Romeo and Juliette thing with her being the daughter of migrant workers (undocumented, by the way) and him being the son of the largest orchard owner in the county. The pictures from their wedding day are absolutely stunning. I've never seen two people beaming at each other with so much love.

And from what Chris says, every day since then has been abject misery for them both. I hate to make an example of their misfortunes, because when they're apart from each other, they're both kind, gracious people. It's only when they're together you see how volatile marriage has made them. But that gets me wondering about the one happy moment they shared, that blissful, perfect wedding day. Do they look back on it with embarrassment? Ask themselves *What in the world was I thinking?* Do they feel guilty for being so naïve?

And how does God feel about it all? Of course, he's right there with us when we go through our good times and our bad times, and I like to picture him empathetic enough to weep with us when we weep and rejoice with us when we rejoice. But what if what we're happy about is going to turn into destruction in a matter of weeks or months — or hours if you're Chris's parents? Right now, imagine there's a couple getting ready to join their lives together, and it's the most perfect day of either of their lives. But if God knows that in two years she's going to be in the battered women's shelter and he's going to be behind bars, is the omniscient Almighty still delighting in their happiness today?

You could ask the opposite question, too, but that gets even more convoluted. What if there's a sick baby on a ventilator, but because of what happened to that family, someone ends up getting saved, for example? Could you therefore go on to say it's a good thing that baby's so sick? What if she dies? What if that newborn will pass away tonight, but a year from now, after walking through hell and grieving her blasted heart out, the child's mother is going to give her life to Christ? Does that mean we should be happy the baby's dead? Does that mean God refuses to mourn with that child's family while they're sobbing into each other's shoulders?

I doubt it, but I wonder sometimes.

And then I realize it doesn't matter. It doesn't change anything.

God sends his rain on the righteous and the unrighteous. He shines his sun down on the wicked and the just. That's the way the world's gone from the time of Noah on. And that's the way it's going to continue. Some questions don't get us anywhere. They only make us dizzy or despondent.

But I do still wonder from time to time. Wonder what God thought the night Chris took me out for my twenty-first birthday. We were spending the summer before our senior year back in Orchard Grove, but he drove me all the way to Spokane. I should have known something was going on. Should have read it in his nervous chattiness, in his perfect grooming. Chris never was one to take his appearance all that seriously. He wasn't cut from the Abercrombie mold. His style was casual and easy, his hair always a tad on the long side, not because he liked it that way but because he hardly ever took the time to get it cut. He was far more comfortable in an old jersey than anything else, but tonight he was wearing a collared button-down, no tie, but perfectly pressed.

I should have known then. And maybe the drive to Spokane could have given me the perspective I needed. Given me time to think about what I was doing.

But we were so young. And it had been almost three years since my last crash, so I truly thought it was all behind me.

He didn't tell me where we were going. I hadn't even known the Spokane Theater Troupe was putting on any summer shows. I was so busy spending every waking minute with Chris, breathing Chris, loving Chris. What did I care about summer shows?

But he knew this was one I wouldn't want to miss, and we pulled up in front of the theater with fifteen minutes to spare before the start of the Saturday matinee.

To Kill a Mockingbird. I'd already told Chris way back in tenth grade there would never be a single work of American literature more perfect. More flawless. He must have remembered that conversation because that's the show he took me to. Spokane's not Seattle or San Francisco or New York. If we had been in a bigger city we might have seen more impressive stars, but it still would have paled in comparison. The Spokane theater seats a little more than a hundred. That's all. And it was in the midst of that small, intimate audience that my soul was tantalized by Harper

Lee's tale of justice and oppression and hatred and racism and childhood innocence, all wrapped into one glorious masterpiece.

I'm convinced that I could spend the rest of my life as a Broadway groupie, and I'd never come close to experiencing a show so impressive. So flawlessly executed. We were right there. Breathing with Scout, idolizing Atticus right along with her. Weeping for the injustices, hating the perpetrators, begging for a different outcome even though we all knew how the story was going to end.

Flawless. A single moment in time where if I could relive any one day of my life, that's the one I would choose.

Glorious. The love of my life sitting next to me, the greatest American novel ever written impeccably performed for us and a small handful of others.

Torturous. Because that one night set the rest of my life on an irreversible track that would bury both Chris and me in the depths of grief and torment, sweeping us down a floodway of sorrow that no amount of love, no degree of romance could have prepared us for.

CHAPTER 8

After the show, Chris and I went out to Paradise Bistro. I was a little surprised, because Annie's was a fancier restaurant and where we'd celebrated my birthday the summer before. But tonight it was Paradise, and when we got to our table, there was a small crystal bottle waiting for us.

"What's this?" I picked it up. There was no label.

Chris grinned. "Raspberry cordial."

I didn't even know the stuff existed outside of Prince Edward Island. I suppose I could have guessed, but the only time I'd heard of it was in *Anne of Green Gables*. Chris knew that was one of my favorite books, not because Anne is so bewitchingly charming and imaginative but because it's probably the sweetest romance in all of literature. Anne Shirley and Gilbert Blythe. Seriously, do you get more sublime than those two?

Well, that wasn't the only surprise Chris had prepared. I can only guess how long he spent planning it all out. Because after he poured me a glass of raspberry cordial, he took out a package.

It was a long box, so at first I thought it might be jewelry even though I couldn't figure out why. Ok, so we did read *The Necklace* together in eleventh grade, and I guessed he might have attached some strange significance to it, but there are so many better Guy de Maupassant stories he could have chosen from.

Well, it wasn't a necklace. It was a fountain pen, a Lamy 2000, the kind I'd drooled over for months. And he'd even had it inscribed with a series of letters.

I t d t m m m, T l w m a b m l.

I felt the smile creeping to my face, wondering about this game he'd planned out and put so much thought into.

"Can you guess it?" he asked.

I stared at the inscription. "Must be a poem."

He leaned back in his chair. "How do you know?"

I shrugged. "There's a comma and then a capital. Second line in a poem. But which?" I stared harder. The first word might be *I* or maybe *It. I trust … I travel …* No, that didn't make sense. *If?* I've always loved that line from Anton Chekov: *If my life can ever be of any use to you, come and take it.* But that wasn't a poem, and it didn't work with the rest of the letters.

If … If what?

There's Rudyard Kipling's poem, but that's something a father would write to a son on graduation day, not what a boyfriend would inscribe on a birthday present. Hmm …

If …

I let my eyes travel ahead to the three *M*s.

Meet me. Move me.

Marry me.

No. That wasn't it.

The second line proved much easier to solve. Once I figured out the last four words, I worked backwards to see if the rest would fit. It did. *If these delights thy mind may move, Then live with me, and be my love.* It was from *The Passionate Shepherd to His Love*, the kind of poem I would normally find too quaint and simple if it weren't for this painting I once saw. In it, a young shepherd boy and small shepherdess are caught out in a rainstorm. He's taken off his coat and is shielding her from the downpour as they run to shelter.

I must have googled five dozen different descriptions of that image over the years, even called the museum where I first saw it in a traveling display. I can't for the life of me find out who painted it or get my hands on a copy. It's like a phantom, existing only in the recesses of my memory banks. That picture has remained my favorite piece of art, perhaps for no other reason than its perfect elusiveness. I can never hear the *Passionate Shepherd* poem without thinking of it.

Chris couldn't believe I'd figured the lines out that quickly. "How did you do it?"

I shrugged. "Because you already know what I like." I was so happy I'd solved the clue and exultant about my new gift, I didn't stop to wonder why Chris had gotten out of his chair and leaned down over me from behind.

"Ok. Let's see if you can decipher this." He took the pen, my brand new Lamy 2000, and set it in my grasp. With trembling fingers — why didn't I ask myself then why he was shaking? — he moved my hand to form four simple letters on the wrapping paper.

I stared. "What's this?"

"Don't you remember Kitty and Levin?" His cheek was so smooth against mine, his body so near I felt each and every quiver. He pointed to the letters. "Isn't this how they did it in *Anna Karenina*?"

"How they did what?" I was whispering. I remember that part so vividly. But why was I whispering?

"How Levin proposed to Kitty."

I stared a little longer at the letters. It looked like his handwriting, not mine, but more unsteady. More uncertain. Those four letters in Chris's slanted script.

He was on his knee.

The ring was in his hand.

I told him my answer. I didn't write it. I spoke it out loud.

"Yes."

Such a small word. I can still recall with perfect clarity the way it somehow warbled in my throat. I was still trying to whisper. I can't remember why.

But I told him yes.

I couldn't have replied anything else.

Not that I would have wanted to.

And even though I'm far from the biggest Jane Eyre fan you'll ever meet, you'll pardon me when I steal her words to tell you about the next stage in our better-than-story-books, soon-to-be-curtailed happiness.

Reader, I married him.

CHAPTER 9

You want to know why I refused the first time you suggested I write all this out? Want me to tell you? Look at me. Look at me right now and you'll know.

Look at where I am.

The women's shelter. Again.

The women's shelter in God-ought-to-forget it Orchard Grove, Washington, land of apple trees, cowboy wannabes, and conservative fogies all lining up for Sunday services. All ready to prove to God they're giving him their best. Their best clothes, their best accessories, their best behavior.

Didn't I warn you? Didn't I tell you this is exactly what would happen?

I couldn't do it. I started writing about our wedding day. It seemed the most logical step in the story, didn't it? The next stage in the saga that you were so eager for me to scribble out.

You told me for months I should do it. And I argued, and

I cried, and I swore to you that if I put pen to paper and got out even the first little fragment of our convoluted history, it would be the end of me. Maybe you thought I was being melodramatic.

You were wrong.

Dead wrong.

You know the worst part about being delivered from that demon of suicide or whatever it was you did to me that day in church? You probably think you saved my life, junk like that. You know what you really did? You took away my only consolation.

Suicidal thoughts gave me hope. Maybe you think that's just the sign of how sick and twisted my mind had become, and I'm not about to argue with you. But you know what's worse than lying on a cold mattress for a month imagining the different ways you'd kill yourself if you had the strength to roll out of bed? It's lying on a cold mattress for a month knowing that even once you get up, even once you crawl through hell yet another time and survive and start functioning again, it's only a matter of time before the cycle repeats itself.

Another trigger.

Another episode.

Another wasted month.

Wasted year.

Wasted life.

With no end, no reprieve in sight. That's what you did to me. You murdered the only hope I had left, hope that maybe one day I would find the energy to end it all.

Your prayers saved me from thoughts of suicide, but they weren't enough to deliver me from the depression. They weren't enough to keep my husband by my side. They weren't enough to keep me and my daughter together. So it's one point for you, three points for the darkness.

The hopelessness.

The despair.

Sorry, but that's a pretty pathetic track record no matter how you look at it. Maybe that's why I'm so drawn to Poe these days. *And the Raven, never flitting, still is sitting, STILL IS SITTING.* I can hear the desperation, the crescendo in the poet's voice. Can feel it in my spine.

Will you ever leave me in peace?

Will you ever take your cursed memory and go away?

And in the stillness, I hear the response. Know with both certainty and dread that I've already received my answer.

Nevermore.

CHAPTER 10

I've seen so many different counselors and therapists over the last year, it's gotten hard to tell them apart. Their faces, something about their expressions, morph into one another in my mind so I have a hard time remembering if Dr. Klarson is the redhead with the strawberry blonde goatee and the moose head above his office desk or if that's Dr. Carter and Dr. Klarson is the jolly-looking one with the little pot-belly threatening to burst out of his shirt that only manages to stay buttoned by an odd miracle.

Today's meeting is with someone new, a Dr. Jacob (last name, not first). At least I won't get her confused with Dr. Klarson and Dr. Carter and all those other middle-aged men. She's the slim, professional type. Look up stock photos for *business woman* online and you'll see about nine thousand copies of her with various shades of skin tone and hair color. She's got the whole look down — dark nylons, high heels that scream femininity mingled precariously with professionalism. Tailored skirt suit, size eight if I had to guess, even though she'd be a lot more comfortable in a ten. The only distinction between her and any other businesswoman is a purple and black beaded barrette in her hair. I wonder if she goes to craft shows on the weekends.

"Thank you so much for stopping by to see me," she says, as if I had any choice.

I simply nod. My only goal is to get through this meeting so I have a place to live one more week. I've gotten so used to surviving from day to day that the thought of being taken care of for seven feels like the epitome of upward mobility.

Dr. Jacob buries her head in my file. It's short, no medical records for her to sift through since I didn't give the intake folks at Sacred Meadows my real name. I glance quickly at her oversized clock, the kind with imposing Roman numerals marking the four corners, and then back to her. I give this meeting twenty-five minutes max.

Twenty-five minutes and I'll have earned my seven-day stay.

She clears her throat. It sounds awkward. Forced. We're both petite women, she and I, but I outweigh her now. It's the meds. Makes it near impossible to lose those last ten pounds of baby fat.

Not that there's anyone to impress at a place like Sacred Meadows.

"So tell me," she begins. It's just like all those other conversations I've had with all those other strangers who believe that a few fancy letters after their names grants them the right to probe into my psyche. Into my past. These doctors all begin their discussions the same way. *So tell me ...*

She's still looking at my file, and I pick up on the fact that she's lazy. She might dress for the part of a seven-figure executive at some Fortune 500 something-or-other, but she's here at a shelter for battered women, probably taking a huge pay cut or maybe doing this *pro bono* on her days off. That's why she hasn't bothered to read my file before she strikes up this conversation.

She doesn't know me. She doesn't really want to. She's here because she's got a time card to punch or because she's got some sense of duty to the shelter or to God. I'm here because the resident advisor told me I either had to attend group or meet one-on-one with a psychologist. And I've been in places like this enough times to know that group's a joke. All the women ever do is sniff their noses and share their sniveling stories about the horrible men who beat them and bruise them and then come begging on their knees for forgiveness.

Which is why I decided to meet with Dr. Jacob, and I hope she remains as disinterested as she looks. Friday night. Who knows? I don't see a wedding ring, so maybe she's got some hot date waiting to pick her up right at five.

I should be so lucky.

"It says here you're from Orchard Grove? A local girl." She smiles. As if it's something to be proud of. She fumbles past another page. "And you're living with your husband?"

"Lived." I'm quick to use the past tense.

"Of course. That's right." She's staring at the top corner of a blank piece of paper as if my entire life history were revealing itself to her there. "Well, why don't we start with him? Why don't you tell me about your husband. Tell me about …" Her eyes scan the form.

"Chris." His name falls dead from my lips. I wonder what I should say. Does she want the sob story about the central Washington nobody who married her larger-than-life boyfriend only to find out that a wedding ring didn't solve his anger problems? Maybe she'd rather I play the part of the enabler, suffering through her husband's issues because *he's so good to me when he's not angry*. She's heard all these stories. Dime a dozen at a place like this.

I'll tell her something. Anything for the chance to spend a full week here. Sacred Meadow's no B&B, but I've never been all that high-maintenance. I've got a bed, and if I'm lucky I'll find a roommate who doesn't have a passel of scared, whiney brats with her. I receive three meals a day, and all I have to do is see Dr. Jacob once a week and tell her about why I've left my husband.

Easy, right?

I should be so lucky.

CHAPTER 11

Dr. Jacob asks about my medical past. I wonder how much she really wants to know. I'm still not sure if she's interested in my story or if she's just doing her job to get her Brownie points with God. I usually get a pretty good feel for people. Comes from all those novels I read. Dr. Jacob is still something of an enigma, but I don't mind.

Gives me more to puzzle over while she probes into my past.

First it's the pills. She wants to know exactly what drugs I'm on, as if she's some kind of MD and not just a shrink.

Then it's when the depression started, if I've ever felt suicidal. I lie and tell her no.

Then she asks the most stupid question of all. She sits forward in that great big mahogany chair and asks, "What have you found that helps your depression?"

As if I had an answer for her. Although I guess I have learned some things as a result of my battle with this demon. I'm not using that term in the same way folks at Valley

Tabernacle would, by the way. I don't literally think there's a demon sitting on my shoulder, whispering dark thoughts into my ear. Maybe I'm wrong. It certainly wouldn't be the first time. I'm not about to put God in a box, not about to pretend like I know what causes depression or how to get over it. But the way I figure, if it was something as simple as a real and literal demon, I should be able to pray it away, except this sickness in me won't be dismissed so easily. Don't you think I've tried that route?

There are so many things scientists don't know about depression. It's the same with philosophers and theologians, too. If depression could be completely understood, it could be destroyed. Like a virus. There'd be some kind of immunization, some kind of cure. Certain remedies take the edge off, like my meds, but nothing's come close to healing me.

Some people in the general public — the ones who've never walked through the valleys that I have — look at depression and treat it like something so simplistic. I'm talking about the folks who tell me I should just decrease clutter in my life or walk outside twenty minutes a day and I'll be perfectly functional. Normal.

Then there are the people who assume that depression means sadness or grief, but they're dead wrong. I've grieved without succumbing to depression, and I've also been laid up in bed for weeks for no logical reason whatsoever. And depression's not a sign of faulty faith like some Christians claim, either. Trust me. I've looked for those connections, those clues. Don't you think if it was as simple as confessing my sins or making sure I didn't carry around anger in my heart that I would have beaten this thing by now? Don't you think that if memorizing a couple Scripture passages about joy would have given me relief, I'd have learned the entire New Testament by heart?

I don't mean to get so worked up, by the way. I just hate it — and yes, I know that's a strong word, but God uses it in the book of Proverbs all the time, so you really can't tell me not to. I hate it when people tell me what I should be doing to *get over* depression. Like it's some sort of cold or flu virus and if you take the right vitamins and drink enough fluids, you'll be better in a couple of days. Depression's not something you *get over*. It's something you live with. It's part of you, right there in your core. It's so interwound in your psyche that there's really no way to tell where you end and it begins. It's a classic parasite, incorporating into your sense of self so seamlessly that you wouldn't even know who you are apart from it.

Sometimes it lies dormant. I've gone a whole year before without crashing. You can hope it's gone, but deep in your soul you know it's still there. In your darkest thoughts, you can sense it waiting, biding its time. Depression's patient if it's anything. It doesn't need to hurry because it knows that when it comes to claim you, there's no way you can resist. You might fight for a day or two, might struggle valiantly and make it a whole week before you finally crash, but depression knows. It *knows* that your endurance will only carry you so far. It's the trained heavyweight champion of the world going up against an eight-year-old schoolyard bully. When it decides your time has come, you can put up a fight of epic proportions, but you'll still succumb in the end. It sucks your energy dry, feeds on your mental clarity until all that's left is fog and darkness.

And you wait, because your adversary's taught you the art of patient endurance. You wait, because you know the blackness won't last forever. The monster will eventually loosen its grip, allow you to breathe again. Think clear, rational thoughts once more.

Just as long as you don't forget that one day, it will come back to feed on your sense of self until you're so enmeshed in the blackness you're nothing but a shadow. A shadow without a home, without a history.

A shadow without a name.

CHAPTER 12

I wonder what Dr. Jacob is thinking by this point as I ramble on. She probably assumes my depression is all related to my marriage problems. That I made a huge mistake, married my high-school sweetheart, and wound up in the ER or something so many times that eventually I left him in the middle of the night and fled here. It's the type of story she must listen to week in and week out at a shelter like this.

I feel like I should defend Chris whenever she asks about him, but if I do that, she's just going to lump me into the same category as those mousey girls in group, the ones who go on and on about how *he's so much kinder to me when he's not stressed out at work, and I just need to find a way to keep from irritating him.* Says the girl with three broken ribs, a black eye, and a dislocated jaw.

I know I'm being pretty closed off with Dr. Jacob, and I don't mean to. I'm only talking to her so I won't get kicked out of Sacred Meadows. I think we both know that. I'm just here doing my time like she is. Telling this stranger my sob story, getting my meal ticket for another seven days, and finally leaving her office no worse off and certainly no better.

I'm still not sure how much I'm going to tell her. It's all about choices. I have so few of those left to me these days. Even in the dining room, we don't get to pick what we eat. It's not like a school cafeteria where you can choose what kind of sandwich you want or which sides you'll have with it. Here, it's soup. And if it's not soup, it's casserole. You don't select your own sides because they're all cooked together in one blob. The only thing you get to choose is whether you want one scoop or two.

Maybe you'll tell me I shouldn't complain, but you're the one who can drive anywhere you want in your own car and select your dinner menu every single night. Eat out, cook in, you probably have no idea how lucky you are. You've heard about prison inmates, I'm sure, how they get institutionalized so by the time they're released — especially the ones who go in as teens and come out middle-aged — they have absolutely no idea how to function in the real world.

How to think or make choices for themselves.

I've made my choices. That's what landed me here. And

I'll fess up to each and every one. I'm not so jaded and bitter I'll go blaming everything on someone else. That's not my style. Mostly because I still love Chris, at least in a way. Sure, when I say that, Dr. Jacob might roll those big doe eyes at me. Throw a label on my forehead and lump me together with all those other women she talks to at the shelter, the ones who we all know are destined to return to their abusers the second they step out of here.

That's not me. But like I said before, the more I try to defend my husband, the guiltier I'm going to appear, so I'll just have to let my story speak for itself. Right now, she wants to know about our early days. How we ended up married. I can't believe how young we were. How unprepared to forge a life together.

Well, she'll see.

And then she can make up her own mind about Chris and me.

CHAPTER 13

We got married between semesters during our senior year of college. The date's slowly creeping up on us, actually. Almost our anniversary.

Mom was shocked when I told her we wanted to marry in Spokane. She'd always dreamed her little girl would walk down the aisle of Orchard Grove. But I swear the architect who designed that church must have been a grumpy and dour soul. I don't know this for sure, although the congregational records are so exhaustive, I could probably find everything I wanted to know about him in the business meeting minutes if I looked back far enough. The building itself is a squat, imposing, boxy sort of cube with a steeple, utterly lacking in imagination, as if its sole purpose was to remind you that earth's not the place to be hunting around for beauty or grace.

My mom and I have gotten into dozens of spats over the years, but the wedding question was one of the most epic. She couldn't understand why the daughter of the town's first and only Chinese gynecologist would want to get married anywhere else besides Orchard Grove, surrounded by fat gossips and retired orchardists. I tried explaining to her that the purpose of a theme wedding is to have not only the bridal party but all the guests attired a certain way, and stickler as I am for historical accuracy, I couldn't picture Chris's Dickens-inspired frock coat, neck stock, and top hat fitting in alongside men in pressed jeans and collared shirts and ties or women pretending to belong to a 1950s *Good Housekeeping* magazine ad.

It didn't fully sink in until I showed Mom my Victorian wedding dress and the sketches I'd come up with for her mother-of-the-bride outfit. That was what finally changed her mind, truth be told, just like I knew it would. There was no way my fiercely staid and oh-so-proper mother would want any of her missionary league friends to see her in a period getup like that.

After that, she backed out of the wedding planning completely. Daddy's strength was failing with each day, but he could still sign checks, checks my mother would never see since she firmly believed that managing the family finances was beneath her role as a housewife. Daddy set the budget, but we both knew I could at least double the amount as long as every so often I sent him private emails with pictures of the arrangements so he could see how the plans were shaping up.

What we both knew and both refused to say was that the chances of him making it to the ceremony diminished with every doctor visit he took. When Chris and I first got engaged, we planned to marry right after graduation. Then we moved the date up to spring break and finally settled on the week before Christmas.

The wedding itself was everything I hoped it would be. Jinny, the planner, took my fairly rough sketches for a Victorian England, book-inspired ceremony and outdid herself. You can still go to her website and see the work in her portfolio. Maybe it sounds like I'm bragging, but it was Chris and my wedding that really put Jinny's Nuptials on the map.

It wasn't difficult for either of us to decide on the location. Lots of people marry in the Spokane Modern Art Gallery, but we were the first couple — at least as far as the seventy-something-year-old curator could remember — to hold their ceremony in the library where, surrounded by a few dozen friends and a few thousand rare editions, we said our vows. Jinny found beautiful calligraphy prints on white fabric, excerpts from our favorite stories. Through the curtains by the windows and draped across the chairs down the aisles, our wedding guests included Steinbeck, Dostoevsky, Poe, and Hugo. Our unity candle was sculpted to look like two calligraphy pens bent down together in the shape of a heart, and the tablecloth beneath it bore in beautiful script the scene from *Anna Karenina* where Levin takes Kitty's hand and writes out his proposal in abbreviated letters, an homage to our own engagement.

The reception was just as literarily inspired, with beautiful origami cranes folded from the pages of hundred-year-old classics. The only way I agreed to allow books to undergo such egregious sacrilege was when Jinny found an old grumpy heir whose father left him an entire antique library. Most of the volumes were water-damaged and not fit to be sold. I made Jinny promise that after our ceremony, she'd put the decorations in storage. I'd much rather think of those book pages sitting in a heated space unit instead of meeting their destruction at the hands of a selfish ignoramus.

She also took several book covers and made elaborate centerpieces for each of the tables. Every grouping had its own theme. The American classics a la Steinbeck and Hemmingway at the table with Chris's aunts and uncles on his father's side. Victorian-era romances where my few college friends joined our celebration. I asked Daddy what he wanted by his seat, and that centerpiece turned out to be the only one that wasn't perfectly organized by genre, era, and country. He wanted Mary Shelley's *Frankenstein* ("because, let's face it, with my hair fallen out and this colostomy bag hanging down by my side, that's what I look like"), *Moby Dick* ("because even though I could turn this ordeal into my own personal white whale, I'm not going to get bitter like that Captain Ahab fellow"), and what I found to be the most depressing selection of them all, *The Old Man and the Sea* ("because you and I know how hard I've had to fight to make it to your big day, and that's all that matters, not what anyone else thinks about me").

He was there, colostomy bag and wheelchair and everything. He insisted — he and I insisted together, even though Mom was convinced we'd both look like fools — on the father-daughter dance. "I Will Always Love You." Whitney Houston. A strange choice for a wedding, you might think, seeing as how it's a break-up song.

A goodbye song.

But that's what it was, and Daddy and I both knew it, even though we never said so.

Two weeks later, Mom insisted Chris and I go through a more traditional ceremony all over again at Orchard Grove since certain people in town were convinced we were living in sin until we had a proper church wedding. There were no book decorations at this one. No bowties folded out of Hemingway passages or boutonnieres made from the pages of *Wuthering Heights*, no silver candlestick holders in the style of those the bishop gave to Jean Valjean in the opening of *Les Misérables*.

No father-daughter dance either, with Daddy's full-time nurse wheeling him around in his chair so we could both imagine he was spinning me off my feet.

No goodbye song.

Daddy had already soared away.

He was already gone.

CHAPTER 14

I know there's little to be proud of when it comes to depression. Nothing honorable about sleeping twenty-three hours out of every day. But there is a small dignity in walking through grief and not succumbing fully to darkness and despair.

I think maybe one of the reasons I handled Daddy's death without crashing completely was because Chris was so supportive. Sure, he was intimidated. Sure, he felt guilty. Who wouldn't? You marry your high-school sweetheart, and a week later she's so broken-hearted she can't shuffle to the bathroom without crying. But looking back and knowing what I know now about depression, that's a good thing. If I cry, that means I can still feel something. Crying means I have a channel for my sadness.

Weeping may remain for the night, but rejoicing comes in the morning. Or in four or five months, as the case may be.

But I was grateful to have Chris to love me and hold my hand through that time. He'd come home from class (he was the only one of us who was able to finish that last semester), fix us a quick dinner, and spend the rest of the evening cuddling me. Reminding me he was there. He didn't try to make stupid chit-chat. *How do you feel? Do you want to talk about it? You must miss him a lot, don't you?*

He was just there. Like Job's three friends who were smart enough to hold their tongues, at least at the beginning.

I didn't know how to go on without Daddy. I hated him sometimes. He was so strong. He fought that cancer with every ounce of strength left in his frail, hundred-and-twenty-pound body. Fought it so that he could be at my wedding. So he could dance with me in his wheelchair.

Why couldn't he have fought just a little bit harder?

Teng "Donald" Shin, Orchard Grove County's first Chinese gynecologist, died peacefully at home after a long battle with colon cancer. That's what Mom wrote for his obituary. *Long battle.* What a stupid euphemism. *Long battle.* Makes it sound like something you'd read about in J. R. R. Tolkien — elves and dwarves and hobbits fighting orcs and trolls.

Long battle. So what does that mean? That Daddy lost?

People like him don't lose. He made it all the way to my wedding when the doctors only gave him three months after he came out of remission. He stretched out those last and final weeks, striving tooth and nail for his survival.

And Mom goes and writes that he *died peacefully after a long battle.*

Daddy was always the book-lover in the family. Mom was just as happy with her missionary league's Bible study material as anything else, but Daddy was the bibliophile. I'd sit and read to him those last few weeks. Poetry mostly, because my voice couldn't make it through long prose, not when it felt like I had a lump in my throat the size of his second tumor.

Do not go gentle into that good night.

"Daddy, why won't you listen to me?"

Do not go gentle ...

"You don't really want to go, do you? I know you hurt. I know you're ready for heaven. But what about me? You don't really want to say goodbye, do you?"

Into that good night ...

"What about me and Chris? What about the novels I'm going to write? How can you give up and miss all that?"

Rage.

Rage.

But Daddy lived his entire life in peace with himself, with God, and with others. In the end, he even made peace with the cancer.

And that's when I had to learn to say goodbye.

CHAPTER 15

I shouldn't have been so forthcoming with the shrink. Told her so much about my past, about losing Daddy. I regret it as soon as the words leave my mouth. First of all, it's none of her business. Even if I really did come to Sacred Meadows to escape an abusive husband, not just to find a place to sleep, wouldn't our time be better spent talking about that? I watch Dr. Jacob lean back in her chair and study me. I really need to be more cautious. Why did I let my guard down like that?

And now we're back on Chris.

"So your husband was violent with his temper?" Dr. Jacob ascribes to the school of psychology that encourages its counselors to rephrase everything their patients say, making them repeat the same stories multiple times.

"Yes." Much as I would rather be exposing myself to a physical exam at the gynecologist's, I shouldn't complain. Dr. Jacob is only doing her job.

"And did he ever hurt you?" I've answered this question five times just in the past two days since I got here, and I've denied it each time, but now I feel compelled to tell her something that will prove I've got a right to stay here at a shelter for battered women.

"Well, there were some issues in the bedroom." I'm staring at my hands in my lap. Dr. Jacob keeps a selection of stress balls and weighted trinkets on her desk, and I'm currently pulling on the little strands of a funny animal with stretchy strings that poke out like innocuous quills on a round porcupine.

"Do you want to talk about that side of it?" she asks.

"No. Not really."

I squeeze the ball until one of the bug's eyes pop out to the side. I keep on picking at the strings while I wait for the next round of questioning. I'm sure Dr. Jacob can tell I'm shutting down.

"Parts of it were hard, but we had our good times too."

"In the bedroom?" she asks.

"No." I try to hide my surprise that this was her assumption. "No, I just mean in general."

She leans back in her chair. "Tell me about some of the good times, then. What were those like?"

"We went on a vacation once. Nothing much, just stayed at a nice little B&B in Leavenworth. They had a hot tub there with a glass ceiling so you could look at the stars."

"That sounds romantic."

Again, I'm surprised at her choice of words. "I guess. It was just nice."

"And did he get angry at you on that trip?"

I wonder why everything has to come down to Chris and his rage. Doesn't she realize our life, our marriage was far more three-dimensional than she's making it out to be?

"Nothing big that I can remember."

Another pause. At my most cynical, I wonder if this is a trick they teach psychologists who charge by the hour. "And would you remember? If something big happened?"

"What do you mean?"

"Some women, some survivors of abuse for example, find it hard to recall certain details …"

I cut her off before she can say more. "No, nothing like that."

I'm squeezing the little porcupine ball so hard both of its eyes as well as its tail area are bursting out like balloons inflated to twice their recommended size.

"That kind of stuff didn't happen with us," I say.

"I'm glad to hear it."

I should let her change the subject, but I can't let it drop for some reason. "I remember it all. I haven't blacked anything out."

She's not smiling. She's staring at me squarely. "Ok." She pulls her eyes away to take a sip of tea. She's already offered me a drink, and I've already refused, but she asks, "Are you sure I can't get you a cup?"

"I'm sure."

She takes another slow sip. The silence is drawn-out enough that my core has started to tremble. If I don't get myself under control, my shoulders and limbs will start shaking next. I'm glad for the bulky sweater that hides how worked up I am. At least I hope it does.

She reaches across the desk and touches me on my sleeve. The weight of her fingers make me jump in my chair. I yank my arm back and pull it against my chest.

"Are you upset?"

I bite my lip and shake my head. "I'm really tired. I'm ready to be done."

She looks at me once out of the corner of her eye. "I think it might be better if we talked a little more. Ten minutes?"

"I'm sorry." I scoot my chair back noisily. I'm shaking so much it almost falls to the floor. "I'm not feeling well. I really have to go."

I hurry out the room, trying not to think of her worried stare following me down the hall. I take a choppy inhale. Breathe. I just need to breathe.

Back in the safety of my room, I lock the door and slink down against the wall. I cover my face.

Dr. Jacob is wrong. My problem isn't one of too few memories.

It's one of too many.

CHAPTER 16

Another Friday, which means I've managed to stay off the streets for another seven days. Maybe you think that's strange since I'm so close to my mom's I could walk to her place and be there in half an hour. Maybe you wonder why I haven't called and asked to stay there while I get back on my feet. Which obviously means you haven't met her yet.

Mom thinks I'm still living at Chris's place. She doesn't know we foreclosed a year ago. When she complained to me that creditors were calling her house looking for me, I made up some excuse about a medical bill insurance had guaranteed to pay. As if I've been on any kind of insurance except Medicaid. But of course, you can't tell that to the widow of Orchard Grove's first and only Chinese gynecologist. Anyway, the less I think about Mom, the safer I am from another full-fledged attack of depression, so we'll leave it at that for now.

It's Friday morning, and I've got to meet again with Dr. Jacob this afternoon. She wants me to write out my past, specifically my past with Chris. I have no idea how long she expects it to be. I hate these kinds of assignments. I still don't know what to tell her, how much of the truth she wants to know. Still don't know where I can find the energy to make up a story about my husband and the way he may or may not have mistreated me when we were together.

At this point, I'm not even sure it's worth it. I don't have to stay at the shelter anymore. There's a girl I met at Sacred Meadows, Mel. I guess you could say we became friends. She's gotten herself out of here and told me I could stay with her if I wanted. She's doing all right. Looks like she may have even kicked that no-good boyfriend of hers out for the last time.

Funny coincidence is we actually went to high school together even though she was three years ahead of me. When we met up again at the shelter, it was awkward at first. I knew she looked familiar, and I could tell she recognized me too, but this isn't the sort of place where you just walk up to someone and strike up a friendship like if you'd bumped into each other at a coffee shop.

But anyway, we started hanging out in the cafeteria, eating our bland casseroles side by side. She'd dropped out of college, too. And if that's not enough to have in common, her mom's a widow living in Orchard Grove Heights. Small world, eh?

So Mel's been out of the shelter since Wednesday, and she's doing pretty well for herself. She finally told her deadbeat of a baby daddy to get lost, and who knows? Maybe this time he'll stay gone for good. She's sweet to invite me to move in with her, but it's not just altruism. She's a bus driver, which is somewhat surprising because she's five-foot-nothing and all of a hundred and ten pounds. And she sits behind the wheel of this huge yellow school bus, schlepping loud, snot-nosed brats around. Has to get out of the house at 5:30 every morning, and her kids' daycare is charging her a fortune for the early hours. So she told me that if I watch the kids while she's on the road, we'll count that as my room and board.

Win-win, right?

So I'm thinking about it. I know she could use the help. Three kids, two still in diapers. And there's no way she'll ever get a nickel out of Kai, that no-good ex of hers. I just don't know if I can handle being around kids right now, especially the baby. She's just two months younger than little Gracie …

I think it might be too much.

But it's nice to have a fallback plan. Some sort of option. Because if Dr. Jacob puts her foot down, if she realizes I don't belong at Sacred Meadows, at least I'll have somewhere to go. I just have to make up my mind before too long or else Mel may find someone else.

Not that I know of too many people desperate enough to share a trailer the size of a studio apartment with a colicky baby, whiney toddler, and painfully inquisitive preschooler. But you never know. I'm not usually one to sit on my hands waiting for life to take care of me. So I'm leaning toward moving in with Mel, but like I said, we'll see what happens.

I just hope she doesn't get so nosy with her questions about my past. Mel's the poster child for an abuse victim, but I'm not. I came to Sacred Meadows because I need a place to sleep, a chance to get back on my feet. My being at this shelter has a lot more to do with my issues and faults than anything Chris said or did to me. See, I told you I could take responsibility for my own actions. I'm not so big of a mess that I'm only looking for a scapegoat. But sometimes I wonder if our marriage was doomed because of who we were intrinsically or if it had more to do with the myriad plot twists that life hurled our way. I guess there's no way to know for sure, is there?

I had a dream about you last night. Weird, isn't it? Dreamed I was back at Valley Tabernacle. Chris wasn't there, which is funny because he was always more into that Holy Ghost stuff than I was. Always a lot more comfortable at your church, whereas I'm probably bound to attend places like Orchard Grove for the rest of my life. How's that proverb go? *Like a dog returns to its vomit ...*

Maybe that's why you took his side. Maybe that's why you told me I just had to submit to his authority and everything would turn out ok. Maybe that's why I'm here, trapped in this shelter for battered women, even though my husband never hit me.

Not even once.

CHAPTER 17

Dr. Jacob is wearing wide-rimmed glasses today, the kind that would make most women look dowdy, but she's well-dressed and young enough to pull it off, even though they slip down her nose like a pair of spectacles as we talk about my past.

"So you both went to different colleges?" she asks as she reads what I managed to write about Chris.

"Yeah, but he transferred to Spokane our junior year."

She nods without a hint of surprise, so I wonder if she's already read that part and is just saying something to fill in the silence.

"And your episode with the depression? You think that was because you'd been apart for a year?" There's a slight trace of incredulity in her voice. I try to guess her age. Mid-thirties? Has she ever been married? Is she another one of those shrinks who thinks ours is just a tragic case of young love gone wrong?

"There was more to it than that," I begin, but she's already moved on to the next part.

"*To Kill a Mockingbird*?" She raises her eyebrows, but I'm not sure why. I decide not to say anything else unless she asks me an actual question. I hate this part of writing. It's one of the reasons I dropped the creative writing minor in school. To sit still while strangers dissect your soul, to know that after a few minutes of silence comes the inevitable brutalization of your manuscript. Everyone telling you what to cut out, what to add in.

I'd rather subject myself to a tooth extraction every day of my life than endure this degree of scrutiny.

But at least the humiliation of writing all this out helped me make up my mind. I'm leaving the shelter first thing tomorrow and moving in with Mel, at least for a little bit. I got in touch with her earlier today. It's all planned out. So I'll have a place to stay as long as my nerves can handle sharing a trailer with all those kids. I don't know how long it will last, honestly, but if I want to stay out of Sacred Meadows, I've got to try to make it work.

And it will be helping out a friend, too. That's what I keep saying to psych myself up to become a live-in nanny for three needy children who aren't my own.

I'm helping out a friend.

Dr. Jacob clears her throat. It's the only habit of hers that isn't decisively feminine. "Well," she begins, "I can see you spent a lot of time on this." She doesn't know I whipped it out in about fifteen minutes. After writing everything here to you, scribbling a page and a half for the shrink was easy as reading a Hemingway short story after you've just finished *War and Peace*.

She sets my papers down on the table in front of her. Here it comes. How I got it all wrong. The list of things I left out that should have been in. The even longer list of things I put in that should have been left out. It's like I'm sitting in *Creative Writing 101* all over again.

"It's a lovely story, at least the parts you've included here." Her voice trails off, like she's inviting me to jump in and add something. Like what? She offers a conciliatory smile. "You were very honest."

I want to laugh. If she only knew. I have a lot of character strengths, but honesty isn't one of them.

Dr. Jacob leans back in her chair. Takes off her granny glasses. "I'd love to hear more about what happened right after you and Chris got married."

Apparently, honesty isn't her strongest virtue either. I don't reply.

"Would you like to make that your assignment for next week? Write out what came next?" She asks the question directly, but there's a gentleness in her voice. "Or maybe you could tell me more about Justin?"

When she mentions his name, my spine tenses. "Actually, this is my last night here."

"Oh?" Some people can cram so much judgement into a single syllable. Take my mother for example. But Dr. Jacob just says the word and leaves it at that.

"Yeah," I continue. "I've decided to move in with a friend for a little while. She needs a babysitter. We're going to see how it works out."

"What about your depression?"

"What about it?"

"Do you feel ready to take care of kids all day? It can be very tiring."

"Yeah." I'm only partially listening. I'm making a mental list of what I've got to do so I'm ready to leave Sacred Meadows after breakfast tomorrow.

Dr. Jacob smiles warmly. "Well, if you decide to write more of your story out and don't mind an audience, you're welcome to contact me through the shelter."

I have a hard time deciding if she's just being polite or if this is a valid invitation to share more of my life with her. I offer a non-committal, "I might do that," suffer through a few more questions that don't really get us anywhere, then stand.

I can't get out of here soon enough.

CHAPTER 18

I doubt even God wakes up at five in the morning. I remember back when I was a kid. Mom would burst through my door like a tsunami every day at six sharp, straightening up my piles of laundry, clucking her tongue over the wadded paper scraps on my nightstand, grumbling in Cantonese as she tidied up the clutter on my desk. Maybe that's why I have such a hard time staying organized today. Mom always handled all that stuff for me.

It's not like she wouldn't still do that for me now, actually. I can't tell you how many times she calls to try to convince me to move in with her. She always makes it about me, which is why I refuse. If she were to come right out and say something like, *you know, it's awful lonely here, and I would love to have you come spend more time with me*, I might feel more inclined. Some mothers are masters at subtle manipulation, but I'm pretty sure the word *subtle* isn't even in Mom's vocabulary (English or Cantonese). It's just as well. Me living under the same roof as my mother is a toxic combination and has been ever since I hit puberty, which as luck would have it was the same year she started getting hot flashes. I'm surprised Daddy survived the two of us.

More accurately, I'm surprised we survived each other.

So here I am at Mel's. I got settled in over the weekend, and today was my first shift watching her kids while she did the early-morning bus route. I don't think I anticipated the amount of sheer energy it takes to listen to a baby scream. There was nothing wrong with her. I kept her dry and fed all morning long, but other than a twenty-minute nap around nine, she fussed the entire time. Mel says she's going through separation anxiety, which probably explains why little Jasmine was perfect once her mom got home. She promptly took a bottle and lay down for a two-hour nap. Lucky me, she woke up in time to say goodbye to her mom as soon as she had to go out again to take all those school kids home.

It's evening now, and neither Mel nor I have energy to cook anything. Our agreement was I'd watch the kids in exchange for room and board, but I think she was expecting the entire package deal. If she wants a maid and a chef as well as a babysitter, she should go find herself a housewife. Or maybe one of those stay-at-home dads.

I'm exhausted. Physically and mentally worn out. It'd be one thing if it was just Jasmine's crying I had to contend with, but Gabby (the toddler) is in the process of getting toilet trained (actually, Mel's in the process of trying to make Gabby get toilet trained), so if I wasn't bouncing a screaming baby, I was wiping butts or singing little nursery-rhyme songs with a two-year-old who's too afraid to sit on the kiddy potty alone. And the entire day — I mean it literally, the *entire* day — Bowman followed me around like an obnoxious stray puppy who only knows how to use sentences that begin with the word *why*. He's already five and smart enough to find the contacts in my cell phone and nearly prank call my mother. That kid needs to be in school, but he missed the cutoff for kindergarten by just a few weeks.

His poor mom.

They say that whatever doesn't kill you makes you stronger, and if you're someone like Mel, they're probably right. I don't know how she managed to keep her kids alive on top of working those insane hours and dealing with her ex. She's had to learn to be tough. Life hasn't given her any other choice. That's why she can handle a bus full of fifty rambunctious kids or all of Bowman's incessant questions without losing her mind. Not me. I'm just now wrapping up my first day on the job, and I'm already thinking about quitting.

Of course, I might not be the babysitter right now, but I'm still here. Stuck in this tiny trailer. I'm happy for Mel getting Kai out of her life and all, but man, I wish she could afford something bigger than a single-wide.

Dinner tonight's Spagetti-Os straight from the can. I can't believe I'm about to say this, but I actually miss the casseroles at the shelter. I don't know why I complained so much there. Sacred Meadows was good for me. I needed that rest. I'm doing a little better now. I think writing out some of my story has helped. I guess that's why you told me to do it in the first place. At least it gives me something to focus on while Mel chases the kids around the apartment at night and tries to get them ready for bed. The way the two-year-old cries for her daddy, you'd think Mel was the most awful mother in the world for taking her kids away from him.

I can't stand it anymore. I can't handle the noise. I tell Mel I'm going out for a walk even though the sun's already set and her trailer's far from the so-called nice side of Orchard Grove. I don't care. I'll take my chances. I've got to get out of this house. Give my ears a break. Mel asks me to take the baby in the stroller, but I mumble something about walking down to the liquor store on the corner. I don't plan on getting a drink. I'm just trying to get away from the kids. Only for a little bit. I'll be there to help Mel in the morning when she has to get up before the crack of dawn and drive the school bus. But until then, I'm off the clock.

Twenty minutes. Just twenty minutes to myself, that's all I ask.

God knows I've earned it.

CHAPTER 19

There's something about depression, this self-propelling spiral. You start feeling tired, isolated, lonely, so you respond by locking yourself in your room and withdrawing even more from the world. The experts tell you to engage, find a hobby, call a friend, even take yourself out for a walk, but they don't realize that all of those activities require energy. Energy you don't have when the depression's sucking you dry.

Or they tell you to clean up. *People who live in cluttered houses are three times more likely to develop depression, studies find.* Did anyone stop to think that maybe the reason depressed people have dirty homes is that they're too exhausted to clean up?

So much of depression treatment these days is putting band-aids on the symptoms. Have you noticed that? Like telling the woman who's isolated herself from the world that all she has to do is join a pottery class or sign up for Pilates and she'll be back to her old chipper self. Or making folks who are prone to depression feel even worse because their homes aren't picture-perfect every moment of the day. The way I see it, you're not entitled to tell me how to help myself if you haven't struggled with depression firsthand. I'm not talking about feeling a little melancholy every now and then or developing a minor case of the blues. I'm talking about crawling inch by inch across the grimy bottom of a seemingly endless emotional pit where you sink into the muck like Jean Valjean in the sewers beneath Paris and there's no foothold there to pull yourself out.

Once you've experienced depression like that in its rawest, truest form, you're not about to go blabbing to others or telling them how to make things right. That's like giving a blind man written instructions on how to read Braille.

I haven't warned Mel yet. About the depression, I mean. I really should. But so far, it's just been casual comments and an encrypted allusion or two. One day we'll have to have that heart-to-heart — if I'm still around by then. I'm pretty lucky to be getting room and board free, but I honestly don't see Mel as the kind to be totally supportive and understanding the next time my brain decides to shut down. She's had a difficult lot — you've got to give her that. And sometimes that makes people compassionate and soft around the edges, and sometimes that makes them hard. Like leather. Mel's the leather type. If you were to hear her story, you'd know why. Like I said, I don't judge her. But I know

I need to think up some sort of contingency plan because my guess is the next crash won't be long in coming.

Thinking about my past with Chris hasn't helped either. I don't know what you were thinking when you told me to write everything out. What good did you expect would come from it? From rubbing salt into old wounds? The funny thing is now that I've started, it's almost all I can think about, especially when I'm out of the house and don't have Jasmine's incessant screaming or Bowman's relentless questions grating my ears.

It's a shame things turned out the way they did because Chris and I had such a good start. Such a solid foundation to our marriage. Isn't that what youth pastors and Christian parents are always telling their kids? *Put Christ at the center of your relationships, and everything will work out in the end.*

Well, we did everything right. Waited to have sex until our wedding night, the works. Do you know how hard that is to do in this day and age? Do you know how many Christians treat premarital sex like it's no big deal? I'm serious. All the conservative fogies at Orchard Grove would be shocked to read the statistics, they really would. That's not how Chris and I did it, though. We'd made ourselves a commitment, and we stuck to it. I'm not saying we were totally platonic or anything like that. Passion is still passion no matter what your religious convictions are, and we were two young, healthy kids madly in love with each other. So do you have any idea how much restraint it takes to do it right?

And you'd think after all that — after we jumped through all those hoops people hold up for teens who want to follow Christ into their twenty-something years — you'd think God would somehow bless us or reward us for our obedience. Guess it goes back to the whole thing about the rain falling on the just and the unjust. I swear that's got to be one of the most depressing verses in all of Scripture.

The night's getting cold. So far the winter's been a particularly nasty one. And here I was thinking global warming was going to mean I could stop worrying about things like a scarf and gloves.

I pop into the liquor store at the corner of Mel's trailer park. She really should start saving up to move her kids to a better neighborhood. I know she's got to go where the assistance will take her, but if she started saving up now …

Well, it's none of my business. I doubt I'll stick around long enough to see her life change at all. Time to be moving on soon. Get myself settled, hopefully before my brain shuts down again. I can do it. I know I can.

One day at a time, right?

That's what I keep telling myself.

One day at a time.

CHAPTER 20

I get back to Mel's trailer and pause at the front door. If that baby's screaming, I'm not going in. Thankfully, I don't hear Jasmine's colicky shrieks. I walk into the little five-by-five entryway that serves as the living room, dining room, and playroom all in one. And now that I've moved in, this will also become the guest bedroom once Mel brings the air mattress out. The place is far too small for five people to share, but I guess I'm in no position to complain.

Mel's in the hallway shouting directions at Bowman. "No, those are the hand wipes. I need the ones that say baby wipes."

"Which are the baby ones?" he shouts back.

"Look for the letter B." Mel's got Jasmine draped over her knee and is trying to clean out an explosive diaper without putting the child on the floor. I don't blame her, not after seeing what bugs are infesting this place. Set the baby down for half a minute and the cockroaches might carry her off.

"Which one's B?" Bowman yells from the room.

"The one with two bumps!" Mel's only paying partial attention to him since Gabby's on the kiddy toilet shouting that she needs to *go number two.* "So go," Mel sighs, resignation ripe in her voice.

"But that makes the bowl *dirty*."

I figure I should pitch in, and helping Bowman find baby wipes is the task least likely to drag me into contact with bodily fluids. I pull the box from the shelf and hand it to his mom. "Thank you," she breathes like I'm a stewardess on an airless plane and I've just strapped on her oxygen mask. I'm about to back my way into the kitchen when she looks up from the mustard-bomb of a diaper.

"Oh, your phone was ringing while you were out."

Great. I swear if it's my mom … I told her I was working extra shifts the past two weeks — she thinks I'm still employed — but that woman acts like she'll spontaneously combust if I let a full seven days pass without calling to check in.

It takes me several minutes to find my handbag in the tornadoesque mess that's my new home. I glance at the screen, relieved that it's not my mother who's been ringing. I stare at the name, wondering if the nighttime cold and darkness are worth the extra privacy.

From the bathroom, Gabby lets out a shrill shriek. "Mom, I got off the potty too soon and now I'm all *messy*!"

I open the front door and shut it gently behind me before hitting the return call button.

"Hello?" His voice is calm. Something about him reminds me of a lighthouse. Solid. Sturdy.

"Hey, it's me." I know every single cell comes with caller ID, but I'm still used to having to announce myself on the phone.

"Yeah, thanks for calling back." Justin's got this laid-back aura about him. If it weren't for his somewhat posh job as the CEO of his own graphic design company, you'd think he was made for life on the California beaches.

I chuckle nervously. I'm not sure why I'm always trying to prove to Justin I'm happy. "No problem. How's everything going?" I don't know if this is just a social call or if he has something particular to say.

"Things here are good. Excellent."

"Glad to hear it." It seems like whenever we talk, it takes a few minutes for us to get going. Drop the nervous pretenses. The scripted greetings.

"How are you doing?" he asks, and since he's the only person from my old life who knows I've been living at a women's shelter, I give him the quick rundown about my new situation at Mel's.

"That's great." The funny thing is I know he means it. "I've missed talking to you." Now that we're warmed up, the conversation flows more easily.

"Yeah, it's been a little while." What's it been? I try to remember. A week? Ten days?

"Too long."

I have to agree.

Thirty minutes later, I'm back in Mel's house. I decide that if I'm going to pitch in, I'd rather spend my energy on this pile of filthy dishes instead of the kids who are even filthier and infinitely noisier.

Once she gets everyone settled and the first load of dishes is drying by the sink, Mel and I sit down on the air mattress, the closest thing to a couch Mel's got here.

"Who was calling for you on the phone earlier?" she asks.

I don't think I'm blushing, but I'm glad her lights are dim just in case. "That? Oh, it was just a guy I know. His name's Justin."

She gives me a playful nudge and wiggles her eyebrows. "Oh, yeah?" Apparently, being a full-time bus driver with a restraining order against your ex and three kids under school age doesn't take away your inclination toward gossip. "And just who is this mysterious Mr. Justin who's calling you so late at night?"

I think it's five percent cute and ninety-five percent pathetic that she's three years older than I am and calls 8:45 late.

"Well?" She elbows me again. "You've got to tell me everything. Who knows the next time I'm gonna get out and enjoy myself a man?"

"It's not like that." Part of me wishes I could concoct some juicy story about me and Justin just so she could experience a little vicarious excitement, but I can't go there. Not tonight.

She's still waiting, so I tell her the truth, at least the abridged version.

"Justin's the father of my little girl. He's Gracie's daddy."

CHAPTER 21

"Is it lunch?" Bowman asks. I don't have to check the time to know we're not even an hour past breakfast.

"Not yet." I hear the annoyance creeping into my voice but can't help it. I'm not cut out for taking care of children long-term.

"Can I get a snack?"

"Not yet." When I'm tempted to envy Mel, who gets to leave the house for four hours twice a day, I just imagine her with that busload of fifty or more kids. I can't have it harder than she does, can I?

But I guess that's a silly way to look at it. We do it so often, though, try to cheer ourselves up by reminding ourselves there are other people suffering more than we are. What's the point? You don't look at a happy couple and tell them, *oh, cut that out. Don't you know there's lots of people out there who have it so much better than you?* That's the interesting thing about sadness (and happiness for that matter). It's not as relative as we like to make it out to be.

You can be having one of the best days of your life and still suffer that bittersweet feeling in your gut, the sense that things can't stay perfect for long. Or you can experience joy in the middle of such intense sorrow you're sure your soul's about to crumble like the pages in a two-century-old book and it's only the grace of God coupled with herculean psychological fortitude that keeps you from melting into your grief right then and there.

I don't pretend to know all the answers. I've learned more about human nature from novels than I'd ever glean with a psych degree. But I think maybe Tolstoy had the right idea when he talked about how happy families are all alike in their happiness, while the sad ones each experience grief in their own way.

Well, Tolstoy would get a kick out of this trailer. Mel's home certainly isn't a hub of peaceful togetherness and brotherly love, especially not today. I've just put Gabby in time-out in her high chair for biting her brother's arm. Not that I blame her. Bowman was playing on her fear of the toilet by chasing her around the house with the plastic lid over his head calling himself the potty monster.

At least the baby's getting used to me. I wonder what's going to happen now that we've trudged all the way to Friday, Jasmine and I. Because now she'll have all weekend with her mommy, so I'm a little worried Monday's going to be a disaster when Mel goes back to work.

For the moment, things are relatively calm. I'm starting to wonder if maybe I've gotten past the worst of working here. But this weekend I've got to get out. I still don't know what I'll do. Mel and her family aren't church-goers. I don't want to make a big deal about it or anything. Christians are always getting such a bad rap for shoving religion down everyone else's throat, and that's not my style. But I could probably use a good, solid service. Those chapel meetings they made us go to at the women's shelter were nothing but fluff, like picking up a book you expect to be an encyclopedic Bible study only to find out it's nothing but a *Pilgrims* magazine's devotional, the kind they keep as bathroom reading at Orchard Grove Bible.

Now there's a church for you. I haven't been in nearly a year, but I know if I ever return, it will be exactly the same as when I was a kid. I'm not talking about the pastor or anything like that (Orchard Grove's one of those special sorts of churches that goes through about a pastor a year and prides itself on how many unworthy men it's permanently disqualified from the ministry), but the people there are always the same. I could go back this weekend to find the exact faces I worshiped next to when I was a high schooler.

A little older, a little more weathered, but it's one of those churches that is deathly stubborn in its refusal to change. I mean, you should have heard the uproar when they thought about switching from piano to a weighted keyboard. And that was only a couple of generations removed from the Great Organ-Piano Debate of 1964.

"Can I be down?" asks the repentant Gabby, so I take her out of her high chair with a warning against biting anybody again.

"Is she supposed to have that?" Bowman asks, and I lunge across the living room (all five feet of it) to take the electric cord out of the baby's mouth.

"Gotta go potty," Gabby tells me, which is her way of saying she wants me to sit in the hall and watch her valiantly sit on her plastic chair (the same one her brother chased her around the house with) for twenty or thirty minutes. I glance once more at Jasmine. As long as the baby's happy and safe, there's nothing pressing I need to get done. As far as jobs go, sitting in the hall pretending to be interested in a toddler's elimination habits doesn't require an awful lot of energy.

Gabby yanks down her pants — after naming every single Disney princess on her pull-ups — and squats on the kiddie toilet. I'm glad I don't remember this phase of my own childhood. I don't really remember anything before first grade, which is why I couldn't say if Chris and I were in kindergarten together or not before his family moved away for those few years.

I hate that I'm thinking about him all the time. It's gotten even worse since I started writing out our story for you. But actually, the depression hasn't been too bad lately. My meds have definitely been helping. The way my mom talks about it, you'd think that anti-depressants shut down every receptor in your brain and feed your cells to little hungry zombie-demons, but it's not like that. You're still exhausted, but at least you've got a little boost to help you work your way through it.

Mom still doesn't know I take the stuff, but it's not any of her business, especially now that I'm on state insurance. That's one reason I don't like going back to visit. Even if she won't ask me directly if I'm on anything, she'll make sure to give me her opinion on pharmaceuticals over a series of daily lectures.

I'm actually surprised she hasn't called me. She's out east visiting my brother, but it's been two weeks or longer since we last talked. That either means she's busy with the grandbabies or she's devising some way to guilt-trip me for my negligence.

"It's not coming," Gabby whines from her potty.

My back's got a kink in it, and I'm ready to get off the floor. "Well, maybe you should get dressed and try again later."

She pouts, probably thinking about the promised Skittle she'll receive after making a deposit in the chair. "I'll try a little longer."

Great. I glance over my shoulder and see that the baby's busy trying to pull up on the TV stand. I can't believe it. Nine months and already acting like she's about to take off walking.

I think about Gracie. It's torture and will leave me despondent the rest of the day, but I can't help it. They're so close in age but completely different. Gracie's not as chubby, but her smile's even bigger, and she has these adorable dimples. My own mom's not the sentimental type, so she doesn't have album after album of baby photos of me like some families would keep. I don't know if my daughter looks like me or not.

Does it matter? What's the point of thinking about her now anyway? Why do I torture myself?

I shut my eyes. I can picture Gracie against my chest. Peaceful. Solid. I thought a newborn would feel more fragile.

My little baby …

No. That's the part I can't forget. The part I can't get over.

I love her so much that my arms ache from longing to hold her again.

I love her so much that my soul stings whenever I look at her photo and realize I haven't been there to watch her grow up.

I love her so much, and she doesn't even know who I am.

CHAPTER 22

"So, you made it through another week with the kids from Hades, did you?"

I smile as I walk down the sidewalk in Mel's run-down trailer park. "It's not that bad," I tell my phone.

Justin lets out a little laugh. "I'll remind you of that next time you text me that Gabby's screaming because you left her alone on the potty to stop Jasmine from eating the dead cockroach she found." He sounds so relaxed. I wonder what his secret is.

"I'm just glad it's the weekend."

There's an awkward silence. I'd forgotten that I never gave Justin an answer yet when he invited me to Seattle. I clear my throat. "So, what was your day like?"

I feel guilty talking to him. I'm not sure staying in close contact with him is such a good idea. I know my mom would flip out if she knew. She's three thousand miles away, but I can already hear her lecturing voice in my head, telling me to stay away from him.

He's talking about his most recent camping trip. When he's not doing his design work, he's got these adventuring buddies who travel all over the Pacific Northwest together. I'm surprised he can stand hiking anymore after what he's gone through, but people deal with losses in different ways.

"… so we had to grab the pop-up tent, and you should have seen his face when I told him …"

"Hold on." I'm sure the story's hilarious, and even if it isn't, I enjoy the sound of Justin's cheerful voice. He's so involved in his tale, I have to interrupt him twice. "Just a minute," I tell him. "Mel's calling me."

I glance at the time. Have Justin and I really been talking for an hour already? No wonder she's worried.

I switch the call. "Hey, Mel. Sorry about that. I didn't realize how late it was …" I stop when I hear someone yelling my name on the other end of the line. "Bowman, is that you?"

Sniffles.

"Bowman, where's your mommy?" I turn around and head toward Mel's trailer. "Where's your mommy?" I repeat.

"Dad took her outside."

Uh oh.

I start to run. "Bowman," I shout into the phone. "Bowman, listen really carefully to me, ok?" I've only seen Mel's ex once when he tried to strong arm his way into the women's shelter the morning after she and the kids made their escape, but with someone like Kai, once is all you need. "Take your sisters into the bathroom, ok?" I can't tell if he's listening above his sniffing and whimpering. "Did you hear? Take your sisters into the bathroom and lock the door."

"Where's my mom?" he asks.

"Get in the bathroom, and lock the door. Do you know how to lock it?"

"Uh-huh."

Good. "Do it. And keep the phone with you." I can't decide if I should stay on the line with him or call 911. I don't want to leave him alone. I'm his only lifeline right now. "Are you in the bathroom?" My lungs are bursting by the time Mel's trailer comes into view.

"Gabby doesn't want to go."

That child and her terror of toilets is enough to make me scream. "You're bigger than she is. Do what you have to do and get her in the bathroom. Lock yourselves in. What about Jasmine? Is she with you yet?"

"No, she's in her crib."

My shins are stinging each time my feet pound the pavement. "So get her out."

I hear shouting. Thank God Kai took Mel outside. At least the kids aren't exposed to his insanity. Not this time.

"I can't pick her up out of the crib. It's too tall."

I don't have time for Bowman's whining. "Get everyone in the bathroom and lock the door," I shout once more before I hang up to dial 911. My fingers are trembling so hard it takes me two different attempts.

"… get my freaking work pants." Kai is yelling, that booming sort of shout without a hint of falsetto. It's all diaphragm, all breathing muscle.

"So buy yourself another pair." Mel isn't helping matters. I wonder if her time away from Kai has made her too bold. Too reckless.

"What is the location of the emergency?" asks a buzzing voice in my ear.

I don't know Mel's street address. "I'm in the trailer park off Sharp. Two lefts after the entrance. It's the green trailer halfway down the road."

"And the nature of the emergency?"

My entire core is trembling. I have to snap myself out of this. Have to keep Mel and the kids safe. "My friend's ex is here. She has a restraining order, but he just showed up."

"And your friend's name?" the woman asks, and I want to scream as loud as Kai. *Who cares about names? Get the cops down here.*

Kai takes a step closer to Mel. I swear if he hits her, I'm

dropping this phone and rushing him. Don't ask me what my plan is after that, because I don't have one, but hopefully the surprise itself will give Mel a sporting chance.

"The name of the individuals involved?" The dispatcher sounds displeased to have to repeat herself.

"Melody Campos," I answer. "Her name is Melody Campos, her ex is Kai. I don't know his last name. Are you sending someone down here or what?"

"We have a car headed toward you right now. Are you in a safe location?"

Who cares about me? She's got to make the cops get here faster. "I'm fine. Just tell them to hurry it up."

"Can you see or hear what's going on?"

"Both." I still don't know what I'm doing standing here chatting with the dispatcher. I should either walk up to Kai and tell him to get lost or run up and check to make sure the kids are safe.

"Can you tell me what you observe?"

I wonder if this woman sounds so robotic even on her days off. "Right now, they're just yelling. He's cussing, saying she kept his work clothes or something like that."

"That's what Kai's saying?"

I roll my eyes. "Yes. That's what Kai's saying." I wonder for a minute if I should put it on speaker phone so she can hear everything for herself. It starts off as sheer sarcasm, my annoyed reaction to the dispatcher's questioning, but then I think that if Kai does go crazy on Mel, I could get the whole thing recorded. I fumble with my phone, trying to figure out how to get the camera to work without disconnecting the call.

Apparently, Ms. Dispatch isn't all that thrilled with my silence. "Has anything changed? Is he still yelling at her?"

"No. He's actually getting in the car now."

"With the woman?" For the first time, I detect a hint of worry in Ms. Robot's tone.

"No. No, she's on the sidewalk. She's ok." I don't know what Mel said to get him to leave. Maybe he knew he only had a few minutes before the police would show up. Whatever it is, he's on his way out. I glance down at the phone so I can focus again on my call. I won't be needing the camera after all. Thank God the kids are safe. Thank God …

The sound of screeching tires stings my ears. Mel screams. It's so fast. Kai's truck is on the curb, squealing away from her. She's on the ground. I can't see how bad it is from here.

I rush across the parking lot and shout into the phone, "Get an ambulance! He just hit her with his truck."

CHAPTER 23

"No." Mel sniffs into the Kleenex that the female officer hands her. "No, he didn't hit me."

Three pairs of cop eyes turn on me. I shouldn't be here. It's eleven at night, but at least the kids are finally calmed down and asleep in their beds.

Interrogator Number One holds a pen poised over a notebook. "You said you saw him run into her with his truck?"

I don't look at Mel. I know enough to predict how this will turn out. I'll tell the cops everything, she'll kick me out of the home, and we'll never talk to each other again. I may have just kept her boyfriend from murdering her, and she's going to hate me for the rest of my life.

"She didn't see anything," Mel protests into her Kleenex. The female officer stands behind her, which I find funny. I know they bring women to domestic violence cases for the extra support and sympathy, but this particular officer looks about as warm and inviting as David Copperfield's aunt

Betsey.

The two men are looking at me. Glaring at me. As if I've wasted their time by concocting some story about my roommate's insane ex trying to drive over her with his truck. "Yes, I saw him charge straight at her."

"And you saw him hit her?" asks Officer Two.

How many times will I have to repeat myself before the night's over? I clench my jaw, certain I'm nailing the lid on both my job as well as my relationship with Mel. What's that they always say about tough love, right?

"Yes, I saw him hit her with his truck."

"Which part of the truck hit her?"

I try to reconstruct the scene in my head. I have to twist my body to the side a certain way. Don't ask me how that helps, but it does. "So, it would have been the right side of his bumper that crashed into her left side."

"Where on her left side?" The officer points toward Mel. "Her leg?"

"I'm not sure." What does he think? That I have night goggles and X-ray vision? "The truck was blocking my view."

Officer One frowns. "The truck was blocking your view, but you say you saw it hit her?"

So we're back to the basics again. "Yes, I saw him hit her. How many times will you make me tell you that?" I realize now that I'm getting more agitated than Mel, and these guys are treating me like I'm on trial for trying to murder my roommate.

"Ok, let's back up." It's Officer One still. He's slightly older and talks slower than his partner. As long as he can hold a tune, I think he could make an excellent Javert in a community theater production of *Les Mis*. "You were standing across the parking lot."

"Right."

He walks over to the window and points. "About where that street light is?"

I have to pause to remember. "No. Further over to the left."

"The left from our vantage point, or the left when you're looking at the building?"

"From here." He nods, as if I've just proved my own guilt. "Ok. And then you say you saw the suspect pull up and drive toward your friend?"

I stared at my hands. Wonder if he'd talk to me this way if I weren't a petite Chinese-American woman with a voice that's far too soft to match my rage. "No, that's not what I said. I said they were fighting, he got into his truck, and he sped toward her and hit her."

"Hit her with the right side of his truck."

"Yes."

"Which right? The passenger side right or the driver's side right?"

I feel like I'm back in fourth grade getting drilled on multiplication facts. "The passenger side."

"But you didn't actually see him hit her."

"Yes, I stood there and watched the whole thing." I don't care that my voice is rising. Who is this man to tell me what I did or didn't see? How in the world would he know?

"So you stood there and watched your friend get hit by her ex in his truck."

"Yes." *Now can we move on to the part where you go after Kai and arrest him?*

"But your friend's not hurt."

Mel shakes her head. She's agreeing with him.

"I guess he wasn't going all that fast," I admit somewhat deflated.

"You said you heard the tires squeal."

"Well, he started out like he was backing up, and then he turned real fast and hit her."

Mel mumbles, "He never hit me," but she's said it so many times we all tune her out.

"So you saw the truck hit her? You saw the passenger side of his bumper actually *hit* your friend and make her fall?"

The words stick in my throat. I feel queasy. "Well …"

The trio of officers exchange meaningful glances.

I swallow, refusing to look at Mel. "I guess I didn't really *see* the truck hit her. I saw him speeding toward her, next thing she was on the ground, and then he drove off."

"I lost my balance," Mel insists. *The lady doth protest too much, methinks.*

Officer Two clears his throat. I assume it's his turn to take a stab at Good Cop for now. "So it sounds to me like what happened was you heard the tires, you saw him going forward, and you saw your friend on the ground, and you *assumed* she'd gotten hit. When like she said, maybe all that happened was she lost her balance."

I feel like we're arguing semantics at this point, but I realize the officers have got me on a technicality if nothing else. There's no reason for me to say anything more, and thankfully they don't push the issue further.

The female officer asks Mel if she wants to press charges, but there's not a single adult in the room who's surprised by her answer. "No, he just wanted his old work clothes. I forgot to give them to him when he moved out." She still won't meet my eyes, but at least the cold haughtiness in her voice is gone.

"You make sure to tell us if he keeps coming around here

bugging you, got that?"

I don't even look up to detect if it's Officer One or Two talking. I've had enough of policemen to last me a lifetime already.

The cops leave, and I don't even argue when Mel stares at the wall in front of her and tells me I've got until tomorrow morning to find another place to stay. "I just fell," she insists once more, perhaps for good measure. "He never hit me."

I don't reply.

I've heard that argument far too many times.

CHAPTER 24

"So you're thinking of leaving Mel's, huh?"

I've got the heat in the house on low even though the night's thirty-five degrees outside. I haven't told Justin I've already left her place. He doesn't know I'm spending Saturday night at my mom's empty house. Thank God she didn't think to change the security code. And that my brother took that job on the East Coast. I don't want to talk to anyone now.

Not even Justin, much as I hate to admit it.

It's not that I think he would judge me. I'm not embarrassed to tell him I couldn't even keep a babysitting job for a single month. That I have no other recourse than to sneak back into my childhood home, haunted as it is with memories. What I don't want him to know is that I haven't gotten out of bed since this morning. That I might not emerge until after the New Year, when Mom's due home and this squatting vacation will come to an end. If he knew the truth, he'd start making the drive all the way from Seattle to come out here and rescue me.

Which I need about as much as McMurphy needed that lobotomy in *One Flew Over the Cuckoo's Nest.*

"How's the job market out there?" he asks. I can hear the worry in his voice, can tell he's trying to mask it. We've talked so much by phone over the past month. I'm learning these nuances of his so well.

I don't tell him what he really wants to know. That the depression is getting worse. That I'm getting dangerously close to the start of another crash. Either that, or I'm already in the early phases of one but lack the mental clarity to see it for what it truly is.

"Oh, there are lots of openings available." I force cheerfulness into my tone, but I know that he can discern my subtle mood changes as well as I can his.

He clears his throat, and I know what's coming. It won't be a direct offer to help. We both realize that would never work. It will be something discreet, his way of trying to save me while still protecting what little pride I've got left.

"I have a friend who's looking for someone to fill an office assistant position. I can give him your contact info if you want."

He doesn't tell me the job's in Seattle. He doesn't tell me that this *friend* he's mentioning is really his business partner, that he's asking me to come and work for him.

He doesn't have to.

There are so many excuses I could make. I could pretend I already have a lead on a good position out here. I could make up some lie about living off my savings and writing that novel I've always dreamed about. As if someone like me had a savings account. Heck, I'd be happy with a couple of five dollar bills in my wallet.

"I don't think I'm ready for that yet," I tell him quietly and wait for his response.

"Yeah, I understand." There's mild disappointment in his voice, but mostly gentleness. "Well, there's always room for you out here if you change your mind," he says, even though he doesn't have to.

I already know.

CHAPTER 25

I've been thinking a lot about Justin since we got off the phone last night. I don't know why I keep on turning down his invitation to head toward Seattle, even if it's only for a visit. But what I told him yesterday is just as true now as it was then. I'm not ready. And it's not just the relationship side of things either. It's more than that. It's the entire history between us.

I'm not ready to confront that yet. Maybe I never will be.

I managed to make myself some dinner last night. That's a positive step. I have no clue where it comes from, but Mom's a major disaster prepper. Has enough canned goods stock-piled in the basement that you could live a decade here and never leave the house. In fact, you'd probably end up gaining weight from all that extra sodium. She's also something of a conspiracy theorist, so my brother and I are the only people besides her who know what's downstairs in that cement basement.

I helped myself to a can of raviolis. I even heated them

up in the microwave instead of eating them straight out of the can. It's a step up from the Spaghetti-Os we always had at Mel's. The good news is that as long as I clean up after myself, Mom will never notice a few missing non-perishables.

My only fear is that one of the neighbors will see me here and say something to Mom when she comes back from dictating my brother's life to him. Jonathan's the smart one. I only made it as far as Spokane, but he got all the way to the East coast. Little did he know that in so doing, he was also inviting Mom to spend one month out of the year with him and his new family.

I've never been out to see him. Wouldn't want to, really. Jonathan's almost a decade older than I am. By the time I was in grade school, he was this crazy punk-star wannabe with his torn-up denim jacket, the works. Drove Mom insane. But he's straightened out since then. Doesn't spike his hair anymore. Let his ear piercing close up. He's an accountant at some big firm out east. Don't ever ask him what he does because you'll be snoring two minutes in.

It's not that Jonathan and I get along poorly. We don't interact at all. Probably because of the age difference, I don't know. I already told you I don't remember an awful lot from back when I was young. My most vivid memories of

Jonathan are of him coming home to visit on his college breaks and getting into fights with Mom.

At least those days are over. This house is so quiet now. It's Daddy's presence I miss the most. Daddy's voice I strain to hear. This morning, I thought I noticed a creaking on the stairs, and even though he's been dead for years now, I imagined it was him coming up to tell me good-morning. To hand me a new book he'd finished and tell me to have it read by dinnertime so we could share our thoughts.

Daddy …

I'm actually doing fine, though, all things considered. I mean, I got myself out of bed and took a shower. That's pretty huge. And I'm dressed. Call me crazy if you want, but I've decided to take myself to church today. It's been several weeks since I've attended a service anywhere, and now that I'm home, I guess Orchard Grove is the place to go.

My reasons aren't entirely altruistic. Mom called last night after I got off the line with Justin. I answered. I couldn't help it. I'm sure a scientist or math whiz could come up with a formula to determine exactly how many calls from your mother you can let go straight to voicemail over a certain amount of time without significantly increasing her chances of having a heart attack. Whatever that time limit is, I exceeded it weeks ago.

So I answered, possibly against my better judgment. It was typical, just what you'd expect. Mom rattled off every way Jonathan's four-year-old isn't as smart as we were as children and how she's worried the baby isn't growing like she should be. Lamenting about how Jonathan married some Filipino girl instead of settling down with a nice Chinese bride. Droning reminiscences about his wild days in high school, how she should have known then he wouldn't amount to anything.

Says the mother of the accountant living in a gated community with his own private pool overlooking a country club.

Once she got all the family disappointments out, it was time to gossip. I swear that woman hasn't read a single novel in her adult life, but she knows exactly what every member of her women's missionary league and their scores of spouses, children, grandchildren, and extended family members are up to. What's more, she thinks I care.

"Did you know that Joy Holmes is expecting another baby?" she asked in a scandalized tone.

At the time, I was still trying to decide if it was worth the mental energy to find some food in the cement bunker known as the family basement, so all I said was, "Really?"

Mom apparently wasn't satisfied with my lack of

interest. "You know, this is her fourth child. And her oldest isn't even in grade school yet. She's trying to make a name for herself. Doing that thing where you write what you're up to on the internet each day."

"Blogging?" I asked, half distracted because I just saw a box of Chris's old letters stored up on my bookshelf behind my Turgenev collection.

"I don't know what those people call themselves," Mom replied with a huff. "As if it were a real job. And all those kids she's supposed to be taking care of. You know, we've got an entire generation of young mothers who do nothing but stare at their computer screens and think their babies are going to raise themselves. She and her husband moved recently, you know. Nice five-bedroom in the Heights. But how does she expect to keep it up when she's typing into her keyboard all day? Her mother said she's actually looking to hire a nanny to help with the kids and the housework."

So there it is. The reason why I'm dressed up in my old clothes from high school, brushing my hair in front of my mirror that still has decals of all the Soul Boyz plastered on it. Don't even ask. Junior high was rough on me, that's all I have to say.

I know Joy. We graduated in the same class, and she has every reason to hate me. If it weren't for me, she would have given the Valedictorian speech, for one thing. Not to mention that she was the runner-up for prom queen, and I was the one crowned. The rivalry goes way past that, all the way back to junior high when we were picked to co-captain the spirit squad. When she had a major crush on Chris before he and I started dating.

And now look at me. I'm squatting in my mother's house, terrified to be discovered. I have no mailing address, no job, no degree. And Joy's got her family, her five-bedroom, and whatever blogging stuff she's into now. And I'm about to show up to church and ask her for a nanny job.

There's karma for you, right?

I may have stolen the homecoming crown from her, but here we are years later and I'll be the one scrubbing her toilets and changing her baby's diapers. If she'll hire me.

Oh, well. I'm not too proud to beg. I need a job, and if Joy's got one for me, I'll take it.

And who knows? Maybe the pastor's sermon will be just what I need to hear.

CHAPTER 26

As glad as I am Mom isn't around, I know as soon as I step into the foyer of Orchard Grove Bible Church that I made a huge mistake coming here. I'm immediately accosted by a dozen of Mom's cronies from the women's missionary league, and they all want to know what I'm doing in town.

"Don't you still live in Spokane?"

"Isn't your mother still out east?"

"Aren't you celebrating Christmas at your brother's?"

At least I don't get a bunch of the men coming up and telling me that they remember me all the way back from when I was *this high*.

I'm asked far too many times about my health because whenever I've dragged myself home to recover from the depression over the past few years, Mom's told her friends I had the flu. Do you know that's our code word in this family? The *flu*.

I'm sorry, she'd drone on the phone to her church-lady friends, *I'd love to attend the fundraiser tea, but you see, my daughter's home for a little while, recovering from the flu, so I better pass.*

We both know it's a stinking lie, but she's got the luxury of being stubborn, so stubborn that part of her truly believes my problems stem back to a weak immune system.

In her mind, it's the reason why I dropped out of college.

The reason why I haven't seen my daughter in almost a year.

All that because of a little virus. I wish to God it was the flu. Take a seasonal vaccination once every fall, keep yourself immune. Some vitamin C and zinc just for good measure, and voila. Perfect functionality.

I sometimes wonder what I would be doing now if it weren't for these crashes. It's counterproductive, but maybe I'm just a glutton for suffering.

Would Chris still be here? Here with me and my daughter?

I wouldn't have to lie to my mom about coming down with a virus once or twice a year. I wouldn't feel like I have to defend my choice to take pharmaceuticals, even though Mom's convinced that Prozac's for overgrown babies who never learned the suck-it-up-buttercup philosophy she's so fond of.

And when I really want to torture myself, I imagine the person I'd be if it weren't for the depression. The person I could turn into if I found the magic drug or guru or prayer recitation that would cure me instantaneously. Back in college — before I dropped out, I mean — I could write a thousand words in an hour. That's back when I was taking those creative writing courses. It's not fast if you compare it to a secretary's seventy or eighty words a minute, but do the math. A thousand words an hour. You work your butt off two or three hours a day, and all of a sudden, you've got a full-length novel out at the end of a month. Obviously there's editing and writer's block and all those annoying barricades to deal with, but what I'm saying is it's possible.

Just look at how many books get released every day by first-time authors.

I'm torturing myself. I really am, but I need something to distract me. Something to get my mind off of church. Off of how humiliating it's going to be to walk up to Joy Holmes, my high school rival, and ask her if she's still looking for someone to vacuum all those floors in her new five-bedroom mansion in Orchard Grove Heights. I see her over there. A daughter pulling on her arm, a baby on the hip, and a boy she's shouting at as he runs in between the legs of all those old orchardists in their Sunday best.

She hasn't noticed me yet. Maybe I should go. But that would give all of Mom's friends even more reason to gossip. By one o'clock this afternoon, Mom will know I was at

Orchard Grove, she'll know what I was wearing, and she'll probably have a pretty good suspicion of what I ate for the past seven days and how consistent my bowel movements have been.

Funny how a church this old can change so little. I recognize nearly everyone. I'm not sure that's a good sign. Aren't churches supposed to constantly add new members to their congregations? Well, it's probably due to demographics more than anything else. Orchard Grove's something of a black hole. Not too many people leave here. Look at Joy and me. The top two students in a class of over a hundred. I could count on one hand the number of kids we graduated with who are out of state. The vast majority are within a fifteen-mile radius of right here.

Kind of depressing, really.

And now she's seen me. There's no stopping it. Joy's smiling and coming this way. Now that she's turned, I notice the baby bulge. The way my mom talks about Joy and her ever-increasing line of offspring, I was expecting her to look older. More tired and rundown. But she's the exact same Joy who stood next to me on homecoming court, smiling through what I'm sure was the disappointment. She looks more like the kind of girl you'd expect to get crowned. Blond hair, not as light as some but enough to give her that Barbie look. At least when she's not pregnant. But she's one of those women who carry it all in her midsection. Looking at her from behind, I wouldn't have had a clue she was expecting if my mom wasn't such a gossip.

She's giving me a hug and sounds genuinely happy to see me. I smile and gush and pretend to be so impressed with how radiant she looks, with how pretty her two girls appear in their little dresses. She's in her second trimester. Just found out last week it's another boy. I try to come up with a way to mention the nanny position, but she's just talking and talking. And it's all about the kids, which I'm sure is all she writes about as well.

As if the one thing the World Wide Web needed was another mommy blogger. Oh, well. None of my business. And if her desire to reach thousands of readers with her touching stories about changing soiled diapers is going to land me a paid position, so be it.

Joy's husband, one of the rare transplants into Orchard Grove County, whispers to his wife that it's time to sit down. She smiles and tells me how good it will be to catch up now that I'm back in town.

And then I'm left to walk myself into the imposing sanctuary of Orchard Grove Bible Church before the service starts.

CHAPTER 27

I find a pew toward the back in case I have to leave early. Just showing up here has got me exhausted. Not to mention dealing with Joy and my mom's friends, all of them as hungry for gossip as Oliver Twist and his orphanage friends were for their gruel. I'll be lucky if I make it past the first few songs.

While one of the elders reads the announcements (which are right there in the bulletin for literate congregants to read for themselves), I glance around. The church's women's missionary league has always done its best to overcompensate for the building's somewhat bland exterior by overloading the inside with every single fake flower, gaudy candle arrangement, and ornately framed piece of junk you can find on clearance at the local craft store. It's even worse now at Christmastime, with every single windowsill laden with garlands and fake holly, and the maroon carpet underfoot littered with artificial pine needles that have fallen from the arrangements.

The piano begins, the exact same hymns I remember from my childhood and a few Christmas carols sprinkled in. Since we never sing through more than one or two verses, we can cram in eight or ten songs. I'm glad when the music dies and we can finally sit down. How did standing during a fifteen-minute set turn into such an exhausting ordeal?

The pastor walks up to the front, all smiles. It's a new guy. Hasn't been here for more than a few months, but Mom's told me enough about him I could deliver his job performance summary at the next church business meeting. Pastor Greg, he's this young man originally from Orchard Grove. Part Latino, part Native, which isn't a mix you see too much around here. He graduated around the same time I did, but he was homeschooled, and back then the homeschool/public school divide was even more impassable than the barriers separating out the whites from the Latinos, the Latinos from the Natives, and the Natives from everyone else.

Which is why I think it's funny Mom loves living in Orchard Grove so much. Maybe she enjoyed the fact that Daddy was the only Chinese gynecologist the town had known. Everyone's searching for some claim to fame, right?

Pastor Greg opens with a little inspiring story he could have picked up from a *Pilgrims* magazine, and I find myself wondering how much longer the church will keep him on. Orchard Grove goes through pastors like some folks go through casseroles at a potluck luncheon. I think they've had five just since the time I graduated high school. There was one pastor run out of town, not because he had an online counseling business *per se*, but because he sometimes talked to his paying clients on Sundays.

Another was forced to resign when his adult son, who was in his thirties or forties by then, came out of the closet, and the preacher didn't disown him the exact same day. (That came later, by the way, just not soon enough for everyone at Orchard Grove.) Let's see, there was a pastor whose wife had that fling with the high-school principal, but that was probably a decade ago. I think it's a once-in-a-generation type of scandal, and good thing too because the average age at the church is really creeping up the scales, and I'm not sure too many of the octogenarians have hearts strong enough to withstand another shock quite that severe.

Pastor Greg's wife, she's this little homely wisp of a thing. Not the kind of trim and curvy you see in Hollywood, either, but beanpole skinny like adolescence just decided to pass her over. She's got a somewhat literary name. Tatiana or Natalia or something stoic and Russian like that. I don't know her history, but if she's got Russian genes, maybe once she has kids she'll go through a second puberty and finally put on some weight. I can see her shoulder-blades through that skinny cotton sweater she's wearing. My mom's told me plenty about her. She met Pastor Greg in LA or some urban center like that then followed him to Orchard Grove. You can tell she's not cut from rural stock, but I can't picture someone demure like her making it in the city either. Just like I can't see her or her husband lasting another year at this church. Of course, twelve months at Orchard Grove is probably equivalent to two decades anywhere else, so there's that to factor in.

It's just that based on what I've heard from my mom, the missionary league ladies aren't all that infatuated with mousy little Katerina. That's her name. I knew I would remember it if I gave myself enough time. It's not that she's standoffish. Reading between the lines, it sounds like she's just a little girl thrown into the position of first lady at Orchard Grove, a role in which even the love child between Princess Di and Jacqueline Kennedy Onassis would fall short.

It makes me sad, come to think of it. Sad to think about how stressful it must be for a young couple like them. I forget exactly how long ago Mom said they got married, but I know it's been less than a year. I look at them and imagine the way they must have been happy and in love in LA, her with her spring sweaters, him with his boyish dimples and charm. I'm sure in her mind he was larger than life. He's quite a bit older than she is. As the story goes, she was a student in his youth group down there or something half romantic, half creepy like that. She probably idolized him.

Maybe she still does. I don't know. It takes some people longer to fall off their pedestals than others.

I remember what it was like to be that young. I remember what it was like to be that blissfully happy until you feel almost guilty that the rest of the world isn't as exultantly joyful as you.

The universe has its checks and balances, doesn't it? I think it's so funny when Christians get all upset about the whole concept of karma.

Everything comes full circle.

There's no true happiness that won't one day lead to utter devastation and loss.

CHAPTER 28

It's impossible for me to sit in Orchard Grove without thinking about Daddy. Thinking about the church wedding he never got to see. Thinking about my first few months married to Chris. I dropped out of college. Only one semester left to go, but I couldn't make it. Mom clucked her tongue, certain my poor taste in husband material had something to do with my failure to graduate, even though hard as she tried that woman couldn't find one legitimate fault in Chris.

I hate how I can't even go to a Sunday service without having all these shadows from the past pressing down on me. Some people keep track of time by the ages of their kids or the dates of major life events. My calendar's tied to the biggest crashes. A few months after we married, I came to peace with Daddy's death. That doesn't mean I stopped grieving. Stopped missing him. But eventually the gaping, bleeding wounds turned into heavy aches. The raw, open cuts in my soul scabbed over, leaving sores and bruises instead of gashes of agony and pain.

I healed in pieces, in faltering steps, in tears and prayers.

I got out of bed.

I ate real food.

I brushed my hair.

I got over the acute stage of grieving, but the next phase was longer, slower. I'm sure some people would say I'm still in it. That phase where the grief is no longer a chasm the size of a cannonball in the center of your chest but an enduring, persistent heaviness that settles on your shoulders and your spine, sometimes radiating all the way out to your limbs.

I didn't regret that I couldn't graduate with my class, not at the time. I was proud of my husband for getting his degree, proud of us for making it through those first months of marriage when I was so sad and Chris's studies got him so stressed out.

Stressed out. That's what I called it when he came home from class and snapped at me because I hadn't gotten dinner ready.

Stressed out when the shirt he wanted to wear wasn't ironed, even though he'd never bothered ironing during the entire decade leading up to our marriage.

Stressed out in the bedroom when I wasn't as involved as he wanted me to be. Because even though we were both committed to fairly conservative standards of purity before our wedding night, he jumped into the marriage thinking that a simple three-day honeymoon would provide me with a crash course adequate to teach me each trick and technique from every book, magazine, movie, or webpage he stumbled across during our days of abstinence.

Chris's schoolwork became a worthy scapegoat, although once he graduated and landed a somewhat lenient job as a courier for an Orchard Grove attorney's office, I realized I couldn't blame my husband's rage on stress alone.

Knowing what I know now, I could have come up with a number of other explanations. Maybe the rocky example that his own parents provided him had warped Chris's sense of what marriage should look like. I might have even gone so far as to blame conservative Christianity or the Proverbs 31 woman herself for deluding my husband into thinking that a godly wife was a perfect wife. But young newlyweds are nothing if they're not narcissistic, so I internalized my husband's rage and assumed complete culpability for it all.

Every part.

Because if I paid more attention in the kitchen and didn't burn his dinner, he wouldn't get so angry.

And if I remembered to tell him when the gas tank was half empty, he wouldn't worry about running low during his long hours on the road.

And if I learned to compromise a little in the bedroom, if it weren't so hard for me to shrug off the prudish, anti-sex upbringing from my past, I could *bless my husband* in all the ways he needed it.

And so my answer was to try harder. Try harder and hide more and more of myself. My husband wanted a perfect housewife and a sensual, experienced, and adventurous lover. And since I wasn't those things going into our marriage, I had to draw on that bootstrap style of religion my mother is so fond of, grit my teeth, and pretend to be whoever it was that he wanted.

We didn't talk about my depression. We didn't talk about Daddy anymore, either. I hated that we were back in Orchard Grove, so close to the store-front office where the town's first and only Chinese-American gynecologist saw his patients for nearly three full decades.

I got a part-time job at the library. Shelving books, opening crates of new arrivals. Feeling like an architect unearthing rare treasures each time I encountered a new author I adored. Eventually working my way up until I was asked to run the monthly book clubs. It was nice to get out of the house, even though I never overcame my fear of using up too much gas and forgetting to tell my husband. I met some new friends, including an eccentric old man who came in every Tuesday at eleven to donate part of his antique book collection to the library.

Chris was working extra hours, trying to save up for law school. Half the time when he came home, he was too tired to start a fight, which I took as a sign of improvement. We didn't talk about the past, but at least the future looked promising in comparison. I convinced myself that once he made it into law school, he'd be the charming, adoring man I married. We could settle down, maybe even get out of Washington. We could be happy.

At least that's what I hoped.

But I was wrong.

Dead wrong.

CHAPTER 29

Pastor Greg is bucking convention, which is never a wise move within the walls of Orchard Grove Bible Church. He's not preaching a typical Joseph-and-Mary sermon like every other pastor I've heard in December. The way he explains it, he's committed to teaching a book of the Bible straight through, come hell or high water or Advent season.

Another reason I doubt he'll be here the next time I'm crazy enough to step foot in this sanctuary.

So in keeping with his sermon schedule, he's in the Old Testament, talking to us about Abigail, the woman who went behind her husband's back to save her household from King David's wrath.

I find it interesting and a little disappointing that someone as prudent as Abigail never finds herself listed among the famous women of the Old Testament. I mean, you've got Sarah and Rebecca and Rachel and Leah — the matriarchs who are revered for bearing sons for their husbands no matter how pathetic or conniving some of them were as mothers. You've got the villainesses like Jezebel and Delilah, women who are downright intriguing for no other reason than their sheer wickedness. And then thrown into the mix are those noble ladies (in deed if not in birth), women like Ruth and Esther and that so annoyingly perfect Proverbs 31 woman.

Each one has their place. You've got the mothers, you've got the villains, and you've got the larger-than-life heroines. But where does Abigail fall into the mix?

Two decades of attending church services, and I've only heard one other pastor who touched on Abigail's story. Abigail, the woman unfortunate enough to find herself married to a fool. The woman who intervened when David and his men had set their hearts on killing her entire household, whose graciousness and tact not only saved her husband's life but eventually landed her a spot as one of David's wives.

Contemporary American evangelicalism doesn't know what to do with Abigail. She's no matriarch. If she bore David sons, they weren't the Solomons or the Absaloms or any of the others who made biblical history. She was certainly no villain, or else David the man after God's own heart wouldn't have honored her by inviting her to join his small harem. But we have trouble placing her alongside those honorable ladies like Esther or Ruth because Abigail's the only woman in Scripture who explicitly goes against her husband's wishes yet isn't condemned for it.

In fact, she's rewarded. According to Pastor Greg, "She knew that her God-given mandate to respect her husband ended when Nabal's actions put her and her household in jeopardy."

I think about my friend Mel, about the way she and her three kids sneaked out of their trailer in the middle of the night to escape from her ex. Then how she made so many excuses to the cops after Kai did or didn't hit her with his truck. How I became the enemy for daring to think about getting the authorities involved in her little lovers' spat.

I suppose Mel could use a sermon like this. In fact, the more I dwell on it, the more I want to take her by both shoulders and shake her. *Think about your children.* Mel's not even religious. She doesn't have the burden of a conservative upbringing that tells her it's a sin to be anything other than the submissive, obedient wife.

"Abigail is an example of a resourceful, godly, and highly capable woman who could very well have ended up killed or raped by one of David's men if she did what her husband expected of her. Instead, she went against her husband's wishes and made peace with the future king."

Greg's getting himself quite worked up as he goes, not breaking into a profuse sweat or spraying the front-row congregants like you do when you preach, but there's fervor and intensity in his voice.

And I'm sitting here wondering how many missionary league women he just offended by using the word *rape*.

The funny thing is I heard another sermon about Abigail back at Orchard Grove years ago, a sermon in which she was criticized and lambasted for daring to call her husband a fool in the presence of another man. "The fact that God spared Abigail's life is a testimony of his grace and forgiveness, which he offers to even the most rebellious of hearts," the pastor had said. He went on to tell us that if Abigail had stayed with her fool of a husband, God would have certainly protected her and given her even greater rewards for her obedience and submission. Of course, this was the same pastor who encouraged the church secretary to take her repentant alcoholic husband back into her home. Two weeks later, they were all dead — the husband, the wife, and their eight-year-old twins — in Orchard Grove County's only murder-suicide in anyone's living memory.

You know, I wasn't lying when I said Chris never hit me. Maybe that explains why I stayed with him. I can't tell you how many times I promised myself that the second he raised his hand to me, I'd be gone. I wouldn't be one of those submissive doormats that lays herself out to get walked on time and time again.

But even now I wonder. Wonder if I would have found the courage to leave if he had beaten me senseless. If my life was in danger. I hate that there's still so much of the victim in me, the part that wants to gloss over Chris's faults and praise him for his efforts to improve himself.

Because he did try. We've all got our demons to fight, and I watched Chris struggle against his with the faith and devotion that would put the most ardent of saints to shame.

That's the part of the story you're most familiar with, I guess. You jumped right in to try to help him when we attended Valley Tabernacle. I don't remember how long the two of you kept up your regular Thursday night meetings, but even now, I'm surprised Chris went through with it. Submitted himself to that four-hour long prayer session where you and the elders laid hands on him and muttered away in tongues for him to find deliverance from the spirit of rage. You ministered to my husband like the most skilled of counselors would intervene on behalf of a relapsing addict. I lost count of how many times you fasted for him. There was one period where you called him every single evening at nine o'clock sharp to listen to whatever confessions he had to offer and to pray for him to find victory from the anger that held him captive.

And isn't it interesting how you and the entire leadership team at Valley Tabernacle encamped around my husband, fought against the forces of evil on his behalf, fasted and prayed and wept for his deliverance, and even then you never once asked me how his actions impacted me personally? If I felt safe? If I needed a place to go? If my husband had ever hurt me?

That first year of marriage is rocky whether or not your lifelong sweetheart has anger issues that he concealed so skillfully during your ten-year courtship. And maybe some people might listen to my story and feel sorry for me. Maybe wonder why I didn't leave him at the beginning or at least distance myself until he sorted through some of his personal issues.

But that would be neglecting to consider the times in our marriage — yes, even in that horrific first year — when we were truly happy.

Happy to take turns reading to one another at night or waiting to hear the finalists for the Pulitzer Prize for literature like some people engross themselves in the Academy Awards or the NFL draft.

Happy to get plugged even deeper into life at Valley Tabernacle, where Chris took over the sound ministry and I was asked to edit and design the monthly newsletter. Even those cruelly embarrassing intimacy issues began to resolve themselves as I discovered that your body and your mind can learn to adapt so that what once was shameful and degrading might eventually become a normal and expected part of life.

I've always thought that our culture puts too much emphasis on black-and-white labels. *There are good marriages and there are bad marriages. There are good spouses and horrible ones.* Isn't the truth of the matter that we're all somewhere in between?

It's possible that Chris and I could have learned to grow even closer in spite of the tumultuous beginning. It's possible that all your prayers and all your pleading with the Almighty might have finally brought about a dramatic change in him, as miraculous as my deliverance from suicide.

But as you yourself already know, our lives were destined to take a much different route.

CHAPTER 30

Maybe I shouldn't say this to you, but I usually lose interest about ten minutes into a sermon. Sometimes I sit and read the Bible, but there aren't any close enough. I'd have to get up and walk back to the entrance where a few extra copies lie. So instead I study the backs of all the heads in front of me. The only one I don't know personally is the pastor's wife, but of course Mom's told me enough gossip about her I could probably write several chapters of her biography.

There's Joy with her squirming son. Her daughters must be downstairs in the nursery. I can't see any of her face from here, but her husband looks stern. At least he does in profile. He lays his hand on the boy's knee, and that gets him to sit still for a full ten seconds.

And now, as the pastor's back to King David's men, I find my mind wandering to a text message I received earlier from Mel. I guess she realized she's got work first thing tomorrow morning and no daycare or baby-sitter lined up.

She didn't go so far as to apologize. It was just a short, *Hey, let me know if you're free this week to watch the kids.* I haven't responded yet. I'm not sure I will. I mean, I know she could use the help, but if she's going to keep letting Kai into her life and putting her children in danger, I can't see how that's a healthy position for either of us to be in. I feel guilty leaving the kids in such a volatile situation, but I really think she's going to have to find someone else.

You know, back when I was a teenager and Orchard Grove was still reeling from that murder-suicide, I held certain assumptions about abusive marriages. I wouldn't look at a woman like Mel and peg her as an easy victim, but Kai is the second psychotic boyfriend she's had to take up a restraining order against. But you see the way she takes care of her kids or the way she can handle herself with a busload full of noisy children, and she comes across as a sharp, intelligent woman. Which she is.

Until she gets around her ex.

And that's another thing about battered wives. I thought they all cowered, but Mel and several of the other women I met during my time at Sacred Meadows have tempers as feisty as the men they're hiding from. It's just that they don't have the muscle power or the size factor in their favor and so they end up black and blue.

Of course, men can end up in abusive relationships too. Like Reginald, the friend I first met when I was still employed at the library, the one who came in to visit every week. Reginald's ex-wife used to bind him to a chair and beat him. She was quite creative in her choice of tools as well. Purse straps, work boots, belts. And just to be clear, it wasn't the kind of beating you'd do wearing spiked heels and leather lingerie. He finally left after she knocked him out with a cast-iron skillet. There was no permanent damage, but he would jokingly blame that incident to explain why he couldn't keep figures straight in his head when he opened a bookstore of his own.

Reginald's old-school through and through. As rocky as that marriage was, his ex bore him seven or eight children before they split up. And he's not some tiny little thing, either. The way he put it was he'd been taught to never hit a woman, so who knows how many years the brutality went on behind closed doors before he finally called it quits? And you know what else? He had to send that woman alimony payments all the way until her dying day. Opening Orchard Grove's first antique bookstore was his present to himself when he learned he didn't have to write that old biddy any more checks.

I feel bad that I don't think about Reginald as much as

he deserves. He's the only one who knows all the details about what happened between Chris and me, which is maybe why I avoid him now. With so many grandchildren and such a large house with plenty of room to spare, a man like that should have never spent a solitary day in his life.

Poor Reginald.

The preacher must be close to wrapping up by now, and before I grab lunch, I'm going to text Mel and let her know I can't watch the kids. Not this week. Maybe if she's serious, we can have a sit-down and set some firm boundaries about her ex being around, but even now I know exactly how it will go. She'll agree to whatever terms I lay out, and then in a week or a month or whenever it is that Kai rolls around again, begging her to take him back, promising her that he's a better person, she's going to buckle under that pressure and open wide the door to let him into her and her children's lives again.

I can't stick around and watch that happen. If I thought I could do any good, I might try to stay for the kids' sakes, but Mel's going to do what Mel's going to do no matter what I say. Maybe you think I've turned cynical.

I think it just means that I've learned a thing or two about human nature.

CHAPTER 31

Now I'm thinking about what I've got to do this afternoon. I told you my mind wanders during sermons. If that makes me a bad Christian, I'll just have to accept it because I doubt there's anything I can do to change myself. Anyway, Justin's expecting me to call sometime after church. It's hard for me to remember exactly when we went from talking once a month to once a week. And now it's nearly every day. How did that happen?

After my marriage to Chris, it's taken a friendship with someone as steady and stable as Justin to force me to realize how dysfunctional I allowed things to get. Or maybe that's the victim in me talking still. What I should say is how dysfunctional our marriage grew due to my husband's rage.

But I'm resolved to remember the good times as well as the bad. It's the least I can do to ward off bitterness. I started attending church when I was two weeks old. I can't tell you how many sermons I've heard on the topic of forgiveness. What you preachers never seem to mention is that it's a cyclical process, something you do over and over again, each time carrying you to deeper crevices in your soul that you never knew existed. You might forgive someone once and think you've done your Christian duty only to find that in a month, maybe two, you're right back where you were, struggling with anger or resentment, wondering how someone could treat you so deplorably.

So you forgive him again until eventually you realize this is a cycle you might continue on until the day you die. The fact that you have to keep on forgiving doesn't mean you didn't do it well enough the first time. I don't think it's a symptom of the state of your own soul as much as it's an indication of how deeply you were wounded in the first place.

My journey to accomplish the intentional act of forgiveness began when Chris and I were still married, and it persists to this day. It's hard because I feel like I'm grieving on two different fronts. I'm grieving the loss of my marriage, and I'm grieving that seventeen-year-old boy, Orchard Grove High School's homecoming king, with his boyish dimples and vibrant eyes. It's still so hard for me to stop blaming myself. If I had been a better wife, if I had prayed more or learned how to fast, if I had done more to make my husband happy, would our story have ended differently?

Would we still be living out that happily ever after we imagined for ourselves at our Victorian wedding?

It's too late now. Chris and I are beyond the point of reconciliation, and I don't say that because I'm a drama queen or because my heart's hardened against him.

I say that because it's the simple truth.

Inasmuch as it depends on you, Paul writes, *live at peace with everyone*. You know, I used to think that reconciliation was a necessary proof of forgiveness, but I know better now. *Inasmuch as it depends on you …*

I'm not saying I was the perfect wife. I'm not saying that my depression or my grieving over Daddy or my inability to maintain a spotless home didn't contribute to the problems in our marriage. But I've made myself a promise. Maybe I'm not coming at it with the godliest of attitudes, but I am where I am, and that's all you can expect from me. And I refuse to apologize — to Chris, to myself, even to God — for my shortcomings unless they are actual sins.

So maybe it was my fault that I never learned how to scrub the rust stains out of a toilet bowl, but God doesn't judge me for the fact that my husband was so disgusted by my deplorable attempts that he yanked the seat off its hinges and smashed it into the bathroom mirror.

Maybe my prudish upbringing kept me uncomfortable

with some of the things my husband wanted to try in the bedroom. Maybe another woman who didn't feel shameful or degraded could have better fulfilled my husband's voracious sexual appetite, but my conscience is clean. The fact that I never fully met Chris's expectations might be the result of inexperience or immaturity but certainly not sinfulness on my part.

I don't know how to describe to you how vigorously I had to fight through two decades of conditioning to come to this relatively simple understanding. The strictest versions of evangelicalism, the kind epitomized by the upstanding folks at Orchard Grove, certainly didn't speed me on my journey, either.

At one point, I was sure that all our woes stemmed from the fact that I'd never learned how to be a proper housewife. I hate to say it, but I was somewhat coddled growing up. Daddy wanted to see me play, and Mom was too much of a perfectionist to leave any of the chores up to me. So when things got really bad between Chris and me, I hopped over to the Christian bookstore and purchased at least a dozen titles on how to be a respectable Christian homemaker.

You know what I learned?

I learned that if you set your alarm an hour earlier than normal, you can get such a head start on your daily duties that by the time your husband comes home from work, he can find not only a clean and tidy home, but a clean and tidy wife who's ready for *anything*. This is the advice they gave the girl who rejoiced on days when she only had to lay down for three naps instead of four during the darkest times of mourning her father's death.

Know what else these eager-beaver authors claimed? That if your husband is struggling sexually, if his list of faults includes lust in any way, shape, or form, it's because you aren't yielding to him enough in the bedroom. And the fact that your husband's degrading treatment makes you feel as exploited as a street-walker? That must be the result of your own frigid sexuality, and what you really need to do is loosen up.

Of course, if you read enough books, you'll find nuggets of truth in spite of obvious flaws. One of the titles was quite helpful. The author's thesis was that God designed marriage to make you holy, not necessarily to make you happy. I think it helps that he was speaking to husbands as well as wives, and he even had a chapter addressed to victims of abuse.

Your God-ordained commitment to your spouse ends when your safety or your children's safety is put in danger. He went on to list several case studies of women who fled dangerous marriages. (As an interesting aside, I've never yet found a Christian book that talks specifically to battered husbands like my friend Reginald.)

Chris and I had been married about a year by then, so this would be after the toilet seat in the mirror incident. After he refused to give me the car keys for two weeks as punishment for the time I forgot to tell him the gas tank was less than half full and I lost my part-time job at the library as a result.

The striking thing is that when I read that author who put his conservative Christian reputation on the line by urging wives to escape from abusive marriages, I never once thought he might be talking to me.

Chris had his anger issues. My enabling tendencies hadn't clouded my reasoning so much that I could deny something as simple as that. But he never once hit me. He never caused me any physical harm, at least never out of anger.

Was I an abused wife? An outsider might think they have a quick and easy answer, but I'm reluctant to take on that label. And I don't think it's just because of some sort of latent victim mentality, at least not all of it.

If what I went through with Chris is actual, *bona fide* spousal abuse, doesn't that diminish the experiences of other women? What does it mean for people like Mel, women who wind up in the ER with broken ribs, who have pictures on their phones documenting the finger-shaped bruises around their necks? If my abuse (if you can call it that) compares to their abuse, then the agony they went through feels somehow cheapened. Diminished.

Once you open the word abuse to mean anything that might cause physical or emotional discomfort, where do you draw the line? I don't know a single person whose spouse hasn't yelled at them at a given point. Hasn't called them a name they later regretted or hurt their feelings in some way. Does the Christian woman who happens to be married to a grouch get *carte blanche* to leave him because his crabbiness is arguably damaging her psyche?

It's a slippery slope once you take any way one spouse might hurt another and label it as abuse. Is any woman in my situation justified to leave her husband? Jesus himself said that Moses allowed for divorce because people's hearts were hardened. I've never yet met a pastor brave enough to tackle that passage from the pulpit, but my amateur attempts at biblical interpretation lead me to conclude that divorce is a necessary institution to give abused spouses a way to escape.

But what qualifies as abuse and what doesn't? You'd imagine it would be fairly straightforward until you start thinking through the nuances.

I know there's a line. During my entire marriage, I told myself that if Chris ever hit me, I'd not only be justified but I'd be wise to leave him. Pack my bags and get the heck out. But even then, it's not like my plan involved hiring an attorney and signing divorce papers that same day. More like temporary separation, enough so that he would realize I was serious about him changing, that if he didn't get a better hold of his rage, I would eventually be gone for good.

The intriguing thing is that most of the battered women I know have similar lines. For Mel, it was if he ever hurt one of the kids. She was perfectly content explaining away strangle marks on her throat, beer bottle cuts on her scalp. But if Kai ever hurt the children, that's when she would go. Which is how we ended up at the same shelter. Her and Kai's sagacious parenting philosophy was to never fight in earnest until the children were asleep. What neither of them realized was that as Kai was kicking her in the kidneys while she crouched in a ball under the table, the commotion woke up their son. Bowman charged at his father with nothing more than a pillow in his little grubby hands, a pillow wet with tears. All Kai did was push him aside, but Bowman tripped and hit his head on the dining room table. Didn't even bleed, but that had been the line Mel was waiting for him to cross. She sent Bowman back to bed, soothed Kai's raging nerves, and accepted his profuse and flowery apologies. Once he fell into his drunken slumber, she and the kids sneaked out, ran to the nearest gas station, and called a cab to take them to the shelter.

Even now, I'm far more likely to note the differences between me and Mel than the similarities. In my case, Chris wasn't a drinker. When we went out for dinner, I was the one to order wine while he was content with Diet Coke. I never had to sneak past him. Even when he took the car keys from me to keep me from going to work, I figured that was his right as head of the household. He'd never really wanted me to get the job at the library anyway, and if I had submitted to his will more readily from the beginning, he wouldn't have been forced to put me in that awkward predicament.

Those are the excuses I made, the reasons I stayed with him as long as I did. And it's not like you helped. You never once told me that Chris's problems were Chris's problems, not mine. Even when I sat in your office for counseling, you told me that it was my responsibility to submit to my husband, to respect his God-given authority, to shut up and pray and let the Holy Spirit work on his anger issues.

I heard it from you so many times that eventually I grew to believe I was the one in the wrong. I was the bitter wife who stubbornly refused to accept her husband's impressive apologies. Because if Chris knew how to do anything, it was apologize. You should have seen the mess of himself he made after he broke the bathroom mirror. Swept me up in his arms. Cuddled me for half an hour, crying into my shoulder, begging me to forgive him.

That's the side of him you saw. The repentant side. The *oh, please forgive me because I'm trying so hard but I'm still a slave to my sin* side. Did you ever stop and wonder what it was like for me? I'm not asking rhetorically either. I really want to know. Did you ever say to yourself, *Wow, I guess all this must be really hard to put up with. Maybe* she's *the one who needs all the prayer and fasting, not Chris.*

Did that come into your head? Because I lost track of how many times you belittled me for not being more forgiving. *True love always trusts, always perseveres.* You told me that so many times I could recite the entire chapter in my sleep. But where's the line drawn? Because that line exists. I know it does. But how far does it have to go before you look me in the eye and tell me enough is enough? Before you give me the freedom to love my husband from a distance. A good, safe distance.

Before you give me the freedom to walk away without acting like I'm the one transgressing God's commands.

Maybe if you'd recognized that line once we passed it, I wouldn't be sitting here with my chest aching over the daughter I've lost. I wouldn't be sitting here surrounded by missionary league women who all judge me, all condemn me. They only know me as that little Chinese girl who married her high-school sweetheart and then got pregnant with another man's child.

CHAPTER 32

And here comes the closing prayer. At least the sermon didn't run overtime. That's one thing pastors learn within their first week or two of ministry at Orchard Grove. You don't make the old retirees sit on the patently painful pews for longer than thirty minutes max. Greg's preaching lasted about twenty-eight minutes, and I could see him up there sweating a little as he raced through his last two bullet points.

I'm just glad it's over. I've got to get home. Got to clean up after my canned ravioli from last night. Got to make sure I don't leave Mom's house a dust speck dirtier than it was when she left for my brother's. I don't have time for Pastor Greg's long, drawn-out closing prayer.

I certainly don't have time for Grandma Lucy to ask for the microphone when he's done.

Grandma Lucy's something of a fixture in our little Christian bubble in Orchard Grove. If you go to church in our town, or you have a neighbor who does, or your niece and nephew attended vacation Bible school here one summer, you've encountered Grandma Lucy.

I swear that woman's a hundred years old if she's a day, and I only say that because she was white-haired and bespectacled when I was a little girl in pigtails nibbling on my Graham crackers and sipping my Tang in the downstairs Sunday school room.

Grandma Lucy's not the typical sort of Orchard Grove Bible Church congregant. She's, well, let's just say that there are at least two pastors who resigned within a month of meeting her. And I don't mean to imply she's mean or rude. She couldn't hurt a fly even if she wanted to because she's something like four-foot, ten-inches when she's not bent over, but she lives with this Holy Spirit flame in her that I swear would have the fire department, the fire marshal, all of FEMA, and Smokey the Bear himself dousing themselves with water if it were something you could literally see and measure.

I'm not saying I dislike Grandma Lucy, either. I'm just saying that you do your best to avoid her on Sunday mornings unless you want an hour-long impromptu prayer session. Because she doesn't sit down and talk to you like a normal person would. She doesn't even talk *at* you like some folks are known to do. No, Grandma Lucy *prays* at you. What I mean is you might think she's just making small-talk when she asks you how your week's gone, so you might answer, "Pretty good. I've got an English paper due on Tuesday," and all of a sudden you'll find her hand hot on your forehead, and she'll be proclaiming RELEASE from all that's standing in the way between you and academic success and CREATIVITY for the paper you've been called to turn in and a SOUND MIND for your studies and future plans, and then the next thing you know, she'll be chatting away about the azaleas she planted in her garden yesterday and how she hopes her baby goats don't eat them.

I know there are some folks at Orchard Grove who are actively terrified of this little ninety-pound grandma, but she doesn't bother me so much. I'm not saying I seek her out or anything, but I just figure that this little country church would be even more dull and dry without her, so more power to her and that hot little hand of hers. But right now, I don't need any extra delays. Maybe Pastor Greg doesn't know it yet. Maybe he's still too green, but if he gives her that microphone, there isn't a single person here who'll be leaving the church before one o'clock.

"Real quick," the pastor says, "Grandma Lucy has asked for the opportunity to close us in prayer today." And it's his use of the phrase *real quick* that proves just how much of a rookie he is here at Orchard Grove.

Grandma Lucy takes the mic, just like I remember her doing on dozens of different occasions when I was a girl here. It's something she's done from the beginning of time, I'm sure, or at least from the beginning of Orchard Grove Bible Church history. Sometimes she does it once a quarter or less. In other seasons it seems like it's every other week. I don't know how long it's been since the last time she's asked to close the service with a prayer, but Pastor Greg hands her the mic without a hint of reluctance, so I'm assuming this is his first experience.

That poor man has no idea what he's in for.

I notice several congregants straightening their spines or coughing quietly because that's what the Orchard Grove women do when Grandma Lucy stands up to pray. It's their way of showing their displeasure that she's never joined their missionary league and never attends their fancy teas or fundraising luncheons. Toward the front, Joy's son is even squirmier than normal.

I know, kid, I want to tell him. *I feel your pain.*

"Thank you so much, Pastor Greg," Grandma Lucy says, and she smiles at him so sweetly. He smiles back, which seals my conviction that he currently has no clue what he's just done. At least the next few minutes will be amusing.

"I want to close us today with a blessing from the book of Isaiah." That's Grandma Lucy's hook. She tells you she wants to offer up a prayer, and then before you know it you're sitting there listening to a twenty-minute Scripture recitation. I swear that woman has entire chunks of the Bible memorized. Psalms and Isaiah seem to be her favorites from what I can recall, but then again, that was a long time ago so maybe her preferences have changed.

"Comfort, comfort my people, says your God. Speak tenderly to Jerusalem, and proclaim to her that her hard service has been completed, that her sin has been paid for, that she has received from the Lord's hand double for all her sins."

I know it's rude to get up and leave. Not even the missionary league women have the audacity to do that, but I glance at the time and decide to give Grandma Lucy ten minutes max. Then I'm out of here.

"He tends his flock like a shepherd: He gathers the lambs in his arms and carries them close to his heart; he gently leads those who have young." The words remind me of the painting I love, the one of the boy shielding the little girl from the rain with such tenderness in his eyes and in his posture. And of course, I can't think about that painting without the painful reminder of the night Chris proposed to me, the inscription on my pen.

If these delights thy mind may move, Then live with me, and be my love.

I suppose if you're looking for sheer poetry, Isaiah's the place to go. But I'm only half paying attention to Grandma Lucy now. I tune her out as best as I can before her words bring back even more memories of Chris. Instead, I think about the rest of my day.

Talking for an hour or two with Justin.

Staring at pictures of my baby girl.

Wishing life hadn't taken me down this course.

Mental fog. Heavy exhaustion.

Lonely days, dragged-out nights.

That's life as usual for me now. That's my life now that Chris is gone.

CHAPTER 33

I glance out the window and see that the snow has started to fall. Fat, heavy flakes. I can never see weather like this without thinking of our trip to Leavenworth.

Chris and I had been married for a year. It was our anniversary. Pretty big deal, considering all we'd gone through in the past twelve months. Me losing Daddy. Him losing his temper. Both of us learning to exist with his rage and without my father.

By the time Chris surprised me with a two-night stay at the Stargazers' Inn to celebrate our first anniversary, I thought things had started to improve. I thought all those prayers you were pouring out on my husband were finally making a difference. I looked back at how much pain my husband's anger had caused and realized you were right all along. I just needed to be patient and wait for God to work in Chris's heart in his way and in his good time.

The B&B was perfect. Chris was perfect. Not a single fight, not a single argument for three whole days. We even talked a little bit about our relationship on the drive there. The snow was falling just like this. Slow. Peaceful. Have you ever noticed how much easier it is to have a deep conversation when you're sitting side by side, not straight across from each other where you have to look at one another's eyes? See each other's expressions, each other's hurt.

He apologized. I don't know if that sounds like a big deal to you, but while the snow floated down around us, he actually apologized for the times he'd lost his temper. We still hadn't gotten the bathroom mirror fixed, but he told me after his next paycheck he'd take me to the hardware store and we could pick something out together, something fancier than the plain piece of glass we inherited with the place.

I opened up a little, too. Told him how ashamed I'd been when I had to quit my job at the library, how I felt like I'd let my boss and co-workers down, how much of a failure I felt like when I just stopped showing up. I still hadn't mentioned Reginald to him yet, but my old library patron friend had recently invited me to work at the new bookstore he was opening. I wasn't sure if Chris would agree, but with the way the conversation was going, I was hopeful that maybe over the next few days I might find the right time to bring it up.

"I think that if I have a set schedule, something where I

have to be there every day, it might help me manage the time I do spend at home better. Help me stay on top of things like the laundry and dishes."

"I know it's been hard for you," Chris said, and he actually asked if I'd like him to take over one or two of the daily chores.

"No, I don't want you to have to do that." But he was so kind and adamant that eventually I dropped another hint about Reginald's store. "I mean, if I ever got another part-time job or something, it might be nice if you pitched in, but right now I don't have anything else going on, so it doesn't make sense for you to do the housework."

He didn't respond, but it was the first time in a few months that I'd mentioned anything about money without him grumbling about what I was spending on books or worrying about the price of gas or about how I could never remember to tell him when the tank needed to be filled.

There were several turning points for us around the same time as our trip to Leavenworth. I remember it was that Christmas when you gave Chris those CD sermons he could listen to in the car while he drove around town delivering papers for work. CDs from the Truth Warriors conferences that had kind of spread across the country, big events in football stadiums where speakers got men all riled up to fulfill their duties as godly leaders. I know some modernized women seethe at the thought of five thousand men getting together to talk about biblical masculinity, but it did Chris some good. I could see he was growing closer to God, although in all honesty, his relationship with the Lord was never the issue. But whatever it was about the CDs, they encouraged my husband, and the difference it made in our relationship was night and day.

In some ways, coming home from our anniversary in Leavenworth was like recovering from my first round of depression. Now that things were better between us, I was able to finally understand how bad they'd gotten. Of course, no marriage is perfect, but there was steady progress, so much so that I began to believe God had answered my prayers to take away my husband's rage. At the time, you'd pushed me toward the *shut up and pray* theology. I still don't think it'll work in every case. I doubt Abigail would have fared too well if she'd ignored the fact that King David and his men were mounting an attack and instead she had just committed herself to fervent prayer. But who's to say for sure? Never put God in a box, right? I know that tactic certainly wouldn't serve Mel very well, although she herself has admitted that even an atheist succumbs to prayer when her husband's beefy hands are wrapped around her throat.

But in my case, I dared to believe that the worst was truly over for Chris and me. A few weeks after we got back from our anniversary getaway, I worked up the nerve to tell him that I'd met a man at the library who wanted to hire me part time at his new bookstore. I think Chris was a little surprised at first that I'd met anybody who wasn't a woman, but once he found out that Reginald was an octogenarian who'd spent over twenty years getting beaten up by his wife, Chris realized our friendship posed no threat.

He encouraged me to take the job as long as I could work in the evenings so he could always have the car during the day. The pay was three dollars an hour higher than what I'd been making at the library, and I'm sure I cost Reginald more money than I ever helped him earn. He never complained, though. I think he liked the company if nothing else. The position was only part time (a few hours each evening and eight hours every Saturday), but I found it was helpful to have a reason to get out of the house. No, I didn't become the perfect Sally Homemaker after that, but I had more energy and more motivation to keep things up.

I started writing a little during that time too. Dabbling, really. I mean, I wasn't even at the *aspiring author* stage yet, I was a step or two behind that. But I'd write when things at the store were slow, and Reginald didn't mind. He encouraged it. Sometimes he'd ask to read what I wrote, and he never criticized even though it was pure junk. I don't have a single scrap of it left, but at least I felt like my life was moving in the direction I wanted it to.

Chris and I continued being involved at Valley Tabernacle. We bumped into a small scheduling glitch when the music team switched their practice from Sunday morning to Tuesday nights, but we made it work. Chris dropped me off at the bookstore then drove all the way across town to church, and after closing Reginald would take me home in his Explorer. It's quite a generic car for a millionaire with such eccentric tastes as his, but he told me in his earlier days (by which I think he was referring to his seventies) he sported an Aston Martin and litigation-crazed drivers tried to deliberately get him into an accident. He was so much happier when he passed the luxury car on to his daughter and started driving her SUV, which he affectionately named Rocinante after Don Quixote's faithful steed.

Have you ever noticed that when things get bad, they tend to fall apart all at once, but they often improve all at once too? That's how it was for us. With me working again, it looked like we might realistically afford a law school deposit once Chris got his applications in. We'd be a year later than we'd originally hoped, but we were a full year wiser as well. I shudder to think what it would have been like if Chris jumped into grad school immediately after graduation when our fighting was so constant.

His anger issues were improving to the point where we had more good nights together than bad. I didn't eye the clock every afternoon dreading the moment my husband would come home. My mental outlook was improving too. No major crashes. Being Reginald's only employee really helped me stay focused and on target. He needed me, even if it was just to keep him company until closing time, and I wasn't about to let him down by checking out of the world for a month or longer.

Maybe the writing was therapeutic too. I don't know. It was all fluff. Dumb romances I'd never show a living soul today. Not even worth saving in case I ever make it big and my first drafts might find their way into some private collection or other. Chris was furiously preparing for his LSATs, I was surrounded by books all evening and getting paid to write nonsense in my free time, and you had mentored Chris to the point where he was finally accepting responsibility for his anger problems and making steady progress.

Maybe it was because things were improving so dramatically that Chris got it in his head it was time to get me pregnant.

CHAPTER 34

It's often the wives who catch baby fever first, but things worked backwards for us. Even before our wedding day, we both knew that Chris wanted children more than I did. As a young, optimistic bride-to-be, I felt so full and complete in my love for my husband I never understood the need to invite another living being into our familial bliss.

Then after the wedding, after the powerful bonds of Chris's anger reared their ugly head, I couldn't fathom subjecting an innocent child to that degree of volatility.

But Chris came from a rather large family. (In spite of his parents' pure hatred for one another, they managed to produce four children). And once you had gotten him so involved in that Truth Warriors movement with their somewhat rigid concept of biblical masculinity, he grew more and more convinced it was time to start a family of our own.

We had quite a few arguments about it at first. What about law school? What about rent? Childcare? I was adamant that I wouldn't give up working for Reginald.

Because as that winter thawed into spring and spring burst into summer, I grew fiercely loyal to my friend, and no amount of sermons or books on wifely submission could convince me to give up my job at the bookstore when it was so clear that my employer needed me. We were kindred spirits, Reginald and I, more than either of us realized at the time. Then again, Reginald was far more perceptive than I am, so maybe he knew before I did.

But still, I refused to give up my nights at his store in order to rock a baby to sleep. I'd never forgive myself for letting Reginald down like that.

If my obstinacy displeased my husband, who'd listened to those CD sermons on biblical masculinity (and the complementary definition of wifely submission) so many times he probably had them all memorized, he didn't show it. "I'll watch her in the evenings." Chris was already convinced our first child would be a little girl. He'd even settled on the name Grace. "That way you can get out of the house a few hours a night, and it will give me and her some one-on-one time together."

"What about Saturdays?"

"I could watch her all day. I wouldn't mind."

Leave it to the dad to forget about a baby's basic need for survival. "What if she's nursing?"

I thought I might have won the argument, but Chris's grand idea was to ask Reginald if I could bring a baby to work with me, and Reginald was so supportive he bought us a two-night stay at Davenport, one of Spokane's most romantic B&Bs — honeymoon suite, fancy champagne, everything.

We didn't get pregnant at Davenport. In fact, my body seemed in no hurry to get pregnant whatsoever. But the extra time gave me a chance to adjust the idea of becoming a mother. Once I got in the habit of going out every evening to work with Reginald in his store, I found myself bored the rest of the day with very little to do other than stare at piles of laundry I didn't have the gumption to fold and put away. Maybe a baby would do me good. I was also beginning to realize that the reason my scribbles would never be worthy of publication was because I had so few life experiences to draw from. I wasn't ready to talk about depression, and I couldn't publish anything about my upbringing without invoking a lethal dose of maternal wrath. (I still have no clue how Amy Tan manages to write what she does.) Maybe having a baby would grant me some additional life experiences that might one day work their way into a novel.

By the time fall rolled around, everyone was infected with baby fever — Chris, myself, and Reginald too. After treating us to that B&B, even though our luxurious stay didn't result in the sort of exciting announcement he'd been hoping for, I think he felt somewhat responsible for the blessed event whenever it did occur. It was endearing. He was already talking to a contractor to have the back office converted into a nursery. I've never witnessed somebody age in reverse, but that's what this as-of-yet unconceived child did for Reginald. He came from a Catholic background, and I made him cry when I asked him to become our child's godfather.

He gave me a raise (since I would soon be eating for two) and refused to let me lift any of the heavy boxes when we got a delivery in. I'm sure that store of his — and the cost of keeping me employed — left him several thousand dollars in the hole at the end of every month, but he had the money to spend on it and he was doing what he loved.

I hate that I haven't gone to see him in so long. It's wrong of me. It really is. Now that I'm back in town, I owe him a visit. He's the only one who loves Grace as much as I do. Considers her as his honorary godchild even after everything we went through.

Poor Reginald.

CHAPTER 35

Grandma Lucy's warmed up, and now she's really going at it strong. I've seen her in action enough times to know exactly how it all works. She starts with a short prayer, intercession for the pastor and the congregants, things like that. Then it's a Bible verse. And pretty soon she's got her hand up in the air, and she's spewing Holy Spirit blessings out on all of us with a fervency that would make even your style of public speaking look as stoic and rigid as good old Mr. Darcy's.

"The Lord takes such great delight in you," she says, and I know that this is her mix of jumbling prayer and preaching and biblical paraphrase all together. "He rejoices over you with songs of deliverance. His delight is in you, the workmanship of his hands, the masterpiece of the artist of artists, the great author and finisher of our faith when we put our trust in him."

I swear I'm listening to King James Mad Libs.

I'll never get people who pray with so much boldness.

Like they know the exact way God will work in a given situation, so that's what they ask him to do. People like you who actually tell God what the outcome will be. I'm not knocking your style, by the way. I mean, it was that one prayer of yours the first day I heard you preach that freed me from suicide. It was like you were convinced that was exactly what God wanted to do, like if he didn't heal someone in your congregation from the so-called demon of suicide at that precise moment, he would cease to be God.

I don't know that I could ever take a leap of faith like that.

But it worked in my case. Like I said, I don't think of killing myself anymore, which leads to a whole bunch of new questions. If God could snap his fingers and *bam!* take away my suicidal thoughts, couldn't he do the same thing with my depression? Did you just not pray hard enough that first day we met? And after that were you so worried about my husband's spiritual breakthroughs that you stopped asking God for mine?

Or maybe God was unwilling. But why? Would it have been that much of a stretch for him to go the entire way and cure my depression entirely?

I'm not like you or Grandma Lucy, people who get words from God all the time, like you're just going about your day and all of a sudden the Almighty himself pops into your brain and tells you whatever message he wants you to have. I guess my faith is a lot more mundane than that, living day by day and trusting that what I read in the Bible is true. So it's not like God whispered something in my ear and told me why he didn't cure my depression completely, but I do have a few theories of my own.

The way I see it, depression is my battle to fight just like anger was my husband's. If saying a simple prayer of deliverance could free me entirely, I'd have no compassion to offer Chris as he warred against his rage.

Because a war is exactly what it was. Just because our subsequent years of marriage were so much smoother than the first, that certainly didn't mean Chris had fought his battle and won. But as dear old Reginald (who happened to be a history buff as well as a lover of fine books), was so fond of pointing out, achieving one victory in battle is a far cry from winning the war.

And war is what we experienced when a few months of trying for a baby turned into a year. And then two. Reginald was as disappointed as we were. I think he was enraptured by the idea of filling in as a surrogate grandpa to a child who wasn't biologically his. A child whose parents didn't care how big of an inheritance he'd leave, who weren't just counting down the days until his death so they could claim his fortune.

So it was Reginald who took me aside one day and told me he'd pay for testing. For Chris and me both. Because as hard as we were trying, as long as we'd worked at it, there was no reason to explain why we weren't already parents twice over by now.

I thought Chris would refuse. The initial procedure to test male fertility isn't invasive *per se*, but it's not exactly free from its own embarrassments. He put those concerns aside and agreed to accept Reginald's generosity. And then came the waiting. I wasn't sure which would be worse to hear — that there was a problem with one of us or that we were both perfectly capable of bearing children as far as the doctors could discern.

If there was a problem, I had a hard time picturing Chris rolling over and accepting that diagnosis graciously. If I was unable to bear my husband the children he so desperately wanted, would he resent me? Even worse, what if the problem was with him? Chris had learned to control his rage so well that he was almost an entirely different man now. The man I thought I was marrying when we said our vows.

What would happen to him if he learned he was unable

to father a child? Would the disappointment and shame undo the years' worth of progress he'd made?

And who could I talk to about all this? I wasn't in touch with any of my friends from high school or college, and my mother was the last person I wanted to sit down with to discuss my reproductive health or sex life. In fact, you and the elders were the only other people besides Reginald who knew about our struggles. Do you remember that night you laid hands on us both? And you prophesied that we'd conceive a child. Even when you said the words, I didn't believe them. I was afraid you were just setting Chris up for even deeper hurt. Deeper disappointment. Because as soon as you proclaimed there was a pregnancy in my future, I knew that meant that if I failed to produce the promised heir, Chris would blame either me or himself for the lack of faith that kept your prophecy from coming true. So I guarded my heart against what you said, but he soaked up your words, grasped at them like a shipwrecked sailor would cling to debris.

As for me, I turned to books. My most recently found treasure was a novelist named Hester Lynne — can you believe it? Hester Lynne. With a name like that, there's no way she could have grown up to *not* write literary fiction, don't you think?

Hester Lynne splashed her name across multiple bestseller charts with her debut, *The Winding Road*, a somewhat rambling, gorgeously executed novel about a woman coming to terms with her infertility. The prose is so exquisite, so *hit you in the gut* real that I didn't even need to read the acknowledgements in the back of the book to know she was writing from personal experience.

I think I'd read her novel three times before the day came for Chris and me to meet with the doctor and discuss the results of our initial tests. Reginald insisted on taking us out to lunch before that fated appointment.

"I want you children to know I'm very proud of you," he told us over our escargot. Even though he had toned down his car preferences, his culinary preferences were as refined and extravagant as his taste in books.

I think Chris and I were both a little uncomfortable over that lunch. It wasn't that I was afraid of life without children. I'd grown used to our baby-free marriage. I wasn't sitting around bored at home either since Reginald decided to purchase a "company car" for me to drive. I was working for him full-time now without having to worry about sharing rides with my husband.

I knew that on a strictly personal level, I could accept a life without a child. But I also knew my husband couldn't. He was still holding onto your word of faith that God would give us a baby. Maybe you don't realize it, but when you say something like that with so much conviction and boldness, it puts a lot of pressure on lay people like us. Because now if it doesn't come true, we're left to ask ourselves what we did to deflect God's blessings, blessings that you yourself promised.

At the restaurant, Chris hardly touched his food, exquisite as it was. I know in some ways, he had grown resentful of my friend's charity. Reginald would rather lavish his generosity on us, a young couple who truly appreciated his friendship, than treasure his wealth up to be divided and fought over after his death. If we received a poor prognosis at the meeting that afternoon, I knew Reginald would offer anything we could ask. Donating the money for an adoption. Covering the expenses for IVF treatment. But I suppose it's hard for a husband to accept that he can't start a family of his own without another man's charity, which is why we were trying (and failing more often than not) to live off Chris's paycheck alone and saving up my income so we wouldn't have to rely on Reginald's goodwill if it came down to that.

Initially, that money had been set aside for law school, but now it seemed my husband would do anything to become a father, even spend the rest of his life driving around town delivering packages for attorneys instead of becoming one himself.

We left the restaurant a little earlier than good manners would dictate, but I knew Reginald wouldn't mind. He was just as anxious to hear the test results as Chris was.

As for me, call it premonition or whatever else you want, but I went into that fertility clinic with a stone as heavy as an encyclopedia settled in my gut.

Afraid that we'd get bad news. Afraid that we'd get no news.

Afraid that whatever the doctor had to tell us, it would awaken the silent rage that now lay dormant at the base of my husband's soul.

CHAPTER 36

I didn't call Reginald like I promised when we left the fertility clinic. I didn't respond to his voicemails either. He'd already given me the evening off. I wouldn't have to face him for over twenty-four hours.

What I would have to face was my husband.

"What a bunch of idiots." It seemed that insulting the doctors who ran our tests was a better alternative than accepting the fact that he couldn't father children.

"Load of snake-oil conmen." Apparently, when the medical professionals told my husband he was sterile, it was easier to assume that they were greedy con artists intent on stealing our money from us (or Reginald) than to accept that they might be telling the truth.

"Brood of vipers, the whole lot of them." Because when Chris didn't know where else to channel his anger, he took up insults from Scripture. Who could blame him if all he was doing was quoting John the Baptist or Jesus Christ himself?

I kept silent at first, which might not have been the best idea. Chris wanted a partner to commiserate with, a sympathetic ear to disparage the doctor who told us he could never father a child. I simply wanted quiet.

"I bet you're happy about this, aren't you?"

I should have known. Should have suspected that once he ran out of New Testament insults for the fertility clinic, he'd have no other target for his rage except me.

"Now you can keep on working at that stupid, moldy bookstore. Isn't that what you wanted from the very beginning?"

I held my peace. I'd learned enough about Chris by then to know that he wasn't trying to hurt me. He didn't mean the things he was saying. Tomorrow, after a good night's sleep, he'd feel calmer. We'd talk about it rationally then.

"You probably prayed for something like this. Probably asked God to keep you from becoming a mom because you know you'd do a lousy …" He stopped himself. At the time, I thought it was a sign of his improvement when he stormed into the bedroom and slammed the door shut instead of finishing his sentence.

And I waited. Hester Lynne had just released a follow-up to her dazzling debut. I felt bad for her, truth be told, since her second novel had been met with mediocre reception to say the least. I suppose that's what happens when you burst onto the literary stage with such a glorious beginning.

You peak before your career ever takes off.

A one-book wonder.

But Reginald had recommended her latest novel, *The Scent of Silence*, and I'd learned to distrust snooty reviewers years earlier.

I was halfway into chapter four and was actually quite taken with the story when Chris stomped out of the bedroom once more. "What are you doing?"

"Reading."

His eyes rolled so dramatically I'm surprised they didn't get stuck in the back of his head. "Reading. That's perfect. Just perfect."

I lowered the book but continued to hold the page in place. "What would you like to do instead?" If there was a testiness in my tone, it had more to do with my exhaustion than any desire to further enrage my husband.

He threw up his hands with a huff. "What do I want to do? I don't know. Maybe have an actual discussion about what those quack-jobs told us."

I set the book beside me on the couch, my finger still marking my page. "Ok. Let's talk. Are you going to sit down?"

His eyes roamed all over the room with a frantic restlessness. "I can't believe you're so calm about this. This is our future together. Our family."

I should have held my tongue. But I was still trusting in the new Chris, the reasonable Chris I had grown comfortable with after that rocky first year of marriage. I didn't realize all the progress he'd made had been erased by one simple doctor's visit, so I told him we could still be a family even if we never had a child.

"Easy for you to say. You've been against the idea of a pregnancy from the beginning. You just went along with it because it was something I wanted." Given the fact that he was basically speaking the truth, I didn't have a whole lot to add.

He started pacing. Back and forth. Back and forth. A lion in his cage.

"We've got to get a second opinion or something. There's got to be some sort of treatment options, ways to …" He waved his hand in the air like he was trying to snatch some pesky word he couldn't recall.

"That's why we made that follow-up appointment," I said.

"They should have talked about that today. Now we've got to wait another week, I've got to take more time off work …"

What I didn't tell him was the reason they made couples wait between appointments was so that people like my husband, people devastated by the news that they were unable to naturally conceive children, would have a chance to process and cool down before jumping into fix-it mode.

"Those idiots don't have any idea what they're talking about."

Part of me was glad he was back to focusing his anger on the medical professionals. I'd already given up any hope of reading more from Hester Lynne that night and allowed myself to lose my place in the book. I made room for my husband on the couch and patted the cushion. "Come here."

He shot me a disdainful look but finally lowered himself beside me with a huff. I wrapped my arms around him and kissed him on the cheek.

"I love you." No matter what would happen, no matter what the news of Chris's sterility would do to him — would do to us — it was essential that he knew. Essential that I tell him.

"I love you," I repeated as I felt his body relax. I kissed him again. His cheek was wet. "This isn't your fault. This doesn't mean we'll never have children. We'll figure something out, ok?"

I wasn't ready to talk about adoption or artificial insemination or anything like that, and I knew Chris wasn't either. Right now, I just wanted him to know that this was a trial, but it was one we could face together.

Chris rested his head against my chest, and I held him while he cried.

CHAPTER 37

Grandma Lucy's harping on the disciples now. She's been going at it and I've been in my seat in the same position for so long that I've got a kink in my lower back. She's going on about how the twelve spent three years walking around with Jesus Christ, the Son of God incarnate, and they didn't recognize him. They didn't know who he really was but spent all their time and energy bickering over trivial topics, like who was the most important.

Theirs was a problem of foolish arguments, discussing things that didn't matter, but have you noticed it's often the *not discussing* things that can be your undoing, not the other way around?

Chris and I went months not discussing.

Not discussing the fact that his form of sterility was irreversible.

Not discussing the fact that his prognosis so threatened his sense of masculinity he felt compelled to prove himself a man even more vigorously than usual until my body felt more like a therapeutic punching bag than anything else.

The one thing we did discuss was how to reverse our childless state, and I threw myself head-first into these early planning stages, certain what my husband was going through was nothing more than a phase that would pass when God brought a child into our lives. Since I had more free time, both at home and at Reginald's, the bulk of the research fell to me, and I pursued it with more energy than I'd ever thrown into any of my studies.

I researched international adoptions, made a list of everything we'd have to save up for, beginning with the initial two-thousand-dollar home visit. Chris refused to accept any more of Reginald's charity, so we were on our own. I came up with a list of the least expensive countries to adopt from, plugged in some quick estimates, and figured that in three years, we might be in a financial position to begin the process, even though it would be another two years or more after that before we could actually bring our child home.

That was the other thing. Chris didn't just want a child. He wanted a baby. I found out that a lot of private adoption agencies are just as expensive as the international ones, and we were told that with such a large pool of prospective adoptive families, we might be pushing forty before a birth mother chose us.

I spent an entire weekend filling out the forms so we could be licensed through the state and took a three-hour class on fostering with the intent to adopt. The plus side was that it was a financially feasible option that we could begin pursuing immediately. Chris was all for the idea, but I had my hesitations. Even if we took a baby straight from the hospital, the child's medical history would still be one big question mark. Chris was so in love with the idea of having an infant to call his own, he wasn't thinking about things like fetal alcohol syndrome or babies born dependent on drugs.

It was Reginald who voiced the most concerns when I told him about our thoughts of adopting through the state. One of his granddaughters had tried to do the same thing and was matched with one healthy baby after another that she was told was legally free, but either the social workers lied to her outright or a member of the biological family found a loophole so that five or six children were placed under her care and then yanked away from her at the last minute before the heartache was too much to bear.

"If it's the money you're worried about," Reginald assured me, "you know that's never going to be an issue."

I didn't tell him Chris was refusing his assistance. I made it out like Chris was on a mission of goodwill, that he'd read about how desperately the state needed foster families and was committed to providing these kids a safe home for however long children's services saw fit to keep them in our care.

"He's a good man, your husband is," Reginald said.

What could I do but agree?

CHAPTER 38

It's amazing what you can get used to when your options are all stripped away. Amazing how quickly I simply rolled over and accepted Chris's anger problems as soon as they resurfaced. How his rough, unloving treatment in the bedroom no longer felt like degradation or abuse. Instead, subjecting myself to his every whim was simply a way I could build up his masculinity, which had taken such a fatal blow at the fertility clinic. I was nervous again, constantly on edge, constantly afraid I wasn't enough for him, anxious he'd come home and find the house or his dinner weren't up to his standards.

Now that I'd increased my hours at the store, Reginald also became the focal point for my husband's ire.

"Doesn't that man know you have a family to take care of?" Chris would shout if traffic kept me out ten minutes later than expected.

"I'm sorry," I'd say. "I must not have been keeping track of the time."

"Tell your boss if he wants you driving that stupid company car, he's got to make sure to always leave you half a tank of gas or more."

"It's my fault," I'd say. "I forgot to tell him the last time it got low."

"Where are all my work shirts? I thought you were going to iron them this morning. Reginald didn't call you into work early, did he? You know how I feel about that."

"No, I'm sorry. I was on hold all day with children's services."

"So use a headset and iron while you talk."

"I'm sorry." It got to where I could say those two words in my sleep, but even then, it wasn't enough for my husband.

"I'm sick of you telling me how sorry you are all the time but then you don't lift a finger to change anything. Your apologies mean nothing to me anymore."

"I'm sorry." What else was there for me to say?

The snow's still falling outside, but it's changed. Heavier now. Gusts of wind swirling it all around. That sense of peaceful tranquility is long gone. This little winter tempest is actually a more fitting backdrop for Grandma Lucy's feverish crescendo. Even while I'm staring out the window,

I'm listening to every word she says. She's gotten so loud it's impossible to tune her out.

"A voice of one crying in the wilderness." I've heard the reference before, read it myself several times. But there's something about the way she says it now. The conviction in her tone. I'd call her bewitching if I didn't think it would insult her faith. "Weeping and great mourning."

As if I'm a stranger to tears and sorrow.

You'd think with my history, my depression would worsen depending on what was happening around me. But once we discovered Chris could never father a child, when the prognosis forced us to trudge through that valley of devastation and loss, my mind was clearer than it had been in years. It must have been some sort of survival mechanism that clicked on in my body, some latent instinct that told my psyche I had better function if I wanted to avoid my husband's wrath.

Not that there was any real way to get around it.

Chris was as devastated by the news of his infertility as I expected him to be. And really, Pastor, I can't help but blame you for some of that. Couldn't you have waited to hear what the doctors said before jumping in and declaring that I'd soon find myself WITH CHILD by the power of the blood of JESUS? Is that really what you think my husband needed to hear at that moment? The same husband you knew was having so many problems with his anger and rage at home?

The months after our appointment at the fertility clinic were a blizzard of barked-out plans. Chris changed his mind every couple days. First off we were going to pay for the home inspection to get the ball rolling on a private adoption. Then we were going to start looking into international grants. A week or two after that, it was back to fostering through the state with the intent to adopt. I did what I could to appease him. I could have told you at that time my husband was incapable of making a single rational decision, but you'd drilled it into my head by then that he was the God-ordained leader of the household and all these important decisions fell on him.

So one week I was on the phone with Agape Adoption Ministries, and the next I was printing up applications for placements through India while at the same time Chris expected me to have turned in the last bundle of paperwork for our licensing through the state.

"I'm sorry," I had to tell him. "The office was closed by the time I got there."

"That's it. You're done at that stupid bookstore." As obstinate as Chris was about certain things, this was the first time he gave me an official ultimatum. Before, it had always been passive-aggressive, like when he hid the keys from me until I lost my job at the library. But of course, that tactic wouldn't have worked in this instance since it was Reginald's company car I was driving.

Maybe you'll take this as a sign that I was nothing more than a rebellious wife, but I wasn't going to give up my job. Not without a fight. And it was epic. Something to make J. R. R. Tolkien burn with envy. I lost track of time, but I know we went at it several hours, which just goes to prove how much my friendship with Reginald had grown to mean to me. By that point in our marriage, I usually gave in after the first ten or fifteen minutes.

"I don't care how old he is or what he thinks he's done for us," Chris insisted. "You're calling him up tonight and telling him you quit."

"So I messed up," I told him. "I forgot one little errand. That's no reason to lock me up in the house all day like I'm some sort of domestic slave."

"Those forms were due at children's services this afternoon. Why do you think I stayed up so late last night signing everything?"

"It was a simple mistake," I told him.

"Yeah, a simple mistake that could cost us our fostering license."

In spite of everything we'd gone through by then, I was still surprised from time to time how melodramatic he could be. "Do you have any idea how desperate they are for foster parents? I could turn in the forms next month and we'd still be approved in twenty-four hours."

"I'm not talking about next month." Chris's voice trembled. I could tell he was trying hard to keep from roaring. You've got to give him that much credit.

"I already emailed the case manager, and she said I can go in tomorrow and drop everything off."

"Well," Chris huffed, "you should have gone in today."

"I did go in today." I'm sure all those authors of those books on how to be a submissive housewife would have been tremendously disappointed to hear the edge in my voice. "I went there right before five. I'd forgotten that they close at four."

"You didn't forget," Chris told me like he was some sort of expert. "Your brain is just so full of those stupid books and that stupid job working for that eccentric old goon that you refused to take care of the paperwork like I asked you to."

"You make it sound like I deliberately sabotaged this whole thing." I was glad we weren't living in the same apartment we'd moved into as newlyweds, glad that at least our voices couldn't be heard by any neighbors.

"Admit it," Chris pressed. "You've dragged your heels about getting this license ever since your boss sold you that sob story about some granddaughter of his."

What do you say to an accusation like that? "I'm sorry. I'll take the forms in tomorrow. I really don't see what the big deal is."

"That's because you don't care about ever being a family!" His voice was nearer to the roaring stage but still not quite there yet.

"I thought we already were a family," I mumbled. It was so quiet I didn't think he'd hear, but I was wrong.

"You want to talk about family?" he shouted. "How about this for family. How about you start acting like a wife and mother instead of some college student wasting her time around a bunch of old books because she's convinced that she's going to become some New York Times bestseller even though she can't even complete the first *chapter* of anything she starts? You want to pretend we're a family? What if instead of twiddling your thumbs at some stranger's moldy bookstore you actually did your jobs around the house?" He shook his head. "Family." He spat out the word like a curse.

I might have let it drop at that point. I was an expert at letting things drop by then, but he had to go and make it even more personal.

"Of course, I suppose I shouldn't be surprised, seeing as how you've got such a big fan-girl crush on some impotent, eighty-year-old retired professor and literary wannabe who pays you twice what you're worth and buys you a car because that's the only way he can get anyone to pretend to love him."

"Don't you dare talk about Reginald that way." I puffed out my chest like some angry gorilla trying to intimidate its opponent. "Don't you dare."

He sneered at me, as if my reaction alone was enough to prove his point. "You call him up and tell him you won't be going in anymore. And tell him he can come pick up that stupid car of his whenever he feels man enough."

I'm not usually a crier. In the heaviness of depression, I'm too emotionally numb, and in times of intense grieving, I'm too focused on keeping my mind's tentative grip on reality to indulge in tears. The only thing that can really set me off is when I'm angry.

That night was the kicker.

"You can't lay a hand on that car because it's not yours. And you can't tell me if I can or can't go to work because it's not your decision. It's mine." Now that I think about it, my tears had as much to do with Reginald and his deep loneliness than anything going on between my husband and me.

"You're nothing but an ungrateful brat." That's the difference between Chris and me. When he's in the throes of anger, his voice gets even calmer, more subdued until it takes on some eerie, other-worldly type of quality.

My voice, by contrast, just rises with my hysterics. "What do I have to be grateful to you for?" I shrieked. If I had something near me besides a couch pillow, I would have been tempted to launch it at his head. "What have you ever done that I should be grateful for?"

Chris balled his hands into fists, but even then I wasn't afraid. Not yet.

"I've given you a home." His voice was deadly calm. "I've paid all the bills. I've let you waste your time at that stupid bookstore …"

I'm not proud of what I did next. I'm really not. But the past can never be altered, can it? I've begged God for forgiveness, which I guess is the most any one of us can do with those mistakes we've made and later regret. The thing about being married, especially if your relationship is as tumultuous and complicated as ours, is that after a few years you learn where to hit your spouse where it wounds the most.

Now it was my turn to sneer. After Chris finished rattling off every single thing he'd ever done for me, I looked him right in the eyes, certain my words would find their mark. "And after all that, you still couldn't get me pregnant, could you?"

He grabbed me by the hair.

"What are you doing?" My heart was pounding, but even though my physiology went through the motions of fear, I don't remember feeling it myself.

"Let go of me." Even as I protested, I kept my voice calm. Tried to deescalate the situation.

Chris dragged me to the front door. It didn't hurt, or if it did I don't remember that part. His hand was on the knob. What was he going to do? Throw me out in the cold?

"Get out!"

I stumbled back. I was outside. Tottering off the porch. I don't remember feeling surprised. I wasn't even angry anymore. I just sat there and thought to myself, *I shouldn't have said that.*

He threw my coat after me — it was the middle of winter — and slammed the door shut, and all I remember is thinking, *At least he didn't hit me.*

CHAPTER 39

Grandma Lucy's droning on about comfort. I'm still staring out the window. The sky has turned dark gray. This little flurry has morphed into a full-fledged snow storm. Good thing I don't have anywhere to go besides my mother's home. Curl up in a blanket and think about what I'd read if I had the energy to pick up a book.

Hester Lynne's second novel, in spite of its somewhat cold reception from the critics, was exceptional. I loved it even more than the first. So did Reginald. This one wasn't about infertility. It was about a baby who died of a congenital birth defect, spurring the young mother on a journey to seek out her biological family. I know when I put it like that it sounds like it must be a real downer, but it's actually quite uplifting. The dead baby's not the focus, by the way, that's all included as back story and isn't even revealed fully until over halfway through the book.

It's too bad I'll never be able to write like that. After all I've gone through, I know I've got a story to tell, but putting it all on paper would take too much out of me. Even these scribbles exhaust me, and they're just for a pastor whose church I don't even attend anymore. I'm not even sure I'll let you read them anyway. What would be the point?

It's funny, though. You were so bold and brash when you prayed for that child you were sure I was meant to conceive, but when Chris came and told you his prognosis, you were silent. Not a hint that maybe you had been wrong. Not a suggestion that maybe God would choose to grow our family in some other way. I'd felt abandoned by you years earlier, all the way back when you didn't even know my name and you released me from suicide but failed to cure my depression. But Chris idolized you. He adored you. In his mind, you were this super saint living on top of a mile-high pedestal, so close to heaven that you could stand on your tiptoes and touch the outer edge of God's robe.

That's why your silence hurt him so much. Who knows? Maybe if he'd felt more support from you during that time, he might not have kicked me out.

We'll never know now, will we?

Once I realized my husband had locked me outside in the dead of winter, I stumbled to a convenience store about a quarter of a mile away. I could have gone to one of the neighbors, I'm sure, but I didn't know anybody in the area, and it was after dark. I didn't want to frighten any of the families who had young kids, didn't want to wake up their sleeping babies or get the neighborhood dogs all barking and yapping.

When I got to the store, I paced the aisles for a little bit, pretending I was looking for something. Pretending I'd have money to purchase it when I found whatever it was.

When other customers came in, I scanned their features, hunting for a friendly Good Samaritan who might let me borrow their cell phone. I still wasn't sure what I was going to do. If I waited another half an hour or so and went home, Chris would probably be over the worst of his rage. I owed him an apology, and even now I'll be the first to confess that what I said to him was wrong. I was egging him on. In fact, I think somewhere in the back of my mind I was daring him to hit me. To free me from my commitment to him, because once he crossed that single line, I'd be gone.

At least that's what I told myself, but deep down I knew I was simply arguing semantics.

I couldn't leave.

I would never leave.

I thought about calling Reginald, but I didn't know his number. I wouldn't just have to ask someone to use their phone. I'd have to ask them to look up the number to his store for me. It was already past ten, but I figured he was probably still there, sitting among the volumes he loved instead of going home to that cold, empty mansion in the Heights.

I don't know if you've ever noticed this, but the folks who shop at gas stations at night are almost always single men. The store wasn't particularly empty, but I didn't find anybody I was comfortable with asking for help.

Besides, I wasn't sure I wanted to call Reginald and invite him into our family drama. Maybe the phone issue was a convenient excuse. Reginald had his suspicions about Chris and me by then, but at the time I still felt like I had a reputation to maintain, a shred of dignity however thin I was meant to preserve.

The only problem was I couldn't spend all night in the store. After the first ten or fifteen minutes, the clerk started following me with his eyes. I'm not the sort of character that tends to invite suspicion. Petite Asian woman? It's not like I'm regularly profiled or mistrusted. But I'd arrived at the store on foot, not by car, and my coat was dirty from landing in an old snow pile when Chris chucked it at me. It was enough to make the clerk wary, I think. Either that or he was staring so hard to see if I had a wedding ring, but I'm also not the type to get hit on very much either. I swear if I had a doppelgänger, she could make a magnificent spy. I can blend into nearly any setting, I'm demure enough I never arouse anyone's suspicion, and even though I'm no eyesore, I don't attract a whole lot of extra male attention, especially when I'm wearing a dirty, oversized coat.

Whatever his reasons, the clerk's probing interest weirded me out enough that I decided it was time to leave. Forget about calling Reginald. This wasn't his battle, and it would only serve to delay my reconciliation with Chris. I just had to wait it out a little more. It wasn't that late yet. Ten-thirty tops. I'd wander around a few more minutes, get home before eleven, and Chris would let me back in.

Of course he would.

My husband had anger issues, but he wasn't unreasonable.

As I walked around outside, I used the extra time to start planning my apology. Practicing the part where I would swallow down my pride and accept Chris's berating. I don't care who you are or what you've gone through. Nobody should talk to their spouse like I talked to him. It wasn't Chris's fault he couldn't father children, and I was wrong to attack him where he was weakest. I just needed to stall for a little bit longer, then go home and humble myself enough that Chris would let me crawl into our warm bed so we could both sleep off all that adrenaline.

I've never been a fan of walking for exercise. I don't see why people run off to malls to power-walk or what the appeal is in circling the same route time and time again trying to get your heart rate up. It was cold, and I fought off the resentment I felt toward Chris for leaving me out here like this. When my toes started to sting, I almost turned back, but I wanted to stay out a little longer. Maybe he would worry about me. Maybe he'd hop in that stupid car of his that'd cost us so many arguments about who did or didn't remember to fill up the gas tank. He was expecting me to come back, come wandering in like a bedraggled, repentant puppy.

I could withstand a little more of this blasted cold just to play it out a few extra minutes.

The more I suffered, the more he'd regret kicking me out in the first place.

It was passive aggression at its finest. And it worked — far more effectively than I would have dared to imagine.

CHAPTER 40

"Weeping and great mourning." Either Grandma Lucy's repeating herself now or I'm having a crazy case of *déjà-vu*. "The voice of a mother weeping for her child." She just won't stop talking. Won't shut up. "Weeping tears of sorrow and grief."

I've known those tears. Known them far more than I would care to admit to anyone, even you.

Especially you.

"Refusing to be comforted."

I've read the verse before, so I'm prepared for what she's going to say next. What I'm not prepared for is the way her words invite a fresh wave of grief to come crashing down over me as I sit in that hard, uncomfortable pew.

"Refusing to be comforted because her children are no more."

I spring to my feet, not sure I'll make it to the bathroom in time. I never used to throw up. Even as a kid, my stomach bugs almost always found me sitting over the toilet bowl instead of heaving into one. But I threw up six or seven times the night Chris kicked me out, and probably more because there are certain parts of what happened I don't even remember.

What that Sacred Meadows psychologist Dr. Jacob said about blackouts is true. Sometimes your brain turns itself off to block memories. You'd think it was a merciful gesture, sparing you from the horrors of what you endured. But that's romanticizing the trauma far more than it deserves. The fear is still there. The injuries are still there. But now you only remember bits and pieces. You don't remember the voice of your attacker, you only remember the feel of the scream trying to lodge its way out of your throat. You can't recall his face, you only know the way his hands feel as they poke and prod and ram until he gets you in the position he wants.

You don't remember the act of violence itself, so when you wake up in the ER with the terrified eyes of your tender-hearted boss staring down at you, there's nothing in your memory to draw on to explain why you're there. Why your body feels like a pulverized melon. And the physical pain isn't the worst of it, because as broken and bruised as you feel on the outside, you know your soul has endured infinitely worse injuries, except your brain won't tell you what they are.

"Reginald?" For a minute, I imagine I must be hallucinating. The suffering in my friend's face is unmatched in any painting or any sculpture of the crucifixion that I've ever seen.

He tries to smile at me, but Reginald's always been one to bleed out his emotions, which is why his children and grandchildren all learned so readily to take advantage of his generosity and compassion.

"I got hurt." I'm not sure if this is a question or a statement, or maybe a plea for more information to explain why I'm here. Why my throat is so raw. My legs and core so sore. My mind terrified and confused like I'm Anna Karenina in that foggy train station.

"Shh." He runs his hand across my forehead, and I see tears in his eyes. Actual tears. For a minute, I'm afraid I might be dying. Did I get in a car accident? Did someone run me over? All I know is he doesn't want me to talk. He steps aside gently while a nurse fidgets with me. What are they doing? What's wrong? Why don't I remember anything?

"Shh."

I shut my eyes. I want to tell him what happened. I want to explain to him that I'm going to be fine. He looks so hurt to see me injured like this. I want to soothe his pain. He's such a good friend to me. It's a shame he and Daddy never got to meet. They would have enjoyed each other's company, I think.

The nurse asks me something, but I can't make out the words. Then another man comes in. Is that a police officer? Reginald tells him something, at least I think he does, and the stranger goes away.

Reginald stands close again. I feel safer now that he's near. The only thing is I can't figure out what it is that's made me so afraid in the first place.

"What happened?" I ask, but even now I'm not sure I want to know the answer.

Reginald leans over and gives me a kiss on the forehead. "Shh."

CHAPTER 41

Leaning over the bowl in the Orchard Grove bathroom, I don't even realize these flashbacks aren't real. As far as my mind is aware, I'm still in that County Hospital bed. Still surrounded by worried faces. Worried voices. I don't know how much time has passed. I think I've been asleep, but I'm not sure. I have the feeling that hours have gone by. Lifetimes. I've been asleep, I wake up. I'm stirred to full attention by the sound of Reginald's shouts. It's the first time I've heard him angry for as long as I've known him.

"Get that man out of here." I don't know who he's yelling at or why he's using such an authoritative voice. I want to tell him to calm down, but I'm so drowsy. So weak.

I force my eyes fully open and sit up in bed. Everything in my body feels torn and raw. I lay back down and turn my neck so I can see what's going on.

"Don't let him near her." My sweet-tempered, quiet friend is seething with anger. "Get security and tell them to take him away."

"That's my wife in there!"

My heart races at the sound of Chris's voice. The fear is back. Why would I be afraid of my husband?

"Sir, I need you to step aside."

I don't know who's talking or whether they're addressing Reginald or my husband. A police woman looks down at me.

"Are you awake?"

"Yes." My voice is scratchy. I have vague memories of yelling. No, shrieking.

Fearful shrieks.

Pained shrieks.

"Your husband is here to see you."

Again I try to sit up, but my whole body is a convoluted mess of pulp and exposed nerves. "Ok."

She puts her hand on me, but I don't feel afraid. I don't pull away. "We don't have to let him in if you don't want us to."

For some reason, I'm fixating on the fact that I can't sit comfortably. Is that why they're not letting Chris in?

"Do you want me to ask him to come back later?" the woman asks. Kindness and authority merge together in her tone.

Outside my door, I hear Reginald telling someone, "He shouldn't be allowed within a hundred yards of her."

I gain a slightly less vague sense of what's going on. "No," I croak, and at first the officer thinks I'm talking to her. She frowns sympathetically and is about to talk into her little radio, but I hold out my hand to stop her. "That's not it," I say. "It wasn't him …" I falter. Because I've put enough forensic pieces in place to *know* what happened to me, but I'm still not ready to accept it. Not ready to confront it yet.

But I can't have them go on thinking it was Chris. "It was someone else."

A frown. I can tell she doesn't want to believe me. "You're certain?"

I nod. "I'm sure. It wasn't him. He's not the one who did this to me."

CHAPTER 42

The snowfall's turning into a true blizzard by the time I reach home. After leaving church I walked the whole way back in the gray, gloomy weather. Justin would worry about me if he knew. I should tell him the flashbacks are getting worse.

He's the only one who would understand.

Once inside the entryway of my mom's house, I'm hit by a wall of memories that rush me at once, each one vying for my focus and attention. Like the jade-colored ceramic jug that stands a yard high in the front entryway. Last year when I came to visit, Mom still hadn't removed Daddy's cane, but now it's gone and all that's left is a little umbrella that I'm sure never sees a drop of rainfall. Mom hates the rain and would rather hole up in the house for three or four days at a time than run errands in a *downpour,* her word for anything from a slight drizzle to a flash flood. She and I are both alike in our disdain for going outdoors in bad weather.

I still don't know why I stayed out that night. I should have gone home. It's not like Chris would have refused to let me in.

I made a promise to one of my psychiatrists — not Dr. Jacob, this was long before her time. So long ago that I don't even remember if I was speaking with Dr. Klarson or Dr. Carter, but I promised him I would never blame myself for what happened to me that night.

Not that it's easy.

I wanted to make Chris sorry. I wanted to punish him for throwing me outside like that.

But, as Dr. Carter (or maybe it was Dr. Klarson) pointed out, I didn't invite my attacker to come and grab me.

I still don't have all the memories of what happened. Actually, I'm not sure that's the right way to put it. I'm guessing that the memories are there, that I could find them if I really had to, but there's a wall. A locked safe I can't access.

Chris was mortified. I think once the security guards let him in, and Reginald saw the way he mourned over me, how torn up he was, there's no way anyone could have accused him of the attack. The police ran DNA, and of course it wasn't his. Why would he assault his own wife in a public alleyway?

And so Reginald let it go. I still didn't tell him Chris kicked me out. As far as Reginald knew, I was restless at home and went out for a walk. He'd been trying to call me, you know, Reginald had. He wanted to see if I could come in an hour early the following day. One of his granddaughters was turning twenty, and he wanted to take her and her boyfriend out. I don't know where they were going. Probably out for lobster and caviar at Reginald's favorite restaurant. As far as I know, the owner still keeps a small photo of him on the patrons' wall of fame in the entryway, but of course I haven't returned there since the day of Chris and my appointment at the fertility clinic. When I didn't answer my cell or the home line, he finally got worried and went looking for me.

My injuries weren't that gruesome as far as that kind of attack goes. Nothing more than what you'd expect, I guess you could say. I spent longer talking to the policewoman and her partner than I did with the nurses. I went home that same night, but only after Reginald made me swear on the name of every saint he could think of that I wasn't afraid to be alone with Chris.

There were never any charges pressed. They never found the guy. At first, Chris fixated on my attacker with a vigilante-style hatred that started to frighten me. I wasn't scared for myself. As much as I may have wanted Chris to feel bad for throwing me out of the house, I never would have wished the degree of repentance and mortification that man went through. There was never a husband better to his wife, more attentive and doting and affectionate than Chris was to me those first few weeks after the assault.

He cradled me in his arms, whispered prayers over me, took care of all the house chores and everything else while I recovered. It was the mental injuries that took longer to heal than the physical ones. If you thought I was a mess after Daddy died, you should have seen me then. And for some reason or other (not that I was surprised), even though the whole town knew what had happened to me, everyone at Valley Tabernacle remained silent. Maybe you didn't want to invade our privacy, but what you really did was leave Chris and me to try to heal on our own.

Just like with Daddy's death, healing did come. It came in staggering, faltering steps. The nightmares diminished. After the first week, I could sleep through the night without waking up more than two or three times.

Sex was out of the question. I think both Chris and I realized that right from the beginning, and he never pushed it, just told me that I could tell him when I felt ready. He waited for me with the patience of that teenage boy I fell in love with so many years earlier, that boy committed to abstinence and purity.

Reginald hired a housekeeper to take care of me and look

after things when Chris went back to work, and he was thoughtful enough to find an efficient, middle-aged matron who didn't coddle me or bother me unnecessarily as she went about her duties. Reginald stopped by several times a week, bringing me new books. I still hadn't finished Hester Lynne's second novel, so he asked my caretaker to read it to me, and when I told him she was as expressionless as a computerized voice-bot, he treated me to the last half of the novel himself.

He did his best to avoid any run-ins with Chris. I don't know if Reginald was embarrassed for accusing my husband at the hospital or if he suspected I hadn't told him the full story of the night of my attack. It didn't matter. When Reginald was with me, I felt as cherished and spoiled as the daughter of a king. When Chris was with me, I was grateful for the softness that now infused everything he did.

Softness when he talked to me about his day.

Softness when he asked me what I'd been reading.

Softness when he complimented me for venturing out of bed, for regaining my strength and reclaiming my sense of normalcy.

He actually wanted me to go back to work at Reginald's. "I think having a routine would be good for you, and I know how much you love those books."

I told him, like so many other things by that point, I would let him know when I was ready. And again, he was the epitome of patience. "Take all the time you need."

I think in some alternate universe, that could have been the dénouement of our roller-coaster story. I think if events hadn't conspired against us the way they did, I might have kept on healing, and he might have kept on growing in his ability to love me gently and tenderly like I needed. Our story, as tragic as it is, certainly isn't one of not trying. That man did so much penance — penance every day as he baptized me with his remorse and sometimes his tears. And he took responsibility for his role in what happened to me. If anything, he carried it too far, refused to let go of that guilt even when forgiveness was offered.

But even that we could have endured. Could have learned to put it all behind us.

He was so good to me. So gentle. So tender. That's why it took me so long to work up the nerve to tell him the whole truth.

So long to admit to my husband that I was pregnant.

CHAPTER 43

"I'm sorry I haven't stopped by to visit any sooner."

It's Sunday afternoon, and after one long nap and two failed attempts to get myself out the door, I've mustered the courage to take Mom's car out — blizzard and all — to visit Reginald. The store is closed on Sundays, which is why it had to be today.

I don't want anyone else around.

"I miss you." I'd forgotten how comfortable silence is here.

I tell him a little bit about the past months, keeping out the parts that would get him worried. I tell him about working for Mel, about my lead for a potential job as a nanny for an old friend from high school. Once I got over my puking flashback at Orchard Grove this morning, I was in no mental state to ask Joy for anything, but I can look for her online if I want. After all, she's got that mommy blog. Can't be that difficult to find.

It's hard to be back in Reginald's store without thinking

about the past. Reginald and I grew even closer, if that were possible, after my attack. He was thoughtful enough not to fuss over me, not to act embarrassed around me or treat me like I was some entirely different person he didn't know what to do with.

But he was gentler, too. It was a few weeks after I came back to work when he pulled me aside and asked in a deeply concerned voice, "How is your husband?"

Up until then, I tried not to talk too much about Chris at work. For one thing, my husband hated Reginald, insanely resented him. Always the enabler, I also wanted to downplay my husband's anger problems, so I never mentioned them to anyone, not even Reginald who was the closest thing I had to a friend at that season of life.

Reginald told me that the night of my attack, Chris had been nearly inconsolable. Reginald found him trying to punch a hole in the ceramic tile in the men's room at the Orchard Grove County Hospital. I guess his only thought was to find my attacker and kill him. Reginald finally took Chris's car keys from him, said he was terrified my husband was so angry he was about to get himself in a wreck.

"I'm just glad to know I was wrong about him. Glad to know your husband would never hurt you."

Oh, Reginald, if only you knew.

I found out I was pregnant about a month later. I didn't go to the doctor. Didn't take any tests. I avoided reality for as long as I could, so that I was two weeks into the second trimester when Chris finally asked me if I was gaining weight. I think he had realized it by then as well, but he had just as many reasons as I did to deny what was right there for us to see.

Reginald was the first person I told. His eyes were darts of sorrow that pierced my soul when he asked, "What are you going to do?"

It sounds silly, but Chris and I hadn't even asked ourselves that question yet. Hadn't even realized it was a question we should be discussing. We were still reeling from the attack itself. Still trying to learn how to function in a world where things like that can happen to a woman who's out for a walk in the dark.

"What do you think I should do?" I asked.

"What do I think?" The smile lines around Reginald's temples broke out into calm, inviting tributaries of warmth. "I think you should take plenty of vitamins."

I smiled. "You know what I mean."

He sighed but didn't offer any answer.

I felt compelled to fill the silence. "I haven't even asked Chris yet. How he feels about the baby, I mean."

"Children are a gift from the Lord." Reginald was bent

over a box of books, smiling at them as he took them out one by one.

I didn't know how to say all that was in my soul. Didn't know how to tell someone as good and kind and caring as Reginald that I wasn't sure I could love this child. There was no way either of us would consider abortion. Even at the ER, Chris told the nurse not to give me the shot that would reset my hormones. Back before we even tried having kids, he didn't want me on birth control because of the potential for a chemically-induced miscarriage.

On my good days, I knew that this child was innocent, that what happened to me wasn't her fault in any way. But I didn't even know the race of my attacker. Maybe you think that's bigoted for me to say, but why don't you try getting yourself raped and then wait nine months to see what color skin the kid you've conceived comes out with.

I sound terrible. Hearing these thoughts, seeing the words come out on paper, I realize what an ogre I was. But I didn't know. Didn't realize the love that would flow through my veins and into little Gracie when I felt her kick for the first time. Didn't understand how soft her skin would be, couldn't imagine the gentleness of her small, trusting snuggles as she dozed in my arms.

All I knew was she was conceived by the man who'd hurt

me more personally, more violently than I'd ever been injured before, and I was afraid that once she came out I'd remember what her father looked like and despise her with all of my being.

It was Reginald who changed my heart. Reginald who taught me how to love this little baby I hadn't even met yet.

CHAPTER 44

Reginald's a quiet man. Doesn't offer advice unless you come straight out and ask for it, and even then he usually teaches you in stories instead of sermons. Maybe that's why I love him so much. Why I miss him.

I'm sitting in his back office, reminiscing. "Do you remember the story you told me about Julie?" I ask.

The memories are heavy and bittersweet. Reginald's daughter was raped by a high-school boyfriend. She's middle-aged now, so of course back then it was quite a scandal. I know a lot of families, folks like the old apple farmers at Orchard Grove, who would kick a daughter out for less, but Reginald stood by her.

"Marta and I had separated by then," he told me, "and sometimes the kids would come live with me, and sometimes they'd go live with her, and it was constantly changing. But Julie was always with me, never with her mother. To her dying day I think Marta blamed me for what happened to our daughter. And I let her go ahead and think that. Better her mom blame me for being a lousy father who wasn't paying any attention than for her to go and make Julie feel even more ashamed than she already was for something that wasn't her fault.

"I told her, the day she came and confessed she was pregnant, I told her that I had always asked the Almighty to let me live long enough to become a grandfather. Well, it was happening a littler earlier than I might have expected, but who was I to balk at God's timing?

"I didn't know the father had raped her. Not at first. You know, parents didn't talk about that sort of thing back then. If a girl got herself pregnant, that was just her fault. Boys had it easy, you know. Their dads might give them a lecture, the moms in town might not want them hanging around their daughters anymore, but that's about the worst of it. But Julie, she went through a hell like you wouldn't believe. You think *Scarlet Letter*'s rough, you should have seen how those kids at Orchard Grove treated her. But she finished up her senior year. I was adamant about that. Talked to the principal so she could take some of her classes at home with me because she was so ashamed of herself, especially as she started to get bigger.

"It wasn't until she was round as a beach ball and due to pop that baby out any day when she told me what that boyfriend of hers had done. You should have seen me. I was younger then, you know. Wasn't so frail. And it took her a lot of convincing to keep me from heading right over and teaching Mr. Loose Zipper a lesson for what he'd done."

"But she stopped me. I was the only one at the baby's delivery. Her mom wouldn't have anything to do with her. Kept up that animosity until her dying day. But I was there. And I'd watched my little girl struggle with so much hurt and confusion and sorrow and shame — not to mention how traumatic it is for a girl that young to have to deliver a child in a room with those doctors and nurses and her old man right there. But they laid that little baby in her arms, and you could see the change in her. It was as if the Almighty himself reached down from heaven and breathed comfort and healing into her soul.

"You think Hester Prynne went through a renewal in that Hawthorne book? That wasn't even close to the way that precious baby transformed Julie's life. And in a day, my daughter went from a broken, torn-up little girl to a woman full of grace and love and forgiveness. Eventually found herself a nice Catholic boy who loved her little baby like his own. They're living over in Cape Cod now. Got six kids altogether. A beautiful, loving family."

I didn't know what to say.

And with someone like Reginald, that was just fine.

CHAPTER 45

I'm sitting in Reginald's favorite chair, hating myself for not coming to visit him sooner. And why not? Because I was ashamed of the mess I'd become? I should have known Reginald would never think less of me. He and Harper Lee adopted a very similar mentality: *Don't judge someone until you've worn that person's skin and walked around in it for a while.*

I'm comfortable with Reginald's silence. Sometimes we just sit, sometimes I tell him what's going on.

"Justin wants me to call him this afternoon," I say. "We've been talking quite a bit lately." I don't tell him how much. I don't tell him how long. I don't think Justin and I have had a phone conversation in the past two weeks that didn't last at least forty-five minutes. Thank God for all that Seattle traffic he's got to deal with. Gives us the perfect opportunity to catch up.

And it's not like I have anything better to do with my time.

"He's invited me over for Christmas," I say. "I'm thinking about going."

It's times like this I wish Reginald would give me his opinion, but even if I asked him for it directly, the silence would persist.

So instead of telling him my future plans, I talk about the past. "You know, I never told you this, but that story about your daughter Julie gave me a lot of hope back then. Hope that maybe I could learn to love my little girl."

I remember heading home from Reginald's store the day of our long talk. Prayed for quite a while. I've been a Christian basically my entire life, but I've never really grown that much in my prayers. Never really progressed past *Give us this day* or *Now I lay me down to sleep*. But I remember having a talk with God that evening. Telling him that if he really wanted me to, I could try to love that child growing in my womb.

Know what? It worked. I'm not saying it happened right then. Not saying that as soon as I opened my eyes and said *amen* that she kicked in my uterus or something and I was filled with all the maternal instinct a woman could ask for. No, for months I was victim to the hormonal hysterics that raged chaotically throughout my body. To long battles with insomnia where I lay next to Chris in bed and wondered what we were going to do with this child.

Did I really want to be a mom? Did I feel ready? Does any woman? I don't know. It's not something we all get together and talk about, you know. Especially in Christian circles, it's just expected that if you're married and pregnant you must be excited to have a kid. I can't tell you how many women at your church were hugging me, congratulating me. Women who knew I'd been raped. Even if they weren't aware my husband was sterile, they could do the math if they wanted and guess there was a decent chance the baby wasn't his. Women who'd never talked to me before or spared me a second glance were now my best friends, asking me about the most intimate details of my life from my sex drive to my levels of flatulence.

Did any of them think to ask me if I wanted this child?

It was you, actually, that God used most to change me. You and Reginald, I guess, and the story of his daughter Julie. Do you remember that night after Bible study when you asked me if I'd like to go in your office and pray with you? I forget where Chris was. Maybe out working late. I don't remember. But you said you sensed I could use some prayer, and you brought me into that mahogany and leather office of yours that even years into your ministry smelled like a new furniture store.

I sat down, and you started to pray for me. Except it was

different this time. Quieter, for one thing. No spittle projections flying across the room. No beads of sweat on your forehead.

And no ultimatums. That's what I remember most. Because you were famous for telling God what to do. I would never presume to pray like that, but the night after the Bible study, you were softer. Gentler. And you asked God — you actually asked him, which is maybe why it stands out so much in my mind — to heal me from my scars. Do you remember? Those were the exact words you used. Which is interesting because physically there wasn't anything wrong with me after the attack. I'd gone for all the checkups, everything. No HIV or STDs, no further complications. But you prayed for my scars. And I got a picture in my mind. I'm sure you'll think it was the Holy Spirit, and I'm not about to argue with you. Never put God in a box, right? But the picture was of this wound running from my mid-belly all the way down past my navel. And I could see the damage, the tearing, the ugly puss that you don't even need a medical degree to realize are signs of infection.

And there was heat right there on my body in the place I was imagining, and when you said that word *healing*, something happened to me. My stomach burned hot, but not in a painful way. Not in a way that I started to worry for the baby I was carrying. It was the exact opposite. It was like God himself was taking a heat lamp and radiating warmth and love and goodness into her. Infusing her with his Holy Spirit. Pouring out grace upon grace, blessing upon blessing on us both.

I started to cry, but these weren't tears of shame or anger or fear.

They were tears of release.

To this day, I'm not even sure I can articulate exactly what it was you released me from. My shame, maybe? Shame at the violence that had been done to me. Shame that I didn't love my unborn child the way a good mom was supposed to. Shame that the being inside me felt like some sort of invasive foreigner.

I'd been carrying around the trauma of my assault for seven months by that point. Seven lonely, terrifying, brutal months. Chris had tried to support me through it, but he was disengaging. It was more than he could handle. He was out until ten or eleven at night, not even working late or pretending to work late. He was just out. I didn't even think to ask where he was. That's how disconnected we'd become.

Sex was still unthinkable. I've been as chaste as the Virgin Mary herself ever since the night Gracie was conceived. Maybe that's more information than you wanted to know, but we may as well get it all out there in the open.

Because like I've already told you, there are lots of people I could blame for what happened to me. My rapist, obviously. Chris, for throwing me out in the first place, not to mention all the other ways he'd learned to hurt me by then, even in spite of how hard he tried to support me right after the attack. But when I think of all the people I've got to forgive, you're sitting right there at the top of the list. Problem is, I can't pinpoint why. Can't articulate exactly how your actions wounded me.

I put it all out on paper, and it doesn't seem like such a big deal. So you prayed for my suicidal thoughts to go away (which they did), but you didn't cure my depression. How would you have known? And how can you be the one to blame?

You enabled my husband, took all his sincere-sounding apologies to heart and left me to fend for myself, but so what? After the night of the attack, Chris stopped yelling at me. Eventually stopped interacting with me at all, at least on any personal level. Anger stopped being the problem the moment my husband brought me home from County Hospital. At least for a while. And besides, who could blame you for trying? You were Chris's biggest supporter, the one who walked with him more faithfully than anyone else to help him overcome his rage.

Strange as it sounds, it was actually that prayer of yours, the one you spoke over me while my husband was mysteriously *out*, that gets me the most upset. Because up until then I would have been content with giving Gracie up. I would have been relieved, truth be told, to let someone else have her.

But that night when you prayed for my scars, when I felt the comforting healing the Holy Spirit was pouring out on me and the delight he took in my unborn daughter, I learned to love her too. With all the intensity, all the instinctive, sacrificial, protective love mothers have lavished on their children from the time of Eve throughout human history.

I'd read testimonies by that point (as I'm sure you have too) about women who carry their rapists' babies to term, how the pregnancy and delivery become one big exercise in faith and forgiveness and healing. In my mind, that was just good fodder for *Pilgrims* magazines. Inspirational bathroom reading.

I never thought it would happen to me. And certainly not so dramatically.

But by the time I came home from that prayer meeting, I was changed. I could honestly look myself in the eye and say, "I love my daughter." I wanted to meet her. Wanted to be her mom. Wanted to love her.

Which is what made the last two months of the pregnancy such a living hell.

CHAPTER 46

"I'd forgotten how much I would miss working here," I tell Reginald as I sit in his office and stare at all his books. *The Winding Road* lies bookmarked on the table. I pick it up. They've released it with a new cover now in honor of the Hollywood film they're making of it. Pretty exciting, really. I know Hester Lynne would have been thrilled to see her name on the big screen like that.

What a dream come true.

A harrowing tale of love, passion, and the pain of infertility, says a New York Times review.

It's ironic, isn't it, that after suffering so much with his own sterility, after dragging me through years of turmoil because I wasn't producing him a child, it was Chris who decided that he didn't want to keep Gracie after all.

"I've been thinking," he began, and he had this real serious look on his face. I swear I expected him to tell me he'd been having an affair. That would certainly explain all the late nights out.

I put my hand on my abdomen. There was hardly a time in the last trimester when Gracie wasn't moving. A little dancer who insisted on entertaining herself all hours of the day (and night) with her skillful acrobatics.

Chris sat down across from me. I couldn't remember the last time we'd had a serious conversation like this.

"I've decided we should put her up for adoption."

A single sentence. A pronouncement. Because even through my hysterics, my tears, my protests, Chris saw himself as the God-ordained king of the family. Saw himself as the one and only individual capable of making such a momentous decision. Looking back, I think he was trying to assert his masculinity the only way he knew how. God hadn't enabled him to father a child, so he'd go ahead and yank my baby straight out of my womb and thrust her into the arms of strangers.

"I've made us an appointment with a counselor from Agape Adoption Ministries. She's coming over tomorrow to talk to us about some prospective families."

I couldn't handle it. Couldn't take it. And at that moment, I hated you with more hatred than I thought could abide in a Christian soul.

It was you. You who gave my husband all these ideas of godly leadership. You who got him so wrapped up in his

Truth Warriors conferences, who convinced him that a decision as final as choosing to give your wife's child away to complete strangers was his and his alone. No need to consult me, no need to give me any sort of warning. Chris was finally getting the baby he'd always wanted. Hadn't you yourself prophesied about my pregnancy?

And now, just a week or two after I'd learned to love this daughter of mine, just a week or two after you'd prayed for me to find true healing, just a week or two after the compassionate touch of the Holy Spirit calmed my trauma and the pain of my past, Chris shattered my newfound peace with a single declaration.

I yelled. Shrieked is probably the more accurate word. Pummeled him with my fists when he tried to get me to calm down. And I won't apologize for that. Not after what he did. What kind of sick and twisted joke was this? If Chris wanted to give the baby up for adoption, why didn't he say so right away? Before I felt her move, before I named her Gracie, before I learned to adore her?

I hated him. I know it's sinful for me to say, but I still do. Things could have been so different. In spite of all our pain, in spite of all our trials, the previous few weeks had given me hope that we might one day learn to be happy.

To be a family.

Chris. Me. Our daughter.

Sure, she might not come out looking like him, but she was mine.

We would learn to make her ours.

We would learn to love her.

We would learn to heal.

But all those hopes were dashed, and not even my hysterical cries could change my husband's mind.

CHAPTER 47

Reginald took me into his home. I was so broken, I couldn't even face my husband. I was convinced at first it was all some cosmic practical joke. Or maybe some sort of divine test. Surely God wouldn't drag me through the horror of rape, teach me to love this child conceived in my moment of greatest anguish, and then let someone like Chris rip her out of my life. It would have been less painful if he'd sliced open my abdomen and yanked her out of the womb with his bare hands.

Reginald told me that I could stay with him and offered me a salary as his live-in domestic assistant. He never told me I should leave my husband, but he made it clear that the decision was completely up to me. Even with Reginald's religious stance against divorce, I could have gone that route with his full support, both emotional and logistic. Every once in a while, he'd even run ideas by me about the best place to set up a nursery. There was no pressure. No expectations. But if Chris didn't change his mind about the adoption, how could I even think about going back to him?

My mom, of course, had quite a lot to say when she learned I'd left my husband. She didn't know the half of it, and I wasn't going to be the one to tell her. I never got a straight answer out of him when I finally asked about it, but I think Reginald changed her heart. One day he found me crying so hard I was about to choke on my own vomit after getting off the phone with her. He comforted me, got me cleaned up, and spent the next thirty minutes on the phone with his door shut.

Mom never pestered me about leaving Chris again.

Of course, you had your own opinions on the matter. Actually stopped by Reginald's house to remind me that my husband's authority was given by God, that to step out from the umbrella of that protective covering was like a fireman rushing into a burning house without any of his safety gear.

It was Reginald who kicked you out. Remember that? He's about half your size, but what could you do?

That's the last I've seen of you. I wish to God I could say *good riddance* and forget you completely, but the damage was already done.

You have no idea what it's like to be *under the protective authority* of a rage-insane husband in addition to an overbearing, power-hungry preacher. Because the more I've thought about it, the more I've really looked back at our relationship from that day you prayed that prayer of deliverance IN JESUS' NAME, it was all about control.

Controlling my thoughts so that I couldn't even see clearly regarding Chris and his blind rage.

Controlling my hopes when you prayed that God would teach me to love my child.

Controlling my spiritual destiny when you told me that, hard as it might be, if I wanted to be right with God, I'd have to go back to my husband's home, submit to his authority, and let him take my child away from me.

You know how earlier I talked about a line? A line that if Chris passed it, I'd feel justified for leaving him?

Well there was a line for you, too. And you crossed it the minute you told me I should think of giving my daughter up just because the poor child reminded my husband of his own impotence.

I was done. Done with you, done with your church, and done with Chris.

I'm not saying I made the right decision, but it was a decision that I alone could make. Not you, not my husband, not anyone else.

Gracie was my baby. And nobody could tell me what I could or couldn't do with her.

I sigh while I sit in Reginald's chair. It's been a long afternoon. I really should be going. Don't ask me what the rush is for. But Justin's expecting me to call, and I know sitting here in this empty store with all these heavy memories can't be good for my mental outlook.

"You know what?" I tell Reginald. "I don't think I ever thanked you. For opening your home to me. For being the only person in my life who didn't turn their back on me when I left my husband."

He doesn't answer.

The silence persists.

I reach out and touch the silver urn, say a little prayer for my friend, and let myself out of his store.

CHAPTER 48

I'm back in my mom's home. The snow's let up a little, but I'm careful to slip my shoes off before stepping into the entryway where I might leave some sort of incriminating mud print.

I'm going to have to confront Mom eventually. Tell her that I don't even own a house anymore like she thinks. Tell her about the bank foreclosure, everything. Then again, she probably knows. I swear that woman could have marketed herself as a Chinese Miss Marple for all the snooping and investigative work she does.

Not to mention her *maternal instinct*, which is so uncanny. That woman is either a *bona fide* mind reader or some sort of computer hacking genius who can spy on you through your smartphone and keep track of every conversation.

Maybe both.

She's never been excited about me and Justin. Then again, when has that woman ever been excited for anything good that's come into my life?

The night I told her Chris and I were engaged, she said very dubiously that she hoped we would turn out happier than his parents, because who's ever met a more bitter couple?

I told her Chris didn't want me to keep my own child, and she said, "Why would he when he knows you're only itching to put her in daycare so you can go back to work like some worldly career woman?"

I told her I was separating from my husband, and she mumbled about how difficult it is to always have the right answers but be cursed with children who never listen.

"And what would your father think?" she had to add. But I already know the answer to that. Daddy would understand. I wouldn't even have to tell him about Chris's anger problems or the rape that led to the conception of this child. All he'd need to know is that I love my baby, and nothing could change that.

Nothing at all.

Except for Chris's absolute genius at apologies.

Except for my own indecisive wavering.

Except for the fact that I still loved my husband, hard as that may be for some people to understand.

It's a decision I'll always regret. A decision I can never live down.

With only a month left in the pregnancy, I went back to my husband. *Like a dog returns to its vomit.*

CHAPTER 49

My heart jumps just a little when my phone rings, but as soon as I see the caller ID, my enthusiasm wanes. Mom can leave a voicemail message. We just talked last night. I've got at least until Christmas Eve before I have to interact with her again. Doubtless she's already heard that I showed up at Orchard Grove today. She probably got phone calls from five or six different ladies from her women's missionary league.

I can almost hear in my head the message she's leaving. *It was interesting to hear you went to church today. I'm glad to know you've decided not to keep your back turned against the Lord anymore. Or maybe you went to impress that friend of yours. How are you two doing, by the way? Did you already make plans to spend the holidays with him in Seattle?*

With Chris totally gone, all I have to do is forgive him for things done in the past. With my mom, it's different. Because she still does what she can to wedge her way into my life. Still offers up those thinly veiled judgements over every choice I've made.

She never understood a thing I did. Why I married Chris in the first place. Why I dropped out of college. Why I left him or why I went back.

But if you were to hear the way he apologized to me when I was at Reginald's, you'd understand.

I already mentioned how Reginald kicked you out of his home, and good riddance to you. I should have known then that you'd find some way to get back at me.

You talked to Chris about what happened. Of course you did. Insinuated that Reginald was keeping me locked up in his house against my will, probably hinted at your suspicions of some sort of infidelity. As if Reginald and I could have … Well, whatever. Small people and their small minds.

It was enough to get Chris worried. Not just jealous, but seriously worried for my safety and well-being. He waited for a time when Reginald was taking one of his granddaughters out on a shopping spree to buy new clothes for horse camp, and then he asked if he could stop by.

Some people would wonder why I told him yes, but they're forgetting how close we'd been for so long. I'm not talking about the first two trimesters of the pregnancy or anything like that, or any of those times in our early marriage before his temper got the best of him. I'm talking about all the in-between times, the sweet times, the loving times. Did you think that even going through what we had was enough to make me forget?

And I missed him. Reginald was my closest friend in the world, but he wasn't my husband. Reginald made me feel safe, but Chris made me feel adored. At least he did that afternoon when he came to visit me.

He wrote me a letter. Spent hours working on it, he told me later. You should have heard him when he read it out loud. Should have seen the tears in his eyes. Heard the choke in his voice.

I can't picture life without you, my darling. You're my heartbeat, my oxygen.

I kept up my guard at first, just to see exactly where he was going, but he ended with an apology. *I can't believe how blind and selfish I've been. This whole time, I've been thinking about this child as something* other, *but she's part of you. And by God's grace, you've found the love in your heart to call her your own, to cherish and adore her. I see now what an impossible predicament I put you in, and I'm going to let you know how sorry I am for it for as long as I'm alive. I had no right to ask you to choose me or your daughter. I had no right to tell you what decision you had to make.*

I'm sorry. So terribly sorry. I see now that I can't ask

you to stop loving your baby, just like nobody could ask me to stop loving you. The past few weeks have been the worst of my entire life. I miss you so much. You weren't wrong to walk away. In fact, I'm glad you did because now I see how senseless life would be without you.

I know I've hurt you. I've hurt you so deeply. But if you could find it in your heart to forgive me, I want to ask you to come home. Both of you. You, my princess and bride, and the child that you love. The child that I've grown to love, too. The child that I've decided before God to raise as my own.

It was enough. I can't tell you how much I'd missed him when I'd been staying at Reginald's. I let Chris help me pack my suitcase that same afternoon.

By the time Reginald got back from squandering several thousand dollars on a spoiled granddaughter who didn't even bother showing up for his funeral, I had moved back in with my husband.

CHAPTER 50

"Well, hi there. I was wondering when you'd call." Justin's entire demeanor is so confident. I feel stronger every time I talk to him.

I tell him a little bit about my day, about church (minus the Grandma Lucy drama or the anxiety flashback in the bathroom), and about going to visit Reginald's store.

"I'm still bummed I never got the chance to meet him," Justin says, and we leave it at that. We both know I can't talk about Reginald more than a few sentences at a time. Not if I want to be upright and functioning the following day.

"So what great plans do you have for yourself now?" he asks.

I fumble through some sort of reply that makes it sound like I'm busier than I am. That makes it sound like I've got any plans at all. A week and a half before Christmas, and my social calendar is about as full as Ebenezer Scrooge's.

I know what's coming next. I'm not even surprised when Justin says, "You know it'd be great to have you spend the holidays out here."

Great? Maybe. You never know until you try. But trying takes courage. Trying means opening yourself up to the risk of disappointment. It's safer to go through life like Mr. Skinflint himself. Safer to keep everybody at a distance.

Even the man who's raising your child.

The child you love more than anything else on earth.

"Well, I'm not trying to force you into anything until you're comfortable," Justin tells me, "but I'd sure love to have you come out."

It's not the first time a man I've cared about tried to convince me to trust him, to give him a chance. After I moved back in with Chris, he spent every minute at home proving how much he'd changed. How deeply he'd grieved over his past mistakes. How he was learning to love and accept Gracie as his own.

And maybe you'd like me to end the story there. With Chris and me in our nice little home, with a baby on the way. A baby we'd both learned by God's grace how to love, a baby God used to heal the divisions between us, a baby who was destined to draw my husband and me so much closer together.

If this were some fluffy Christian novel, that's probably how most authors would end it. A nice little morality tale. A warning to pro-choice readers who think that getting rid of a child conceived by rape is an acceptable decision.

Wouldn't it be nice to tie it all up with a little bow like that? *And they all lived happily ever after.* Do you know how many Christian novels end that way? But then look at the Bible. I mean seriously, how many people can you say lived out their happily ever after? There's Ruth and Boaz, but they're the only two people I can think of who had a nice, steady, stable life once they got past the rising action of their storyline.

Everyone else? David died with his house in shambles, his kids fighting and bickering and raping each other. Paul and all those early apostles got crucified or sawed in two or burned in oil or beheaded. Job ended up with more kids and more riches, but who's really going to read his story and think that he got the better end of the deal?

I think that's why if I ever write fiction, I'd make sure to give my ending enough satisfaction and hope — maybe a *hint* of a happily ever after — without being so cliché or trite I made my readers want to barf.

Do you know how long our little domestic harmony lasted once I went back to Chris? Seven days. Seven stinking days.

And not seven days in heaven, either.

It was more like purgatory. Except that, at least from what I remember Reginald telling me about it, most people who believe in purgatory say it's something like the waiting room to heaven.

As for me, I was headed for a direct descent into hell.

CHAPTER 51

It was a Friday. I remember because Chris and I had such a good week together I was trying to come up with something special we could do over the weekend. Nothing too huge because I had no energy left after building a baby for eight months on top of dealing with all the stress of our relationship. And nothing too fancy because by the time I reached the last month of my pregnancy, all I could fit into were some denim overalls I'd picked up at the thrift shop.

But I wanted to do something. Chris had changed so much. He would rub my belly, sing to our little baby. At some point during the past week, he'd stopped referring to Gracie as mine and started using the plural possessive. I couldn't even pretend to imagine what my husband had gone through. Watching your wife suffer through the devastation of rape, learning to love the child conceived through such violence, swallowing your pride and agreeing to call her daughter your own.

He was trying. God knows how hard he was trying. But beneath the surface, all that stress had to go somewhere. You can't be as tightly wound as Chris and go through half the turmoil he did without having to bury down some major psychological angst. Angst that would one day find a vent.

Unfortunately, that vent was me.

You'd think after all we'd gone through, life would have given us both an extra dose of perspective. I mean, after you've suffered through the disappointment of sterility and the trauma of your wife's rape and the shame of a marital separation, you'd think that finding your gas tank was only slightly above the quarter-full line wouldn't be that big of a deal.

Unless you're Chris.

You should have seen him go at it. Screaming at me, cussing like Peter in the high priest's garden. For being such a Holy Ghost boy on Sundays, that man could swear like an HBO scriptwriter every other day of the week.

And what gets Chris more upset than when I forget to tell him the gas is low?

Except I did tell him. That's the thing. Just the day before when I got back from my prenatal appointment. It's not like Reginald would have cared, but I didn't like to drive the company car unless it was for work, so I had taken Chris's to the doctor's, and when I got back I mentioned the gas was low.

"Ok, just remind me in the morning."

And that's what I forgot to do. Apparently even someone like Chris occasionally forgets to check the gauge until it's running on fumes. Which in his mind means he's got less than a quarter of a tank. I swear he could have driven halfway to Wenatchee before it ran out, but that wasn't the issue.

The issue was I hadn't told him the gas was low. Except I had, just the day before, only he didn't remember that much. So the entire ordeal was my fault, the fact that he had to change his route, go a few miles out of his way and fill up so that if traffic had been bad he might have been two or even three minutes late to his scheduled drop-off.

And yes, that's the inciting event that did our marriage in, that sealed the lid on the coffin of our relationship.

Because he was so upset he wasn't thinking clearly. Because with all the stress he'd been under with the pregnancy and the separation and everything else, Chris's store of self-control was now as empty as his gas tank had been.

He yelled.

He threw one of the dishes.

He ripped up the newest book I'd started reading.

And then he hit me.

CHAPTER 52

Ok, so maybe *hit* isn't the best word. It wasn't exactly with his hand. And I don't think it was intentional. But he was so out of control even before it happened that I was getting a little worried. Thinking about that husband who made Orchard Grove history when he came home and murdered the church secretary and their sweet little twins with a crowbar.

And I made myself and my daughter a promise. If I made it through this skirmish alive, I would leave Chris. Pack up and leave, only this time I wouldn't look back. Why had I been so stupid by returning here in the first place? Thinking my husband could change.

I prayed, asked God just to get me out of this situation one last time. Asked him to intervene, and then Chris started to come straight at me, and I saw the rage in his eyes, and all I knew was that I had to get out. Replays of the news segments from Orchard Grove's only murder-suicide flashed through my brain. I needed the keys. Get the keys, get in the car, get myself away. It didn't matter where I went. As long as I was gone.

I made a dash for the front door. The keys were in my grasp. I don't know what happened next. I can't remember. I think I tripped. I must have fallen. I landed on the floor.

My first thought was *he's going to kill me.* I couldn't keep my eyes open. Couldn't look at him. I'm ashamed to say I don't even think I had time to worry about my baby at that point. All I knew was my life was about to end.

He was apologizing. Telling me how sorry he was. Looking at his hand like it had just done something horrible.

"It's ok," I told him. I hated to see his tears. "It was just an accident." I bit my lip to keep from crying. I couldn't even remember why I was afraid anymore. Afraid of what? The husband who knelt by me and sobbed out his heartfelt apologies?

"It was an accident," I repeated.

"You should go see the doctor," he told me. I couldn't figure out why. I'd just tripped. That's all. I didn't even hurt. But he kept persisting. "Tell them you lost your balance. Make sure everything's … Here. I'll drive you."

He tried to help me to my feet. I didn't want to touch him, but I had to. I was too pregnant, too heavy, my back too stiff with sciatica at that point to get off that floor by myself.

"Let me get you to the doctor's," he insisted.

I told him I'd drive myself. It would be all right. I didn't mention that I wouldn't want him to waste the gas. "I'll take the work car," I said and let him walk me to the door.

"Make sure you let them know it was an accident." His voice was choked.

I got behind the wheel, which is a much more difficult feat to accomplish when you're eight months pregnant, but I managed. Tears streamed openly down my husband's cheeks. "I'm so sorry."

I forced myself to smile at him. And after I rolled out of the driveway, I looked back once. Looked back to see Chris standing there with the weight of all his sorrow and all his remorse so heavy on his shoulders.

I looked back because I knew that this was goodbye.

I would never go back to him again.

CHAPTER 53

I didn't go to the doctor's. Didn't think anything was wrong. I'd fallen, that's all. Fallen in an accident.

Happens all the time.

I drove around town. Ended up all the way out on Baxter Loop. Nearly hit one of the goats that had escaped from its pen and was happily crossing the road to get to the fuller undergrowth. I was crying so hard by then my vision was totally blurry. Knew I'd have to stop.

I'd been to Grandma Lucy's farm before. Back in grade school, we'd take field trips there from time to time, learn how to milk the goats, sample some of the cheeses and yogurts. This was the first time I could remember stopping by as an adult.

Mrs. Gregory, Grandma Lucy's plump niece who lives with her, bustled out of the house when I pulled up, wiping her hands on the sides of a checkered apron. "Well, look who's here!" she exclaimed, even though I'm pretty sure she had no clue who I was.

I gave a quick smile as best as I could. All I really needed to do was collect my thoughts, give my brain a five- or ten-minute distraction before I got on the road again. Don't ask me where I expected to go after that. I was sure that by nightfall I'd end up in Reginald's guest room, but I wasn't ready to face him yet. Wasn't ready to tell him about my failure.

Mrs. Gregory was all smiles as she wrapped her arms around me and hugged me like I was some 19th-century heroine who'd just returned home after a transatlantic voyage. "My, but you've grown so big," she exclaimed, and I didn't know if she was referring to my swollen abdomen or if she really did remember me coming here as a child. I guess being the only Chinese-American girl in a town this small makes me stand out more than others.

"Come in." Mrs. Gregory beckoned to me, and I followed her into the little red farmhouse. "I was just getting some refreshments," she told me. "Why don't you make yourself comfortable in the sitting room, and I'll be ready in just a few minutes. Grandma Lucy's already in there."

I'd gotten so used to everyone in Orchard Grove calling her Grandma Lucy that I didn't even stop to think it strange for her niece to use the same title. I wasn't sure I felt like an official visit. Really all I'd wanted was an excuse to look around the little gift shop and then get back on the road. But there I was in

Grandma Lucy's sitting room, which was more like a greenhouse except for Grandma Lucy's rocker and an upholstered loveseat with enormous flower patterns all around.

She turned and beamed at me.

"You've come to visit," she exclaimed, and as antisocial as I was feeling, she seemed genuinely touched that I stopped by. I smiled back at her and figured there were worse places to spend the next half an hour. If Chris got it in his head to come looking for me, he'd never dream of searching here.

"You're due soon." Grandma Lucy reached out her hand, and surprisingly it didn't feel weird or invasive when she patted my belly. "It's a girl?"

I nodded. I was so emotionally exhausted that I didn't think to wonder if she'd heard the gossip through the church grapevine (also known as the Orchard Grove prayer chain), if she had somehow divined my child's gender, or if it was nothing more than a lucky guess.

"Connie's bringing snacks soon," Grandma Lucy said, and I got this eerie feeling that the entire household had been expecting my visit.

Grandma Lucy sat me down in the chair across from her rocker. We were so close, our knees almost touched. She leaned forward and studied my face. "Something is troubling you."

"Yeah," I replied. Grandma Lucy had a well-earned reputation for her discernment, so it was senseless to deny anything.

"There's a violent history between you and your baby's father." She stated it so factually, like she was reading me a press release about Hester Lynne's soon-to-be-released third novel.

The funny thing was I realized she could be talking just as easily about my husband or about the man who raped me. "It's pretty complicated," I confessed.

"These things always are." Grandma Lucy's enigmatic response made me wonder just how much she knew or had guessed about my situation. Part of me wanted her to shut up, to stop prying into my life. The other part of me longed for some word of comfort, some message of encouragement. I didn't want to tell her about Chris. Didn't want to repeat the conversation you and I had recently shared, a conversation where I was told that if I didn't submit to my husband, if I didn't let him be the man of the house and make a decision about my child's future, I wasn't just a sinner but my eternal security was in question. Like I said, at that point in my life, I really hadn't grown spiritually since I'd been a little eight-year-old playing egg toss at Orchard Grove's vacation Bible school. I hadn't studied what the Bible did or didn't say about divorce. I knew it was listed as one of the things God hated, maybe even one of the deadly seven sins or something like that. I also knew that God was a God of love and perpetual forgiveness, so if I found myself unable to forgive my husband when he kept on sinning against me, I could see how I would be somehow falling short.

I've studied it more now, even though I have to admit I've still got my questions. Probably always will. The experts don't even agree. Some say the only time divorce is permissible is when a clear-cut case of adultery is involved. One author I read took his hypothetical example to a pretty ridiculous extreme. He mentioned a woman whose husband was serving a twenty-five-year jail sentence for murdering their next-door neighbor. The wife wanted to know if she'd be justified to divorce her husband. The question hinged on whether the husband had sexually assaulted his victim before the murder. If he'd raped the neighbor, well then, his wife could seek a guilt-free divorce, but if no actual adultery occurred, Mrs. Convict would remain bound to that murderer for as long as they both shall live.

Other authors allowed for divorce in other cases too (such as domestic violence), but they were divided when it came to the question of remarriage. I'm sure I spent over a hundred dollars at the Christian bookstore looking for answers (but even that couldn't keep them from going out of business). Still, no two books agreed with each other.

But those weren't the questions I was thinking about in Grandma Lucy's sitting room. All I knew then was that I had to keep my child safe, and I didn't trust myself to stay away from Chris forever.

CHAPTER 54

I've taken Mom's car out again, snowstorm and all. I know it's stupid of me, but I've decided to leave Orchard Grove for good. With Chris out of my life and poor Reginald dead and gone, there's nothing left for me here except for an infinite supply of maternal guilt as soon as Mom gets back from her East Coast vacation.

Justin asked me again to come to Seattle. His sister's roommate just moved out, but her rent's caught up through April through some strange set of circumstances (which I take to mean Justin is paying his sister on my behalf). If I go now, that gives me four months to get on my feet. If I act soon, maybe I'll even find some kind of retail job. Doesn't every store need extra help at Christmastime?

It's all settled. He's got a meeting first thing tomorrow morning, and the rest of his week's already booked solid, so he's driving out today.

A few more hours, and I'll be saying goodbye to Orchard Grove forever.

But first, there's someone I want to see.

I pull up in front of Safe Anchorage Farm, only there's no Mrs. Gregory in her checkered apron to greet me. Part of me wants to go back to my mom's, but I know there's nothing for me to do there except worry about Justin. At least my visit to Safe Anchorage will give me some sort of distraction.

I knock on the door, hating how timid I feel. I wait out in the cold long enough that I'm embarrassed. They're obviously not home. I turn around but stop at the sound of bells jingling on the doorknob.

Grandma Lucy's there smiling, her hair even a shockier shade of white that it appeared this morning in church. "I'm so sorry to keep you waiting," she says and holds open the door to let me in. "My legs aren't as fast as they once were."

She doesn't ask why I'm here.

"Come into the sitting room with me." She leads the way without looking back to make sure I'm following.

We're sitting in the same chairs again. It's been almost a year to the day since our last visit. The day Gracie was born. The day Chris was ripped out of my life forever. It's not until I look around me, feel the weight of all those memories, that I realize what a mistake I've made coming here. My psyche's already fragile after my little crying fest in the

Orchard Grove ladies room this morning. I don't need to torture myself anymore.

Determined to make this visit as short and painless as possible, I tell Grandma Lucy, "I'm moving soon and just wanted to stop by and say goodbye. Wish you a Merry Christmas."

Grandma Lucy shuts her eyes. She's quiet for so long I'm afraid she might have fallen asleep. When she stares at me, she looks a decade older than I remember. She takes my hand in hers, a hand covered with ridges and wrinkles but surprisingly smooth. She leans forward, so close I can smell some kind of buttery pastry on her breath.

"I'm very, very sorry about your husband."

Don't ask me why I came here, but it wasn't for her sympathy. "It's ok." I hope she'll take the hint and change the subject.

"And how is that sweet little girl? Do you still hear from her from time to time?"

I nod. "She's doing well. It's almost her birthday."

Grandma Lucy sighs heavily. "Is that so? Time sure does race past. Come, Lord Jesus, come," she mutters under her breath, and for the first time I wonder if Grandma Lucy's age is starting to impact her mind and not just her body.

"You know," she tells me, "I pray for little Grace every

day by name." She still has my hand in hers. "I pray for you too, you know. I especially pray that one day you will find your healing."

Now it's my turn to be quiet. I wonder if Grandma Lucy has any idea how awkward this is for me. Thankfully, she breaks the uncomfortable silence with a prayer.

"Father God, you know my sweet, precious sister in the faith. You know all the sorrows she's been through, the valleys, the struggles. You've counted her tears, Lord."

Grandma Lucy's voice is comforting and low, and before I know it, I'm lost in the same room, listening to this same woman, only it's a year earlier. My belly is huge with child and the husband I'm never going to see again is at home praying for me to return.

CHAPTER 55

I swear that if Grandma Lucy were living in the days of the Salem witch trials, she would have gotten herself hanged. There was something mystical, almost unnerving about the way she sat there listening while I told her all my troubles. Told her why I came out to her farm. I hadn't even been this forthcoming before with Reginald.

"So he hit you and made you fall, and that's when you got in the car and drove away?" she asked.

"He didn't hit me." I was quick to correct her. "It was an accident." The word fell flat on my lips.

She nodded, her eyes so perceiving.

Ashamed, I looked away.

"And he doesn't want you to keep this child?"

My abdomen felt hard, like I'd eaten something rotten. Nobody warns you about all those minor discomforts of pregnancy like indigestion. I stared at my midsection. "He didn't want to. But then last week he changed his mind. Said we could keep her."

"But you have reservations now." The observation materialized out of nothing. I never told her that.

"I don't feel right about bringing up a daughter in such a volatile home." There. I said it. Admitted that Chris's temper is actually a problem. Too big of a problem for me to safely deliver a helpless, innocent little girl into our mess.

"But you love your daughter and don't want to give her up." Grandma Lucy didn't have to phrase it like a question. She already knew without being told.

I squeezed my eyes shut. Tried to remember what I ate to make my entire digestive tract harden up like a cement snake. "I can't put her in danger."

Grandma Lucy stroked my hand. I wondered if it was the goat lotions they made there that kept her skin so soft.

"So you've decided to leave your husband then?" There was no judgment in her tone, not a hint of that condemnation you buried me in time after time.

I shook my head. "Whenever I think I can walk away, he apologizes and I go back."

There again. That constricting in my belly. Maybe I did need to go to the doctor. Maybe I injured myself when I fell. I wouldn't admit the full truth to Grandma Lucy, but I was sure she already knew. I reconstructed the scene in my head enough times to remember how it went. I didn't trip in the entryway. Chris knocked me over. I still don't think he meant to. Angry as he could get, he would never try to hurt me. But he did. It was more like a push, not a punch or a slap, but what's the difference?

My husband struck me. He reached out and knocked me over in his anger. He crossed the line I said I would never allow him to cross. The line that said I should leave.

Only now, I wasn't sure I could. In fact, I was pretty positive I couldn't. I could see his tears in my mind. Recall the anguish in his voice, the tenderness. How many times had he apologized to me already? How many times had he promised to change? How many times had I tried to forgive him?

I could say that I was going to leave, but I was like a relapsing addict. Addicted to my husband, broken as he was. And on top of that, there was so much guilt. Guilt because a godly wife would never make her husband lose his temper like that in the first place. Guilt because my husband hadn't committed adultery (at least not as far as I knew), so according to the strictest interpretations of Scripture, I had no justification for leaving him. Guilt because if I could have forced my stubborn heart to submit to my husband's will more readily, we wouldn't have found ourselves in this impossible predicament.

I winced.

"Are you uncomfortable? Would you like to trade chairs?" Grandma Lucy asked.

"It's not that," I told her. "I think it must be something . . ." I stood up quickly. Instinctively. Hot water gushed down my leg like I just peed my pants, only I knew I hadn't. I stared down at myself. "What is that?"

Grandma Lucy squeezed my hand reassuringly. "It's your baby. It seems like today is the day the Almighty wants to introduce you to your little girl."

CHAPTER 56

I never would have thought my body could endure so much. Could stretch so wide. Like a python opening its great mouth and engulfing a kangaroo, only in this case the process worked in reverse.

Grandma Lucy and her niece were home alone without a car, so we called Reginald, who picked me up and took me to County. "Should I let your husband know?" he asked me, and it was Grandma Lucy who smiled at him so sweetly on her front porch and answered, "Maybe a little later, don't you think?"

Getting settled into the hospital was the easy part, at least logistically speaking. I was three weeks early. Nobody was too concerned. I was the only one freaking out. It was all happening too soon. I didn't know what to do. I couldn't make any decisions. Did I want an epidural or did I not? Did I want to sit on the labor ball or recline in the bed? Fortunately, Reginald's multiple experiences with childbirth and his intrinsically gentle nature made him the most suitable birth doula. I'd never actually asked him to stay with me, but he did, standing up by my shoulder whenever the nurses came to check on me even though by the time you're in the middle stages of labor, the concept of modesty no longer exists.

In between the worst of the contractions he held my hand, whispering encouragement in my ear. "You're going to do just fine. This is exactly what your body was created to do."

Says the man who never squeezed a watermelon out of an opening the size of a plum.

When the pain grew worse, he told me to hold his hand, but all I had the energy to do was survive through each individual contraction. He read Maya Angelou to me for a while until the agony was so intense any extra noise made me nauseated.

And then he sat. Sat and waited with the patience of a monument, except unlike stone there was nothing about Reginald that could be called cold or unmoving.

The funny thing about labor is you think it's going to last forever. You think the next contraction will be the one to finally kill you. You think you'll never get over the fear, the trauma, the pain.

But you do.

Gracie was born three minutes before midnight. Everything about her was perfect.

Reginald kissed my forehead and baptized me with his tears. "I'm so proud of you both."

The nurse in the room cleared her throat awkwardly. "Do you want me to be the one to tell her?"

"Give her a few minutes," Reginald answered and kissed my forehead one more time.

I was so exhausted they may as well have been talking about the World Series. I couldn't stop stroking Gracie's face. That skin. I never knew what baby-soft meant before. She took to nursing right away. It was awkward but not painful. Reginald was so much of a gentleman he kept his back discreetly turned until I covered up again and my newborn was sound asleep in my arms.

He smiled at me. So much warmth. But there was something pained in his eyes, too. Something I didn't know how to read.

He stroked Gracie's cheek. "She looks just like you," he said.

I nodded. It didn't matter to me what race her biological father was. It didn't matter to me how violently she'd been conceived. This precious life was my own to hold and love and cherish and nurture. I had never prayed more fervently as on that hospital bed when I asked God to equip me to be a good mom.

I drifted off to sleep and woke up a few hours later. It was the middle of the night, but Reginald was still in his chair by my bedside. "Did you have a nice rest?" He was holding Gracie now, holding her while she lay wrapped up in her receiving blanket like a little baby burrito.

I'd never known my heart was capable of that much fullness. That much love. I was like the Grinch waking up on Christmas morning, or Ebenezer Scrooge in the throes of his conversion.

And then Reginald cleared his throat. "Are you still tired?"

I nodded.

"Go back to sleep," he whispered. "I'll wake you up if she gets hungry. She's a perfect angel."

He didn't have to tell me that. I already knew.

It was right around five the next morning when I slowly blinked my eyes awake. Reginald was still in the same chair by my bedside. I wondered if he'd gotten any sleep at all. His eyes were droopy, the laugh creases more pronounced even though his face was far more serious than I was used to.

"Is she hungry?" I asked and then noticed that his arms were empty. I sat up, underestimating how flabby all my abdominal muscles had grown, but the pain didn't matter. "Where is she?"

"Shh." Reginald patted my hand. "She's in the bassinet right over there. Still resting, although I'm sure she'll be ready for her breakfast before long. I've never seen a newborn sleep straight through the night like that. You've got a real miracle baby there."

I strained my neck to make sure she was breathing. "Is she ok?"

He smiled at me. "She's just fine. But listen to me." There was something in his voice. Something that squeezed the core of my abdomen, floppy and untoned as it was.

Reginald held my gaze. His expression pierced my heart like an inch-deep papercut.

"The nurses and I didn't think we should tell you during the labor. Wanted you to save all your strength for the baby." I could hear his throat muscles work when he swallowed. "But now that you've had a good night's sleep, there's something you need to know."

CHAPTER 57

It's Sunday afternoon. The blizzard outside hasn't even thought to let up. Grandma Lucy's been praying so long over me, my mind's been wandering all over the place. To Chris. Reginald. My perfect little baby on the morning of her delivery.

By the time Grandma Lucy says, "Amen," I realize I've been daydreaming nearly the entire time. I can't remember a single word of her prayer.

She looks at me. I feel like I'm ten years old and my mom is scrutinizing me to see if my hair is combed nicely enough for picture day at school.

"Your road hasn't been an easy one."

I offer a slight half-smile at the understatement.

"But God wants to bring beauty to your pain, reap gladness from the seeds of your hurt." It's nice poetry, but I'm not thinking about that right now. I'm thinking about Justin driving over the North Cascades, wondering how bad the snowstorm has gotten over the pass.

Grandma Lucy strokes my hand. "You will find your healing and deliverance. I'm convinced of it."

I nod, wondering if I used up enough of Mom's gas that I should refill the tank before I take her car back home. Is there anything in Orchard Grove I'll miss once I leave?

Grandma Lucy lets out a sigh. I wonder if she's disappointed in me. It's like she was expecting something more, but I have no idea what that might be, what it might look like. I came here to say goodbye. She's so old I may never see her again. And she did a lot for me last year. Praying for me. Calling Reginald to take me to County Hospital.

I try to remember if I actually got this chair wet when my water broke or not. How do you clean a mess like that?

"I wish I could have met your daughter," she says to me.

The words shoot bitter pangs through my chest. "She was perfect. *Is* perfect," I correct myself.

Another heavy sigh. That's my cue. It's time for me to go. I've got to get ready for Justin. But still I hold back. I realize that there's something I've been wanting to know. Something I need to know before I can have any peace about leaving Orchard Grove. "Can I ask you something?"

"Of course." She smiles. So serenely. I wonder if I'll have anything close to her level of calm when I reach her age.

I fumble over my words. Hate myself for the way my cheeks flush. “Do you think I did the right thing?”

Her eyes soften. Her lips curl into a warm smile. Gentle, like the faintest of breezes on a summer day.

“Father God,” she begins, and at first I wonder why she’s starting to pray when all I asked for was her opinion. “Teach your sweet, precious daughter that you have never taken her out of your sight. Teach her that you are the good Shepherd, that you lay down your life for your sheep, and that nothing can pluck her out of your strong and mighty hand.”

It’s a nice prayer, but it still doesn’t come close to answering my question. Then again, Grandma Lucy always takes a few minutes to warm up.

“Direct her in the steps of your statutes. Guide her in the way everlasting.” Her voice grows in volume. Swells with confidence. “In the shadow of your hand, set her high upon a rock. Keep her safe and sound from the tempest raging about her, from the floodwaters that have risen up to her neck, from the miry pit that’s held her trapped in bondage for so long. For you are her sun and her shield, and you withhold no good thing from her. No good thing.” She repeats the last phrase with special emphasis.

“The locusts have come, Lord,” and I find my mind racing to keep up with her. First it’s shepherds, then its storms and floods and mud pits, and now all of a sudden we've moved on to insects. "The locusts have come," she repeats, "to steal and kill and destroy. The locusts have come and left her devastated, bereft, weeping through her tears and refusing to be comforted."

It's too close to the passage she quoted this morning in church. I feel my body stiffen, but thankfully she moves on, like a hummingbird, except instead of flowers she's flitting from verse to verse, from concept to concept until her spirit lands on the one that grabs her attention.

"You sent your Son, our Messiah and King, to proclaim freedom to the captives, to lead forth the ones in chains, to break the iron bars that hold us prisoner. And so, sweet and merciful Savior, precious Redeemer and Friend, I ask you today to come and fill this room up with the power of the Holy Spirit. We know and proclaim that where your sweet Spirit resides there is freedom, and we know that you've promised that those who put their trust in you will never be put to shame."

It's when she says that last word, it's when she mentions shame that something seems to awaken in my spirit. I think she senses it too because even though she doesn't open her eyes to gauge my reaction, she settles on that motif.

"This sweet and hurting daughter of yours has been a slave to her shame. She has believed all the lies the enemy has thrown at her, lies that the wounds and trials of her life are of her own making, that you're a vindictive judge who's withholding good from her because of the sins of her past. She's been so scarred by life, precious Lord, that she's blind to the loving grace that you long to lavish upon her. The loving grace that can soothe over all her wounds and calm her aching soul. The loving grace that you purchased for her when you suffered and died on that beautiful, terrible cross. She doesn't realize, Lord. Doesn't realize that you've already paid the penalty, already taken away the punishment for her sins, that you absorbed all that guilt when you bled there on Calvary's mountain, that the blood flowing from the wounds to your head, your hands, your feet have washed all her sins away, removed her transgressions from her as far as the east is from the west.

"This is your precious daughter, the one you suffered and bled and died to redeem, but the veil is still over her eyes. The veil that keeps her from seeing the light of your glory, from experiencing the freedom, the forgiveness, the peace that you offer. You tell us in your Word that you came so that we might have life and have it more abundantly, so I speak that abundant life over your child today. I speak abundant life over her baby girl as well. I don't know what plans you have in store for the two of them, but I believe that they are plans for good. That you will redeem the years the locusts have eaten, that you will restore joy and gladness where once there was only bitterness and sorrow. That this young woman who was living in darkness, blinded by her shame and regret, would be transferred right now, right at this moment into your kingdom of light. That the same voice that spoke the sun and the moon and the stars into existence will whisper to her soul *I love you. Before I formed you in the womb I knew you, and I chose you before the foundation of the world to walk holy and blameless in my sight.*

"So I speak that new life over your daughter today. I speak to the darkness and proclaim to it that she is no longer a slave to her fear. I speak freedom over her, freedom from every chain, freedom from her guilt and shame. *For those living in the land of the shadow of death, a light has dawned.* We believe it to be true. Even so, come, Lord Jesus, come."

There's no *amen*, no indication that she's finished her prayer other than the lightness and peace that settles around me while I sit in that gaudy flowered chair.

She takes my hands in hers and squeezes them. "Go now in the grace and love of our God and Father and of the Lord Jesus Christ, the only wise God."

I have no adequate words to return her blessing, but I thank her as sincerely as I can and make my way through the near-blinding snow back to my mother's car.

CHAPTER 58

It's dark when I see the snowflakes illuminated in the headlights as Justin pulls into my mother's driveway. I hate to admit it, but I've been alternatively staring out my bedroom window and then coming downstairs to make sure the porch lights are on for the past hour and a half.

I'm all set to go. There's nothing in me that wants to stay a moment longer than I have to, but I've already offered Justin a short rest here. He's been driving all evening. The coffee's ready, even though I don't know if he likes his with sugar and cream, neither of which has been found in my mother's kitchen for at least the past decade and a half.

I hear his car door slam shut, and I freeze halfway down the stairs. Should I wait for him to knock? And leave him out in the cold? I could go and open the door right away, but then he'd know I was waiting for him.

Of course I'd be waiting for him.

But do I want him to know that? Or will that make me look desperate?

I feel more flustered than I did on the night of my senior prom, mostly because I went to my senior prom with my boyfriend of five years who also happened to be my closest friend.

Justin is … What is Justin? I guess that's what this little experiment in Seattle is meant to determine, isn't it?

I've felt a little unsettled after leaving Grandma Lucy. That prayer she prayed, it was full of so much conviction and faith. I could almost feel the strength of her words infusing inspiration and healing and courage all at once into my body. It's what I'm supposed to do next that I'm still trying to figure out. When you go to a youth group retreat or campout and come back on a spiritual high, pastors and youth leaders are always telling you that if you don't want that feeling to go away, all you've got to do is pray regularly and spend more time in God's Word. But you can do those things, even do them religiously, and eventually the feeling starts to wane no matter what. What does that mean? Is it time to sign up for another retreat? Another mountaintop experience? It's not like I can drive from Seattle all the way back to Orchard Grove and sit in Grandma Lucy's greenhouse every time I need a little spiritual pick me up. Justin goes to church, but I don't know anything about it. I don't know if it's stoic and stuffy like

Orchard Grove or wild and charismatic like Valley Tabernacle or somewhere in between.

But I know something happened this evening. Something so ethereal and intangible that it feels sacrilegious to even try to express it in words. An awakening in my soul, which I realize now has been asleep for a very long time. Maybe my entire life. But what now? Where am I supposed to go from here? If God wants me to put my full trust in him for every single aspect of my life, why doesn't he let me feel his presence like this more often? Why does it feel like something I just have to get lucky and try to snatch when it comes my way since it could be years or decades before the next opportunity knocks on my door?

Speaking of knocking, that's Justin now. He's here. No more standing frozen halfway down the steps.

I hurry downstairs, open the door, and invite him in.

CHAPTER 59

Justin smiles at me over his mug of black coffee. I'm surprised at how young he looks. Even his profile picture online made him appear older.

I'm blushing like a Victorian heroine in a mediocre historical fiction novel. I can't seem to get my words out straight either. It takes me two failed attempts just to check and see if the coffee's all right.

He's all grins, so easy-going. "It's absolutely perfect. Just what I needed."

I realize now that I have no idea what's supposed to happen next. Do we sit here and chat? Do I grab his mug from him as soon as it's empty, wash it up quickly so my mom will never know the two of us were here, and head to the car? What if he needs to use the bathroom? Will he be too embarrassed to ask? Should I be the one to offer it to him first?

"Is Gracie with your sister?" I hate that I can't go two minutes alone with Justin without mentioning my daughter.

He nods. "I thought about bringing her. I know you're probably anxious to see her, but it's a long drive, and she doesn't sleep too well in her car seat." His countenance has changed too, like he's as uncomfortable with the conversation as I am. The problem is when it comes to changing the subject, my mind draws a complete blank.

It makes me miss Reginald so much, his quiet confidence, his gentle and unassuming ways. All that time we spent together, and I can't remember a single instance when I felt awkward or embarrassed around him, which is a lot to say when you're talking about the man who held my hand while I delivered my child.

I still have no idea where I might have ended up if Reginald hadn't taken Gracie and me in. In his mind, it was such a small, simple gesture, and I know there were times he hated himself that he couldn't do any more. At one point, he even offered to adopt my daughter. Not that he expected me to give up custody or anything. It would be the two of us on the birth certificate, him and me, but I knew that his flock of ravenous relations would never forgive him for allotting some of his inheritance to a someone who wasn't a blood relative.

In the end, I know it was for the best. Gracie's had a good life in spite of all her losses and separations. It's been far more stable than what I could have provided for her. Not to say I didn't try. God knows how much effort I put into caring for my child, to do right by her if only to overcompensate for the way everything else in my life had fallen into ruins. Sometimes you have to accept your own limitations. And not just the physical ones either.

Who would have guessed the kind of havoc postpartum hormones can wreak on a depression-prone mind? What biologist can offer the scientific explanation of how sadness and stress can dry up a mother's milk supply only a few days after delivery? You know how you can get a bunch of new moms together and all they talk about are their labor stories and their nursing woes? And it's always complaining about how uncomfortable it is when your milk comes in, how swollen your breasts get, how if you go an extra hour or two without nursing it's like you're about to burst.

I never experienced any of that. I mean, I know I was making something, because Gracie went a whole week before the pediatrician suggested I supplement. She was kind about it too, gave me two big cans of free formula. She didn't realize that I was living with one of Orchard Grove's only millionaire residents in his mansion up in the Heights and I could have asked him to hire a full-time wet-nurse for my daughter if I'd really wanted one.

Bottle feeding made it easier for Reginald to be involved,

but he was getting older. Weaker. I hated to think of him waking up in the middle of the night. And it's not just dumping the formula into the bottle, adding water, and shaking it all up. There's all kinds of special stipulations. Checking that the nipples are properly sterilized, making sure the tap water's been filtered, getting the bottle at just the right temperature even though you're never supposed to use the microwave.

I hated seeing Reginald have to go through so much work at his age, but I was more than dysfunctional by that time. I tried to brush it off, tried to blame it all on the sleepless nights, but even then, as I felt my clarity slipping away, I knew there was more to it than that. I shouldn't have been ashamed to ask for help. That was stupid, but Reginald had already done so much for me, and as far as I like to think I'd matured by that point, I was still subscribing to that bootstrap style of Christianity I'd inherited from my mother and all the orchardists and missionary league women and our scores of pastors who'd gone through the revolving doors of Orchard Grove Bible Church.

It was Reginald who finally came and told me I had a problem. I'm sure it pained him, having to confront me like that, but he loved me and Gracie both and knew that it was a discussion we needed to have.

I'd fallen asleep while drawing the baby's bath. It sounds

worse than it is. Gracie was still in her swing. I hadn't gotten her out of it yet or undressed her. I was going to do that once I got the bath water ready, but after I plugged the tub and started filling it up, I thought I heard a noise from the nursery. I hurried to check on Gracie. She'd fallen asleep in the swing. And she looked so sweet, so peaceful, and I was so thankful for a few moments of quiet. A few moments without this little helpless thing who needed me nearly every minute of the day. I was just going to shut my eyes. Just a few seconds.

By the time Reginald came upstairs, the bath had overflowed. The water line was just a few inches away from his antique chest in the hall. He wasn't angry. There wasn't a single time in our entire friendship when Reginald got upset with me, but he told me that something would have to change.

"Nobody would blame you for being depressed after all that's happened these past few weeks."

"It's hormones," I told him, refusing to admit that what happened with Chris could still impact my life anymore.

He nodded. "Even so, sometimes hormones get you so off balance you can't function without outside help."

I didn't know if by *outside help* he meant a full-time nanny (which I knew he'd hire if I asked him to), a little pill, a month-long stay in a psych ward or what. All I knew was I loved my daughter. Loved her more than anything in the world, and I couldn't even perform the most basic, mundane tasks to take care of her.

We tried a few things, Reginald and I. He made me an appointment with the doctor who delivered Gracie, walked into the room with me and asked her opinion on the benefits of anti-depressants, thus beginning my dependence on pharmaceuticals. I know it's nothing to be ashamed of, but it makes me wonder how moms like me took care of their newborns before the invention of modern drugs. That's also when I started seeing so many different counselors, when I learned the distinction between baby blues, postpartum depression, and postpartum psychosis. It was these professionals who helped me to realize how precariously close I was perched on the threshold of the latter. Apparently, it's not normal for a new mom to cry whenever she hears her baby grunting because she knows that means in a few minutes she'll have a dirty diaper to change. Nor is it healthy to dream every night that your child dies of SIDS, thus absolving you of any further responsibility for her care and well-being.

I knew I needed more help than just Reginald and the Orchard Grove family practitioner could provide. He knew it too. I didn't find out until I talked with his granddaughter after the funeral, but he'd received his diagnosis two months before Gracie was born. He knew even then, even when he was offering to legally adopt my daughter and raise her with me, that he wouldn't live to see Gracie take her first step or say her first word or eat her first bite of solid food.

He was such a gentle soul. A gentle, quiet soul. I can't believe any woman would have wanted to hit or berate him like his ex-wife did. What was most impressive about Reginald, aside from his boundless generosity, was his perfect peace with everything he'd suffered through in his past. "My wife had her share of troubles, but she gave me seven beautiful children, and I couldn't thank God more for the life he's granted me."

I wonder if when I'm in my eighties, I'll be that serene. That free from bitterness.

When I think about where I am right now, I know it would take a miracle.

CHAPTER 60

Reginald and I didn't talk about his failing health. Didn't mention that he'd lost nearly as much weight as I'd gained during the pregnancy. I wouldn't have admitted it even to myself at the time, but looking back I think I knew that whatever decisions I made for Gracie and me, I wouldn't be able to rely on Reginald's generosity for much longer.

I'd been seeing a counselor ever since the bathtub incident. Pretty intensive stuff. Two afternoons a week, and Reginald had to drive Gracie and me all the way to Wenatchee. Orchard Grove's just too small of a town to worry about things like psychiatrists or counselors or mental health in general.

The counselor was really pushing me to consider this fourteen-day inpatient program out in Spokane, three hours away from my daughter. I knew that Reginald would rather die than see Gracie neglected, but I also knew — or maybe sensed is a better word — that Reginald's body would soon betray him. Saw the parallels between him and my father.

I put it off multiple times. Told the counselor I wasn't ready to leave Gracie. I guess like anyone who needs to walk through recovery, the first step is to want to be healed. Isn't that why Jesus asks the lame man, "Do you want me to make you well?" If you're healthy, that probably sounds like the stupidest question in the world. It's only those of us on the other side of the spectrum that really get it.

Yes, I wanted to be healed, but I wasn't about to admit that my child would be better off without me. If the only reason I bore and delivered Gracie was so that someone else could raise her, I should have put her up for adoption like Chris wanted and never left my husband.

The truth was I needed Gracie. She was the only reason I had to get out of bed each day, and I mean that as literally as it sounds.

Reginald didn't push the in-patient program. He told me he'd take care of Gracie if I wanted to go, but he wasn't about to kick me out of his house. And he was everything you would expect from a millionaire godfather with a soul as good as his. He read to Gracie hours a day. And I'm not talking about *Goodnight Moon* or *Green Eggs and Ham.* That child had heard most of the comedies and all of Shakespeare's sonnets by the time she was a month old. In his will, Reginald left Gracie his complete Shakespeare collection. When he wasn't reading to her, Reginald was spoiling her with those fancy, hand-painted toys that are marketed to grow your child's IQ. You'd think with a start like that, she'd be destined to grow up to play Ophelia on the big stage and simultaneously graduate with a PhD in astrophysics and English literature.

There are so many other reasons I have for thanking Reginald, too. Like introducing me to my literary idol. Gracie was about six weeks old, and who was coming to give a talk at the library but Hester Lynne, New York Times bestselling author, on her third book tour? It wasn't that far away, just an hour and a half drive to Wenatchee. Reginald thought I'd be thrilled to go with him, but I didn't feel ready.

I didn't feel safe.

I was so protective of Gracie, too. So anxious about germs and pedophiles and child abductors and dust mites.

So Reginald invited Hester Lynne to visit us in his home.

Yeah, that's about as shocked as I was, too. I realized he had connections all throughout the literary world, but if he was on first-name basis with someone like Hester Lynne, don't you think he would have told me at some point while we were devouring her novels?

The day of her visit, I was as nervous as Anne Shirley preparing to meet her favorite author. Reginald kept watching me with this bemused expression that I couldn't come close to deciphering. Then half an hour before her expected arrival time, Hester Lynne threw open the door to his home, gave Reginald a massive hug, and kissed him on the cheek with a cheerful, "Hi, Grandpa!"

You think you're surprised, imagine how I felt. I mean, I'd known Reginald for nearly all of my married life. We'd read *The Winding Road* and *The Scent of Silence* multiple times together. Dissected them both nearly paragraph by paragraph. Gushed enthusiastic praise over the prose. And this whole time, we were talking about his granddaughter?

"Don't be mad at Grandpa," Hester told me when I recovered slightly from my shock. "I swore him to secrecy, and I'm sure by now you know what a huge gentleman he is."

"But how are you … why are you …" I was so tongue-tied I couldn't even get out a single question.

Hester smiled. My guess is Reginald prepared her to meet a blushing, rabid fan.

I had already come up with a few questions I wanted to ask, especially about her first book. About the infertility if she was willing to talk about it. I should have written them all down, because now that we were face to face, now that I realized she was related to my dearest friend and benefactor, my mind was as empty as Nicholas Nickleby's pocketbook.

She and Reginald talked some about her third novel, which had just released. This one was told from the perspective of an autistic child in the foster-care system. Looking back, there were so many things I could have asked her. How she got into the head of a neglected little boy, how she wrote and researched the autism side of it, how she could delve into such a heavy subject matter and remain the perkiest, most gregarious woman I've met.

She was about my age, give or take. When I asked if she was ever married, she laughed and said she was too busy living her life to think of settling down. Can I begin to describe at that moment how much I envied her?

Eventually we got to talking about her own experiences as a foster parent. As it turns out, she's the same granddaughter Reginald told me about who wanted to adopt but kept running into so many failed placements through the state. I could tell it was still something of a sore subject by the way she talked about the babies she'd taken into her home only to have them snatched away, returned to abusive family members or relatives who were only looking for the monthly payout.

The whole time she talked, Reginald sat beaming until he finally said, "Tell her about the Children's Corner."

Then she smiled too, and her face lit up. "The Children's Corner is a nonprofit I helped start a few years ago when I was between novels. It's something like a pre-foster system. It's completely voluntary. We offer temporary child placement for families who just need a little bit of time to get on their feet as an alternative to state placements."

I was about to ask how many children they served, but apparently Hester didn't need any of my help to keep the conversation rolling.

"You know, sometimes all a parent needs is a couple weeks to really hit the pavement looking for work or finding a place to live. We've got a lot of parents who come to us when they're evicted from their homes. We'll match the children up with host families while the parents work to get settled. Or sometimes it's drug related. Moms who drop off their babies with us before they check themselves into rehab programs. The nice thing is that since the state isn't involved, the parents retain all rights. They can come pick up their children at any time, no questions asked. And we've got some of the most generous, loving volunteers in the world. Most of the placements are short-term, six weeks or less, so that allows even older couples to get involved who might have a heart for this sort of work but maybe don't feel right committing to something really long-term. For health reasons or whatever.

"Or take me, for example. Once I gave up my dream of adopting a baby of my own and threw myself into my writing instead, I honestly didn't have it in me to invest full-time in raising kids. Still don't, but that doesn't stop me from once or twice a year opening up my home, right? And the children, you should see them. I mean, I know there's this whole assumption that anyone in a foster-type system must have fifty-pound chips on their shoulders, right? But, oh my goodness, these children just steal your heart. And the neat part is I've been able to interact with all the different age ranges too. Even when I don't take them into my home, I'm at the center once or twice a week. It's completely optional, but sometimes the host families bring the kids down for a little bit of respite-type care, and we have board games and healthy snacks and outdoor play time. I'm serious when I say I think I could do this into my old age, and it would keep me young. Not like Grandpa over here."

She nudged Reginald playfully with her elbow. He reached over and gave her a strong squeeze and soft kiss on the head.

I stared at my lap. "I just don't think I'm ready to make that sort of decision yet."

Hester looked at me like I'd just admitted I was a Vulcan. Reginald cleared his throat.

I glanced at him imploringly, hoping he'd make her understand. "I just can't do it."

He gave Hester an apologetic glance and rubbed my back. "She's got a baby," he explained. "You know it's not easy for a new mom."

Hester's light complexion reddened. "I had no idea. I'm so sorry. I wouldn't even dream of suggesting …" Now she was the one shooting her grandpa an imploring look.

Reginald smiled and clapped his hands together once. "Did you bring your newest novel?" he asked. "I promised we'd get to hear at least the first chapter in our own private book reading."

CHAPTER 61

Hester could only stay for another twenty minutes or so after she shared the first two chapters of her new book and signed a copy for me. When she gave me her email address and said we should keep in touch, I got the sense she was being perfectly genuine.

I can't tell you how many times I stared at that email address, came up with the dozens of questions I should have asked her when we were face to face. Questions about her books, about her source material, about her life. Sometimes I even tried to muster up the courage to ask for writing advice, but that would be like the author of *Dick and Jane* asking Pushkin for a tip or two on fine literature.

We reconnected during her grandfather's last few days. Several of the relatives came over. The house was full of Reginald's soon-to-be-heirs who'd come to either pay their last respects or get first in line when the time came to divide the plunder.

Hester and I spent two full afternoons together, both of

us and little Gracie. I could tell she was just as disgusted with her relatives as I was. I think the fact that Hester was independently wealthy from her book sales made it easier for me to trust her. She'd take her share of her grandpa's fortune just like everyone else, but it wasn't really going to change her lifestyle.

Some people say literary fiction can't pay the bills, but I guess they don't know about authors like Hester Lynne who get their novels optioned by major Hollywood producers. And even then, even when we were sitting around, giving everyone the chance to give Reginald the kind of loving goodbye a man like him deserved, I never got the nerve to ask her about writing.

But there did develop something of a friendship between the two of us, if you can call it that when one party's completely starstruck in the presence of the other. I think she sensed I was a little idol-worshipy around her, but it never felt like she let that get to her head. She was far more down to earth than I would have expected from a woman whose film adaptation of her debut novel was about to break twenty million at the box offices. She asked me lots of questions about Gracie and about the postpartum depression, so much so that I wondered if I was turning into fodder for her next novel.

We didn't talk about the Children's Corner, the non-profit she'd started, but I kept the information bookmarked in the back of my mind. Sometimes at night I'd lie awake and think about how that would feel. To walk into an office, tell a stranger I didn't have the means to take care of my kid. To listen to my child cry when I walked out of the room.

But then again, Hester was right about its being easier than going through the state. At the Children's Corner, parents wouldn't have to relinquish any of their rights. Her words replayed over and over in my head like some New Age affirmation. *You can come pick up your children at any time, no questions asked.*

No questions asked.

No questions asked.

I knew I was storing the information away. Knew one day I might need to pull it out and examine it more carefully. But right now, I had more pressing things to deal with.

Like saying goodbye to Reginald.

He regained a little of his strength right at the end. So much so that most of the relatives left after waiting it out a few days with nothing to show for their efforts.

Soon it was just me and Hester.

And then even she had to go back to her home in Seattle. Back to her book tours and publication deadlines and volunteer work at her nonprofit.

The night he died, it was just Reginald and me. Gracie was in the nursery. It'd been a long day, but she'd finally drifted off to sleep. I was sitting by Reginald's bedside. We were only about halfway through Hester's third novel, the one about the autistic child. I made myself a promise not to read ahead. I was desperately hoping Reginald and I could finish one last book together.

I followed him into the room, where visions of candy and chocolates tantalized my senses. Teasing me with the promise of delectable pleasure.

"Too wordy," he mumbled.

It was the first time he'd ever criticized a thing his granddaughter wrote.

"Too wordy," he repeated.

I wondered if he was just getting tired. "Should we be done for the night?" I asked. I didn't realize what I was doing then, but I was making my way through Hester's novel slowly. Hoping that Reginald's curiosity about the main character and his pride in his granddaughter would give him enough motivation to keep on living day to day.

I wasn't ready to say goodbye to him yet.

"I should have taken that part out," he said.

"What do you mean?" I was worried his mind might be slipping away even though his speech was perfectly clear.

"She never did like it when I cut out those flowery words. But she's got too many descriptions. Makes her sound stuck up and pretentious."

"Did you do the editing for her?" I asked.

He glanced at me, his eyes widening in surprise. "What's that?"

"Did you help Hester with her editing?"

He smiled. "Help her? How do you think she made it on the New York Times list?" He sighed, the rattle in his lungs shooting barbs into my heart. He took my hand weakly in his. "Don't tell her I told you."

"Your secret's safe with me," I promised. It was the least I could do after everything he'd done for Gracie and me. And he would have done more if he could. I know for a fact that his love for Gracie and me filled his last days with a peace he never would have found from his money-hungry relatives. I wouldn't be surprised if the joy that came from having Gracie around actually extended his life a few extra weeks, but of course the end was still the same. In some ways, it was like watching my father die all over again. But Reginald had lived such a full life, had touched those around him more than he would ever know. When all was said and done, his homecoming was as gentle and quiet and unassuming as he was.

Lucky Reginald.

At least he never lived to see what a worse mother I turned into once he was gone.

CHAPTER 62

Justin and I are on the road now, finally heading out of Orchard Grove. Once we left my mom's, things felt a little more comfortable. It's something I've always liked about car trips. You don't need to make any awkward decisions about whether to make eye contact and for how long. We simply stare at the road ahead of us. The rhythm of the windshield wipers has a hypnotic effect, and I feel ready for this next chapter in my life.

Of course I do.

There's no reason I shouldn't go with Justin to Seattle. Even if we have no future between us, I'll have far more opportunities out there. And if I do have another crash, I may as well do it in a major city. Even that two-week inpatient program I finally checked myself into in Spokane wasn't fully equipped to handle my particular concoction of depression mixed with (borderline) postpartum psychosis mixed with a history of spousal abuse and sexual assault.

Not that I came right out and told them Chris abused me, but all those shrinks, even the ones Reginald took me to see before I finally agreed to in-service treatment, seemed far more interested in my history with my husband than in the fact that I'd been raped.

Justin clears his throat and turns down the music in his car. "I think you'll get along really well with Amy."

"I'm sure I will." I don't know much about Justin's sister, my future roommate. She works in the design business too, not the one Justin started but some kind of company connecting freelance web designers with their ideal clientele. I wonder if everyone I meet in Seattle will end up working in the tech field. And here I am, still wishing we could go back to the days of typewriters and white-out and preferring my fountain pen over any keyboard.

I want to find a way to ask him about my daughter. There's nothing in our past conversations that should lead me to think any topic is off-limits with Justin, but it's harder when you're face-to-face. Or shoulder to shoulder as we were.

We've talked so much by phone, gotten to know each other so well, I think Justin must have sensed what I was mulling over. "Gracie's doing really well these days. Growing healthy. Chattering up a storm."

I try to smile. Try to remember that I gave this precious little girl the gift of life, which is more than some women would have done in my situation. I know Grandma Lucy just prayed over me a few hours earlier that I could find release from my shame, and I'm still hopeful that something really did change in my spirit, but I think I underestimated how difficult this would be. Did I think that because Justin and I hit it off so well when we were living in totally different cities that we could switch to a face-to-face relationship seamlessly?

For a few seconds, I wonder what I'm even doing here. Justin and I have talked on the phone for probably a hundred hours or more if you were to add it all up over the last few months, but does that mean I really know him? What about those news stories you hear from time to time, those online romances gone bad. Justin could be a serial killer for all I know, couldn't he?

No, this may be the first time I've met him in person, but I would have known, would have picked up on it earlier if he were some sort of sociopath. Besides, he had to go through all the screening to take Gracie in. There's no way they would have let him assume that sort of responsibility if there was anything questionable in his background.

Justin reaches out and turns off the music. "You feeling ok?"

I nod and mumble some sort of response in agreement.

"Amy's really looking forward to meeting you," he says. There we go again. Talking about everyone except for him and me and the baby we both want to call our own.

"Gracie's real easygoing," he says, and I'm glad to hear it. Once we get to Seattle, it will be after two in the morning. He'll only have a few hours to sleep before he has to be awake for his Monday morning meeting. At least the snowstorm has let up a little. We're halfway across the North Cascades now. I forgot how carsick I can get on these long, windy roads. The last thing I want to do is ask Justin to pull over.

We've been talking more openly now. He's been chatting away about work, about this big deal he and his partner are hoping to land that comes with some sort of extended contract that will basically set them up for the next decade. I don't think I've got anything akin to a head for business, but I'm inspired by his enthusiasm. There's something in him, his zest for life, his desire to go and seize whatever adventures the universe throws his way, that reminds me of Hester.

I wonder which of her novels he likes the most.

I wonder if she based any of her characters off of him.

There's a lull in the conversation. In the dark, sitting side by side, with the snow falling hypnotically on Justin's windshield, I feel as comfortable as I did whenever we'd talk on the phone. But still, there are some conversations we've never had. Conversations I think we both knew had to wait until we were together.

"I never asked how you and Hester met," I finally say. I've tried doing the math dozens of times to figure out exactly when Justin must have walked into her life. It had to be after her second novel, because that was published before Gracie was born. But after I met Justin, I read through all my Hester Lynne novels again, and the hero in *The Scent of Silence* seems so much like him I'm sure it can't be coincidence.

"We were friends for quite a while. Worked together on a lot of business things. Her publisher hired me to do some design work before her first book tour — banners, bookmarks, stuff like that. I thought I was going to be dealing with just the publisher, but after Hester saw my first concept, she marched herself into my office and demanded a revamp. And that, as they say, was that."

I'm trying to remember how many years ago *The Winding Road* came out. "So how long were you actually dating?"

"Dating?" He laughs. "I'm not sure Hester and I dated at all."

"How does that work?" I'm trying to catch his amusement, but I only feel lost.

"We had this business relationship going on for a couple years. I admired her for being so straightforward about what she wanted, and she liked my designs once I was willing to take my marching orders from her and not the publisher. She did nearly all of her online marketing herself, so we were in touch quite a bit about her webpage, social media images, all that. So we had this working relationship for years, then one day she showed up in my office. She had this cute little baby in a front-pack and said she hadn't had any adult company in weeks and wanted me to join her for dinner that evening and a walk along the pier.

"Two weeks later, we were married."

I smiled, wishing I'd had more time to get to know Hester, wondering if Justin was grieving the same way I'd been grieving for Chris.

"What about you?" he asked. "What's your story?"

"About what? How I met Hester?" I knew she was secretive about her co-writing relationship with her grandpa, but certainly she would have told her husband of all people.

"No," Justin explains. "I mean how'd you find yourself ..." He clears his throat. His confident, jocular voice falters.

"Yeah," I tell him. "I get what you mean."

What Justin's trying to ask is how a mother like me could end up handing her baby over to be raised by someone else.

CHAPTER 63

Before he died, Reginald transferred some money into my bank account and made sure his relatives knew I was expected to stay at his home for at least a year rent free. Nobody could sell it or move in before then.

The first thing I did was hire Gracie a nanny. Mrs. Danvers was a round, matronly woman in her sixties with nothing to do all day but sit around and fret about her grandchildren who lived too far away for regular visits. She was warm and efficient, and I hated to admit it, but she cared for Gracie far more effectively than I could have even on my best days. I once had a nightmare that Gracie called her *Mama*.

Thankfully, Mrs. Danvers stayed out of my way for the most part. She kept up the home with the assistance of Reginald's old housekeeper, and she never made me feel bad for needing the assistance of live-in help in the first place.

The first few weeks after Reginald passed were hard, but I don't know if it was because he was up there in heaven praying for me or what, but the depression never got as bad as it did after Daddy died. Maybe it had to do with the meds. I don't know. The doctor said it would take a while for the Prozac to level out in my system. Maybe it kicked in right when I needed it the most.

Life wasn't easy. I don't mean to imply that, but I was still functional. Still got out of bed every day. My guess is if you were to take all the time I spent caring for Gracie and all the time Mrs. Danvers spent doing the same, it would have been right around a fifty-fifty split.

Not too bad for a mom who's suffering from borderline postpartum psychosis, right?

And then Mrs. Danvers asked for two nights off.

Just two nights. So she could drive down to Oregon to visit her daughter. It shouldn't have been a big deal. She even offered to help me find a respite worker, but I was feeling more optimistic than perhaps I should have. Thinking that a mom with a three-month-old should be able to handle her own baby for a weekend.

I look back at myself and realize how much of my mothering I did on autopilot. Don't ask me why it's such a vivid memory, but I still remember changing one of Gracie's poopy diapers while Mrs. Danvers was gone. What makes it stand out to me was Gracie was screaming. She had pretty bad diarrhea, which gave her an ugly rash. And I guess the ointment or the baby wipe was stinging because she was crying so hard she nearly started to choke. It wasn't like I could just let her sit in that mess. I had to clean it up, but what I remember most vividly is my daughter crying, obviously in pain, and I was completely stoic. I couldn't have felt sorry for her if I wanted to. Maybe it would be different if I'd even felt mad at her or disgusted or inconvenienced. But I felt nothing.

Absolutely nothing.

Mrs. Danvers couldn't come home soon enough. And I mean that quite literally, because it was the day Mrs. Danvers was due back in Washington that I nearly killed my daughter.

CHAPTER 64

Gracie and I had been dozing in a rocking chair Reginald had bought for me as one of my many baby-shower presents. It had been a decent day. There were two times I'd had to put Gracie down in her crib and let her cry because I couldn't keep my eyes open anymore, but at least my mental outlook was all right.

Or so I thought. Like I said, I went through that period really subdued. It was the opposite of mood swings, an emotional flatline. But I was doing all right. I was almost done with my nannyless weekend, Mrs. Danvers would return first thing tomorrow morning, and all I had to do was keep my daughter warm and fed and clean until then.

You'd think that wouldn't be too hard of a task, right?

I was napping with Gracie. We'd fallen asleep reading a little picture book Reginald had put together for her before he died, some of his favorite fine art prints with little poems he'd written out just for her. We read that book by "Grandpa Reggie" each day without fail. It was the only aspect of parenting that I refused to let Mrs. Danvers jump in and take over no matter how exhausted I was.

A noise woke me up, and I heard footsteps coming down the hall. Coming toward the nursery.

"Ready or not!"

I hadn't seen Chris since the day of Gracie's delivery. Had done my best to move on with my life, a life without him and his unpredictable eruptions.

"Ready or not!" He said it in a singsong voice. Was he trying to creep me out?

Don't come near me. But the words caught in my throat. My vocal chords were paralyzed. Why couldn't I speak?

The nursery door opened. He had a crowbar in his hand. His forearm muscles were so tense I could trace his individual veins. "Ready or not, here I come."

I screamed and threw Gracie down, covering her with my body. He might kill me, but he would never hurt my daughter.

Gracie was squirming. I tried to dig deeper into her. *You're in danger, little baby. Lie still and Mommy will protect you.*

She was thrashing and crying. I couldn't get her to stop. *Shh. Don't you know he'll hear you?*

Except there was no he. There was no Chris. Only me.

Me smothering my little girl, who choked and shrieked and writhed beneath me.

When I realized what was happening and got off from on top of her, she had rug burns against her cheek and forehead.

I stared at her in horror. Just touching her made my skin burn, made me realize what I'd done. I was hysterical. I couldn't even comfort her. I left her screaming there on the floor, choking on her pathetic cries. I'd never heard a baby sound so terrified.

And the monster she was terrified of was me.

I was sobbing. Screaming. Any latent questions about whether this was some sort of postpartum depression set off by hormonal imbalance or full-fledged, genuine psychosis were permanently put to rest. I didn't know what else to do. I ran the shower, let the water scald me until my skin was as red as my daughter's cheek. Once the hot water tank emptied, I stood there under the icy spray until every nerve ending in my body was numb.

I got out, dried myself off, and opened the medicine cabinet, trying to convince myself that it wasn't me. It was the meds. A side effect from the drugs.

I wouldn't ever do that to my daughter.

But her persistent screams from the other room told me that I already had.

CHAPTER 65

I checked myself into that in-patient psych hospital the next day. Called Hester Lynne. I didn't know who else might help. I was too distraught to give her any details, just told her I was struggling with the depression a lot more than normal and wanted to put Gracie in that program.

That nonprofit Hester helped to start.

She drove out to meet me that very morning. Brought the permission forms, the legal documents, everything. Told me now that she was done with her book tour, she'd take Gracie into her own home if that was all right with me.

She even drove me all the way out to Spokane on the completely opposite side of the state from Seattle to take me to the in-patient program.

I'd love to tell you about my time there. You'd think after that I could probably work with someone like Hester, and we could put together a pretty gripping novel. Except I don't remember any of the details. It was like that emotional numbness I'd been feeling since Gracie's birth turned into a full-fledge emotional coma.

I slept. I remember that a lot. And gained fifteen pounds, but that's because they put me on something a lot heavier than Prozac, something lithium based. I don't know if you've researched neuropharmacology at all, but that lithium stuff will knock you out like a lobotomy. At least, that's what it did to me. I don't know what it's like for other patients, but I'm not exaggerating when I say that the first day on it, I slept twenty hours straight.

There were specialists there by the dozens. Psychiatrist meetings, group sessions. Like I said, a setting that I'm sure would be fascinating if you were reading it in a novel and not existing in it yourself.

Because existing is about all I was doing. Existing from day to day, biding my time until I could leave the program. Pick up my daughter. Hug her close to my chest once more.

Except the psychologists were concerned. You probably already know this, but postpartum psychosis is the driving force behind all those stories you hear of mothers drowning their kids in the bathtub or strapping them into their car seats and driving them straight off a cliff. And apparently it starts off with symptoms very similar to mine. Emotional numbness. Occasional hallucinations. Fixating on your child's death.

So when my discharge date came closer and closer, I put it off. I wasn't ready. Wasn't ready to reclaim my daughter. Ready to be the mom I should have been to her from the beginning.

Demographically, there's no reason I should have turned into such a pathetic parent. I mean, my mom has her issues for certain, but she and Daddy had a decent marriage and gave me a comfortable, happy home life. As far as I know, none of the extended relatives or anything have dealt with this kind of crippling mental illness. Where did it all come from?

Sometimes I'd like to blame everything on Chris. Maybe all that constant rage made something snap in my brain. It's possible, I guess. And by the way the psychologists kept wanting to probe into my failure of a marriage, I suppose that was probably the working hypothesis they were going with, too.

I wish it were as simple as that, but I know it's not. Just like it's not as simple as me praying for more joy or more love for my daughter.

Love for Gracie was never a problem. From the day you asked God to heal over my scars, I loved that child.

Maybe too much. Maybe I should have listened to Chris. Let him talk me into finding her an adoptive family. God knows her life would have been more stable than it has been now.

I didn't realize Hester had that hiking accident until about an hour after I was discharged. My fourteen days in-patient time had stretched out into a month and a half. A month and a half with no internet, cell phones, nothing. How was I to have known about the accident?

I found out when I reclaimed my cell phone. I didn't know how I was going to get all the way from Spokane to Seattle to pick up my daughter, so I had to call Hester and make arrangements.

"Hello?"

I still remember the pained sound on the other line. Why was a man answering Hester's phone?

"I'm trying to get a hold of Hester Lynne. Is she there?" Who was I talking to? Did she have a boyfriend? Who was that child babbling so happily in the background?

He cleared his throat. "Can I ask who's calling?"

What was this? An interrogation? "I'm Gracie's mom. I need to talk to her about my baby."

"Oh." An uncomfortable silence. Another subdued cough. "Listen, we've been trying to get a hold of you."

I didn't know who this *we* was he was referring to, but I didn't care. I had to get to Seattle, and I had to get my daughter. What had Hester said about the Children's Place? *You can come pick up your children at any time, no questions asked.*

"I don't know how to say this," he began, and my heart must have dropped two or three inches in my chest. "Hester was in a hiking accident last week. A pretty bad one."

What kind of hiking accident could be so serious? I mean, I've heard of shin splits, but how could something like that keep me from my daughter? I wasn't thinking clearly. I couldn't understand his words. "Is she ok?"

Now I realize how hard a conversation this must have been for him, but I didn't know Justin then. Didn't stop to think about what he was going through, losing his wife after two short weeks together.

I didn't find out until later that I called the afternoon of Hester's funeral. Her husband had only returned from the gravesite an hour or two earlier. That's why I'm still so amazed at the compassion I heard in Justin's voice when he said, "I'm really sorry to be the one to tell you this, but Hester is dead."

CHAPTER 66

I couldn't accept it. Wouldn't accept it. In fact, I had such an epic meltdown there in front of the hospital that they encouraged me to re-admit myself for another few days.

Days that turned into weeks.

I called Justin a couple times from the hospital. Had to get special clearance from the psychologist in charge and everything. But I had to know about my daughter. Not that I had any reason to worry. Justin and some of the workers at the Children's Place had done everything in their power to find me after Hester died, but the only emergency contact I'd listed was my mom, and I hadn't told her I was checking myself into a psych ward. Hadn't told her I was placing my baby in temporary custodial care, so you can imagine what an earful Justin got when he reached her.

Reginald was gone, Hester was gone. I hadn't told anybody else where I was going or how to get in touch with me. How was I to have known my child's temporary guardian was going to stand beneath a seventy-five pound boulder while hiking up some picturesque waterfall with her brand new husband?

Thankfully, Justin had been carrying Gracie in his hiking backpack, not Hester. I know it's a selfish way to look at it, but that could have been my daughter killed.

I told myself it was my fault. Blamed myself for not having some sort of premonition. I shouldn't have ever given Gracie up, no matter how temporary it was meant to be.

Over the phone, Justin assured me that he'd gone through the same screening as all the other host families volunteering for the Children's Place. Told me how after Hester died, he'd started looking after Gracie until they could get hold of me. He never actually used the word, he had far more tact than that, but I hadn't been on the phone with him five minutes before I realized that he loved my daughter.

Perhaps more than I ever could.

Which is why I didn't head to Seattle immediately. Which is why even after I got discharged from the hospital, I kept my distance. Stayed in Spokane for a while, hopped from place to place until I finally made my way back to Orchard Grove. Why I dragged my feet so long when he first asked me to come to Seattle.

I knew from almost the very beginning that Justin was a better parent for Gracie than I could ever hope to be.

CHAPTER 67

I didn't mean to fall asleep in Justin's car, but I woke myself up mid-snore.

Real sexy.

"I'm sorry," I apologize.

"Don't be," Justin says and smiles when he hands me a tissue so I can wipe the drool off my face.

"How much farther do we have to go?" I ask, worrying that I sound like a petulant child in the backseat on an extended family vacation.

"About an hour."

"Sorry I haven't been better company." There I go apologizing again.

Justin turns off whatever audiobook he's been listening to. "Don't worry about it. Gave me some time to catch up on my reading."

"Oh? What are you reading? I mean, what are you listening to?" With audiobooks, I never know which verb I'm supposed to use.

"*Scent of Silence*." He smiles somewhat sadly as he names Hester's second novel.

That's why that thirty seconds of prose sounded familiar.

"What do you think of it?" I ask.

He shrugs. "I'm only up to chapter six. I've got ten more hours of listening left."

"Haven't you read it before?" I ask, incredulous. If I were to marry an author, I certainly wouldn't do it before I'd read each and every one of their books.

A little laugh escapes. "She always gave me a hard time about it, too. But I do most of my reading on audio."

His confession reminds me how recently it's been that he lost his wife. Just last summer. In a stupid hiking accident. What a tragedy. What a waste.

"Do you like listening to it?" I ask, hoping I'm not being too nosy. "Or does it just make you miss her that much more?"

He wipes his forehead, where a stray strand of hair has fallen in front of his eyes. "Both."

We sit side by side without talking. I'm about to ask him if he wants to listen to *The Scent of Silence* together when he surprises me by asking, "Do you think it gets easier with time, or do you think that's just what people tell you when you're overwhelmed and grieving?"

I decide to be honest with him. “I have no idea.”

He sighs. I know so much about him already from our phone calls but there’s plenty more I still have to learn. Was Hester his first love? Was their whirlwind romance as passionate and adventurous as it sounds?

Is it easier to lose someone you’ve only loved for a short time? Or maybe it’s harder since you still see them through those rose-tinted glasses. You haven’t had the chance to let familiarity creep in and erode your affection.

“Can I ask you something personal?”

I already know what his question’s going to be. The conversation was bound to turn this way before we reached Seattle.

I nod and find that I’m clenching the strap of my seatbelt. I force my fingers to relax.

“What was it exactly that happened to your husband?”

CHAPTER 68

I stare straight in front of me. Bright snowflakes in the headlights zoom toward us like racing stars. My mind is foggy from my little nap, my spirit reluctant to think about that chapter of my past.

Justin's never asked me before, at least not for any details. But I knew it would end up like this. Knew if I came out to Seattle, it's what we'd end up talking about.

It was Reginald who told me. Reginald who gave me the scant details that even now leave gaping holes in the narrative. I've pieced together his side of it and merged it with what Grandma Lucy and my mother later said, but even now there are so many things I haven't figured out.

What did Chris do after I left home? After he hit me for the first time?

While I was sitting in Grandma Lucy's greenhouse, where was my husband? How did he feel? What did he think?

When my water broke and Reginald came to take me to the hospital, Grandma Lucy and her niece started to pray for me. And at the same time, Chris got worried. He eventually called Reginald's house, but Reginald didn't answer. By that point, he was already with me, either at County Hospital or on our way there.

Another hour passed. Chris still didn't know where I was.

Well, you don't go into labor in a town as small as Orchard Grove without people finding out. To this day, I don't know how the news got on the church prayer chain, but it did. It wasn't Grandma Lucy. She knew enough about the precarious nature of my relationship with Chris that she kept her mouth shut. I assume she would have told her niece to do the same thing, but who knows? People swing by Safe Anchorage Farm all the time. Maybe it was a woman from the missionary league stopping by to purchase some goat soap and the niece let it slip, unaware that just a few minutes later my husband would be getting a call from my mother demanding to know why she hadn't been informed I was in labor.

Well, he hadn't been informed, either.

He charged over to County. Demanded to see me, but Reginald had already warned hospital security. They wouldn't let him in. Reginald said he stepped out and confronted Chris himself, but I can't recall him leaving my side during the entire labor. Of course, it's possible that it happened that way.

I just don't remember.

What I do remember is Reginald's tender face staring at me the next morning when I woke up in my hospital bed. His soft kiss, the way he held my hand like he was afraid he'd bruise my skin.

"The nurses and I didn't think we should tell you during the labor. Wanted you to save all your strength."

My throat was dry. It's such a small detail, but it was as parched as the riverbed running through Orchard Grove in the summer when the heat gets up to a hundred and five.

He stroked my cheek. Stroked my cheek and told me, "Your husband was in a car accident. He's gone."

CHAPTER 69

See what I mean about gaping holes in the storyline? I don't know if Chris got into the accident leaving the hospital or trying to come back later in the day. I don't know if he was so distracted that I'd left him that he wasn't driving safely, or if it was one of those bizarre coincidences.

Someone who hasn't lived through the ecstatic beginning all the way to the explosive end of a tumultuous marriage might expect me to feel relieved.

I actually had a counselor suggest that once. "Did you feel safer knowing he couldn't bother you or your child anymore?"

Yeah, last time I talked to that quack.

Because my husband died thinking I'd walked out on him. Which is what I was planning to do, but in the back of my mind I knew there might eventually come a time for reconciliation.

I've turned my back on you and your stupid church and leadership team who left me alone to suffer through my confusion and grief, but I haven't turned my back on God. You may think I'm an unrepentant sinner, that my marriage failed because of my innate stubbornness, but you never lived with Chris. You never found yourself lying on the floor, unable to get yourself up without his help because he knocked you down when you were thirty-seven weeks pregnant and forty pounds heavier than normal.

You may judge me — in fact, I'm sure you still do — for walking out on Chris that day. Maybe in your mind, I caused him so much psychological despair that he got himself into a wreck and died.

You know what? Go ahead and think that. I'm done trying to prove to you that I've made the right choices. Know why? Because I'm humble enough to realize that I might have made the biggest mistake of my life that day I walked out on Chris. You never thought you'd hear me say that, did you? That's because you deluded yourself into imagining you had me all figured out. Labeled me as a rebellious wife, all but left me to rot in hell if I were to turn my back on my God and my husband.

Well, guess what. I may have left my husband, but that doesn't mean I've walked away from God. And it certainly doesn't mean I wished for Chris's death like that one counselor suggested.

You have no idea what sort of hell and confusion I went through after he died. How could you? In your mind, everything is so black and white. Husbands are good. Wives are supposed to submit. Your pastor is God's mouthpiece so to disobey him is to disobey the Holy Spirit even if your husband is going to lead you into sin. You said it yourself so many times when I was crying in your office. You told me that even if my husband ordered me to abandon my own child, my job was to listen to him, and if what he wanted me to do was outside of God's will, then God would have it out with my husband, not me.

Want to know something? That line of reasoning didn't work out too well in the book of Acts, did it? Or have you forgotten about Ananias and Sapphira? Have you forgotten the way they lied to the apostles about the money they'd donated? If you were their pastor, you know what you would have said to Sapphira? You know what you would have told her? "Go ahead and lie about the money because your husband is the head of your home, and your job is to submit to him as you would to the Lord." Want me to tell you what's wrong with that logic? It's that my husband isn't the Lord and never will be.

Ananias died for lying to God, but the apostles gave his wife a chance of her own. "Is this the correct amount of money you got from the sale of your house?" they asked, and she said it was. Of course, we both know what happened next. She died because of her own sin. Not her husband's sin. See the difference? According to you, all she should have had to do was agree with those apostles, because anything otherwise would be to cast doubt on her husband's honesty. What self-respecting, submissive, or godly wife would do a thing like that?

"Yes, that's the amount of money we sold the property for," she should have said. And according to your gospel, that should have been enough to save her. Except it wasn't, and she was struck dead and buried next to her lying husband.

You think I'm being extreme, but I'm not. Do you know how dangerous your kind of theology is? Do you know how many innocent women and children end up dead like that church secretary and her mutilated twins? Do you know how many wives become complicit in their husbands' sins and crimes because they're told that to do otherwise is to disrespect their husbands' God-given authority?

You'll accuse me of exaggerating, but I'm not. And I'm not talking about people who lived millennia ago like good old Sapphira either. I'm talking about the wife who knows — who doesn't just suspect but *knows*— that her husband is molesting their foster daughter, but she doesn't tell the police because to do so would be to step outside of her role as a godly submissive wife. I'm talking about women like my friend Mel, single women who maybe aren't even saved but the minute they step foot in your stuffy little church, they're going to feel the full weight of your hypocritical judgment, as if getting a divorce is enough to cast you out of heaven forever.

I don't mean to preach at you, Pastor, I really don't, but somebody's got to tell you this stuff. And if it's not me, I don't know who would have the guts to do it.

So go ahead. Prepare your best lecture. Pour out your worst guilt trip. It's nothing less than I would expect. But if my experience happens to save the life of even one innocent woman or child, that's a price I'm willing to pay.

CHAPTER 70

I'm telling Justin about the day Chris died, and I'm surprised at how calm my voice sounds. Like I could be talking about the high-school journalism class we took together or the term paper I wrote one semester on Shakespeare's *Twelfth Night*.

Some people might think it's a good sign that I'm so relaxed, but I'm embarrassed by my own lack of emotions. Am I really that cold? That unfeeling?

Have I even cried for Chris?

I've cried since the day he died. But how much of that is actual grief for my husband? Sure, we were in a complicated relationship, I'd moved out a few weeks earlier and then back in, but we were still married. Is the fact that my husband had issues supposed to make it easier for me to adjust to life as a widow?

Have I cried for him? I don't think I've asked myself that before, and I don't know how to answer. I cry for Reginald all the time. Cry for those stupid relatives of his who were so greedy, so eager to spend his inheritance, but who haven't even thought of planning that trip to the redwoods where he wants his ashes scattered.

I cry for myself far more than I'd like to admit. Cry for the shame of having someone else raising my child because I'm psychotic.

There's that word. I don't know if I'm supposed to own it as readily as I do, but let's call things what they are. A three-hundred-and-fifty-pound man is fat. A woman who's been diagnosed with postpartum psychosis is by definition psychotic.

I'm not saying I'll always be this way. I'm not even saying my psychosis is what identifies me. But it's part of me.

Just like Gracie is a part of me because she came out of my body, and I love her just as much now as I did the day she was born. The fact that she's been living apart from me ever since my first hospital stay doesn't make her any less mine. Doesn't strip away my identity as her mom.

And I guess you could say that in the same way, the fact that Chris hit me the day he was killed in that car crash, the fact that I planned to walk away from him so he couldn't lay a hand on my child doesn't change the fact that I was married to him. That we were once madly, passionately in love.

That the one time he hurt me physically was nothing compared to those previous years of emotional pain and injury.

I can't dissect Chris out of my life as if he were some unwanted mole or a form of tooth decay. Chris will be part of me until the day I die. That doesn't mean I'd be back with him if he were alive today. In fact, I'd like to think I would have kept my resolve to distance myself and my daughter from his rage, but God only knows what would have become of us.

Most likely, the cycle would have continued indefinitely. Maybe you'd say it's a mercy he's dead, but I look at how empty my life has been this past year, I remember the love we once shared, the love that might have been enough to heal over all our past wounds, and I know that you're wrong.

Dead wrong.

CHAPTER 71

I'm not ready for this car trip to end. Once I shared my story about Chris, it's like Justin and I have been trying to fill in decades worth of history into the last forty-five minutes of the drive. I've learned about his pet turtle Moki that he adopted when he was eleven. He's listened to me talk about the play Chris and I started to write in high school, a tragedy so canned and corny that a savvy director could probably convert it to satire without changing a single line.

We've talked about our dead spouses, about what we miss most about them, about the things that drove us crazy when they were still alive. Of course, Justin and Hester had this wild, insane romance that lasted all of a month from the time she showed up and asked him to dinner to the time he was a widower caring for the little girl she'd taken in, while my relationship with Chris spanned far more years filled with far more complicated trials.

I've come to realize that we're both grieving in our own ways. My grief is a lot harder to compartmentalize. I still cry over Reginald at least two or three times a week. And I miss my daughter so much that the fact that I'm about to step into the same house as her sets my abdomen quivering so hard it's probably the equivalent of doing a hundred and twenty crunches in sixty seconds. Even with Chris, I'm not only grieving his death, but the dissolving marriage we both were trying hard to save at different points before his accident.

And I hate to admit it, but I'm even grieving you. The way I lost complete respect for you, the way your church abandoned me as soon as you realized you couldn't snap your fingers and make me go back home and pretend to live my happy little housewife lie. I thank God that I'm free from you now. In a way I think the spiritual abuse you put your congregants through is just as heinous as any crimes that have been committed against me in the past, but I know with the help of the Holy Spirit, I'll learn to forgive.

Learn to let go.

I'm so busy thinking about how many things I've lost in the past year that I don't realize we're in a residential neighborhood until Justin pulls into a driveway and slows to a stop.

"This is it?" I ask, and he must sense my fear because he takes my hand in his. My sweaty, clammy hand.

"We're here. You ready?"

I can hardly breathe. I don't know what to expect. What if Gracie's awake? What if she doesn't remember me? Who am I kidding? Of course she won't remember me. But what if it's worse than that? What if she hates me? What if she's scared of me? What if that tiny brain of hers has some latent memory of the day I nearly smothered her beneath me, and she cries and screams any time I try to come near her?

"I told Amy we're going to keep things really low key, all right? Low stress for you and Gracie both." Justin is speaking encouragement to me as he lets me out of the car and walks me up toward the house, but I can't focus on the words. I can only sense the kindness in his voice.

He has his arm around me. It's nothing romantic. It's just that without his physical support, I literally couldn't walk up these steps to the porch. I pause at the threshold. Do we knock? Ring the bell? Step right in?

Justin reaches out and raps softly on the door. I catch a quick glance at his hand. I want to find out if he still wears his wedding ring or not. I can't believe I didn't think to look sooner.

He's completely unadorned.

He opens the door a crack and whispers, "Amy?"

Nobody answers.

"They're probably sleeping. I'll help you get settled in, and then I better take off."

I want to tell him how thankful I am for everything, but I'm too overwhelmed. This is too much for me. I shouldn't be here.

I think through Grandma Lucy's prayer, the one she prayed over me earlier this afternoon when I sat in that gaudy flowered chair.

You tell us in your Word that you came so that we might have life and have it more abundantly.

There's the slightest trace of whispering coming from upstairs. Justin hears it too. He beckons for me to follow.

So I speak that abundant life over your child today.

My feet are heavy on the carpet. So heavy I feel like an ogre fumbling after its prey.

I speak abundant life over her daughter as well.

It's not crying I hear. Just soft murmuring. A woman's voice and a baby's coos.

A baby much older than my little Gracie.

I don't know what plans you have in store for the two of them …

Justin pauses outside the closed door. "I think they're in there," he whispers. "Do you want to go in?" He sees me hesitate and adds, "Amy won't mind."

He stands back so I'm the one to open the door.

... but I believe that they are plans for good.

The nursery is beautiful. Beatrix Potter decals line all the walls. An intricate mobile with characters from classic children's books hangs over an empty crib.

That you will redeem the years the locusts have eaten ...

A young woman smiles up at me. She has a perfectly chubby, perfectly beautiful baby girl sitting on her lap, grabbing the pages of an illustrated collection of children's poems. Tears stream down my cheeks when I see how calm this child looks. How happy.

"She only woke up a few minutes ago," the woman whispers. "When I heard you pulling up, I thought I'd take her out for a spell."

... that you will restore joy and gladness where once there was only bitterness and sorrow.

Justin gives me a gentle nudge, and I step into the room. I'm like Mary walking into the Secret Garden for the very first time. Or Lucy Pevensie entering the enchanted land of Narnia.

I'm staring at my little girl, and she's staring back at me. She's not smiling, which I didn't have the heart to expect, but at least she's not crying either. She's curious. Like Alice after tumbling down that never-ending rabbit hole.

"Would you like to hold her?" Amy asks.

I don't have to look behind me to sense Justin's encouraging nod of approval.

I reach out for my baby. Except she's no longer a baby, she's a tiny girl. Big enough that soon she'll be celebrating her first birthday.

Her first of many birthdays with her mom.

I have her in my arms. The newborn smell is gone. The skin isn't as soft as I remember, but it's still smoother than anything I've felt on anyone else.

"Hi, sweetie," I whisper. Gracie pouts. She's still not screaming, but I tell myself not to get my hopes up too high. It could take months, maybe even years to reforge the bonds between the two of us. It won't come easily. It won't come without its own share of grief and heartache, I'm almost certain of it.

The pout melts into a cautious smile. She reaches out and touches my chin.

Then again, I've been wrong in the past.

Never put God in a box, right?

A NOTE FROM THE AUTHOR

Before the Dawn is the perhaps the most difficult novel I've written. I went through far more drafts, revamps, and crippling bouts of writer's block than I have in years.

It's not easy writing about depression or spousal abuse for obvious reasons, but I'm thankful to my husband for his continued encouragement, to my prayer team who interceded for me, and to God who helped this project come into existence in spite of all the difficulties and setbacks.

I'm also thankful for my team of editors and beta readers, as well as my son who assists with a lot of behind-the-scenes work on his computer. Thanks also to those of you who lift my writing up in prayer, recommend my books to others, and faithfully buy and read my novels.

The Orchard Grove Christian Women's Fiction books are novels about real women facing real issues. See a full list of titles at www.alanaterry.com.

DISCUSSION QUESTIONS

For group discussion or personal reflection

1. How would you describe your relationship with your mother?
2. Are you as much of a book-lover as the main character?
3. What do you think about the Reginald and his role in the protagonist's life?
4. How would you define depression?
5. In your opinion, is depression different than sadness?
6. How do people in your church or social circles think about depression?
7. Do you know people who think it's wrong for Christians to take anti-depressants? What's your opinion?
8. Have you known anybody who escaped an abusive relationship?

9. Is abuse always clear-cut, or are there gray areas where you'd say it's hard to know if someone is being abused or not? Where would you draw that line?

10. Would you say that what the main character went through in this novel is spousal abuse?

11. Would you have encouraged her to stay with her husband or leave? Or would you have a different recommendation?

12. Under what circumstances (if any) do you think a Christian should seek divorce?

13. Do you think the church is sending a dangerous message to women if it encourages them to stay in harmful relationships? What if the abuse is emotional but not physical?

Books by Alana Terry

Orchard Grove Christian Women's Fiction Novels

Beauty from Ashes

Before the Dawn

North Korea Christian Suspense Novels

The Beloved Daughter

Slave Again

Torn Asunder

Flower Swallow

Kennedy Stern Christian Suspense Series

Unplanned

Paralyzed

Policed

Straightened

Turbulence

Infected

Abridged

See a full list at www.alanaterry.com

Made in the USA
Middletown, DE
04 October 2017